I0823217

Praise for *But Where's Home? A Novella and Stories*

"*But Where's Home?* is literary art that does what the best fiction does. It entertains with equal parts depth and levity, educates, fosters understanding about its characters and setting, and illustrates the beauty, possibility, and power in the written word."—Kristen Gentry, author of *Mama Said*

"In *But Where's Home?*, Toni Ann Johnson brilliantly utilizes the short story form to create a multifaceted portrait of an American family. It's insightful, it's gripping, it's funny, it's unflinching—it's the real deal. Not since J. D. Salinger's Glass stories have I encountered a kindred so alive on the page."—Mat Johnson, author of *Loving Day*

"*But Where's Home?* is an essential addition to African American literature in the new millennium, and Johnson's voice is a breath of fresh air. Readers will be dazzled by both the psychological and the historical scope of this collection."—Jacinda Townsend, author of *Mother Country* and *Trigger Warning*

But Where's Home?

But Where's Home?

A Novella and Stories

Toni Ann Johnson

Screen Door Press gratefully acknowledges the contributions of editorial assistants Akhira Umar and Julian Long.

Publication of this volume was made possible in part by generous support from the Thomas D. Clark Foundation.

Published by Screen Door Press, an imprint of The University Press of Kentucky

Scholarly publisher for the Commonwealth, serving Bellarmine University, Berea College, Centre College of Kentucky, Eastern Kentucky University, The Filson Historical Society, Georgetown College, Kentucky Historical Society, Kentucky State University, Morehead State University, Murray State University, Northern Kentucky University, Simmons College, Spalding University, Transylvania University, University of Kentucky, University of Louisville, University of Pikeville, and Western Kentucky University.

Editorial and Sales Offices: The University Press of Kentucky
663 South Limestone, Lexington, Kentucky 40508-4008
www.kentuckypress.com

Several of the stories in this collection were previously published in slightly different form: "This Side and That," *Transformation: A Women Who Submit Anthology* (Jamii Publishing, Santa Cruz, 2023); "Pride," *Fiction Magazine*, Issue No. 66, September 2023; "But Where's Home," excerpt, *Moria Literary Magazine*, online, May 2023; "Daughtered Out," *Coachella Review*, spring 2021; "This Side and That," *Aunt Chloe: A Journal of Artful Candor*, spring 2021; "Home," *Accolades: A Women Who Submit Anthology* (Jamii Publishing, Santa Cruz, 2020); "Neighbors," published as "The Megnas," *Vida Review*, Issue #2 online, May 2020; "Home" *Serving House Journal* online, October 2018.

Cataloging-in-Publication data available from the Library of Congress

ISBN 978-1-967165-03-2 (hardcover)
ISBN 978-1-967165-04-9 (pdf)
ISBN 978-1-967165-05-6 (epub)

Member of the Association of University Presses

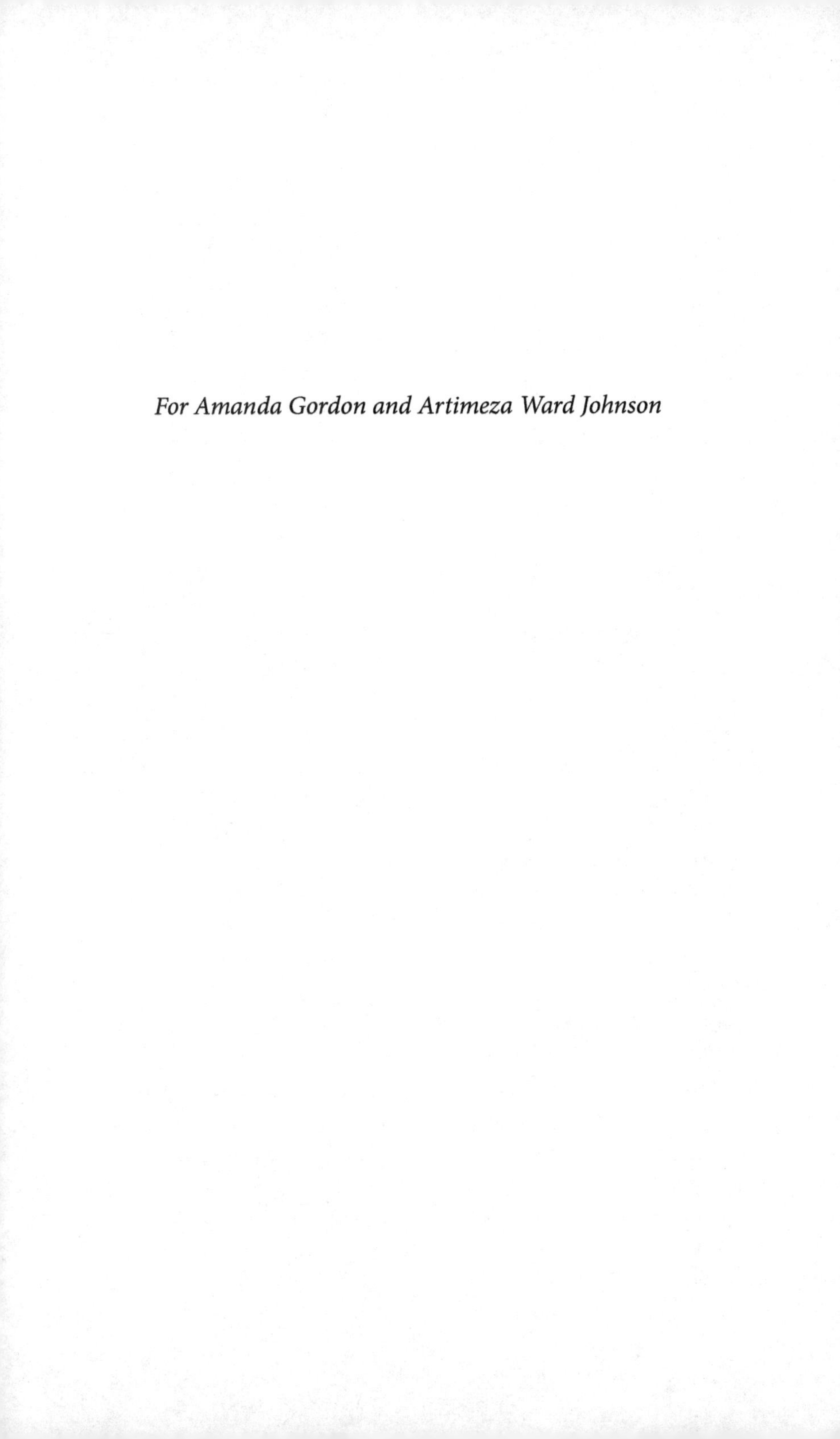

For Amanda Gordon and Artimeza Ward Johnson

Contents

The Family
A Key to Characters

Velma Arrington: Wife of Phil, mother of Madeline, stepmother of Livia, daughter-in-law of Emily, daughter of Althea and Dad, niece of Syl, cousin of Suzy (called *aunt* due to age difference)

Philip "Phil" Arrington: Husband of Velma, father of Livia and Madeline, son of Emily and Lawrence, brother of Lawrence II

Livia Arrington: Daughter of Philip, stepdaughter of Velma, half-sister of Madeline, granddaughter of Emily and Lawrence, niece of Lawrence II

Madeline "Maddie" Arrington: Daughter of Philip and Velma, half-sister of Livia, granddaughter of Emily and Lawrence, granddaughter of Althea and Dad, great-niece of Syl, cousin of Suzy, niece of Lawrence II

Emily Arrington: Wife of Lawrence, mother of Philip and Lawrence II, grandmother of Livia and Madeline, mother-in-law of Velma

Lawrence Arrington: Husband of Emily, father of Philip, father of Lawrence II, grandfather of Madeline and Livia

Lawrence Arrington II: Son of Emily, brother of Philip, uncle of Livia and Madeline

Suzy: Daughter of Syl, niece of Althea and Dad, cousin of Velma (called *niece* due to age difference), cousin of Maddie

Althea: Wife of Dad, mother of Velma, grandmother of Madeline, sister-in-law of Aunt Syl, aunt of Suzy (called *nana* due to age difference)

Dad: Husband of Althea, father of Velma, grandfather of Madeline, uncle of Suzy, half-brother of Aunt Syl

Aunt Syl: Mother of Suzy, half-sister of Dad, aunt of Velma, great-aunt of Maddie

Arrington Family Tree

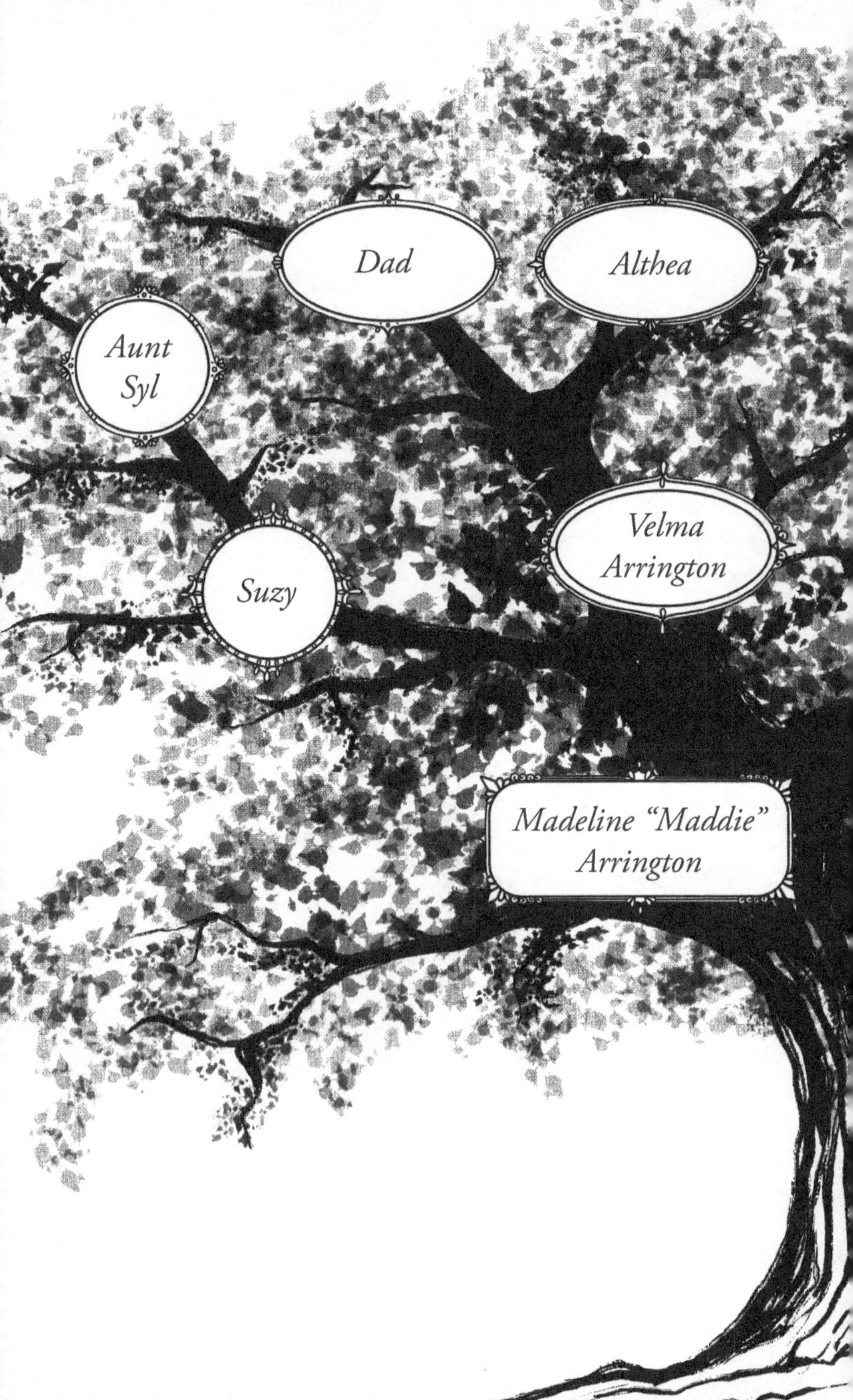
Dad
Althea
Aunt Syl
Velma Arrington
Suzy
Madeline "Maddie" Arrington

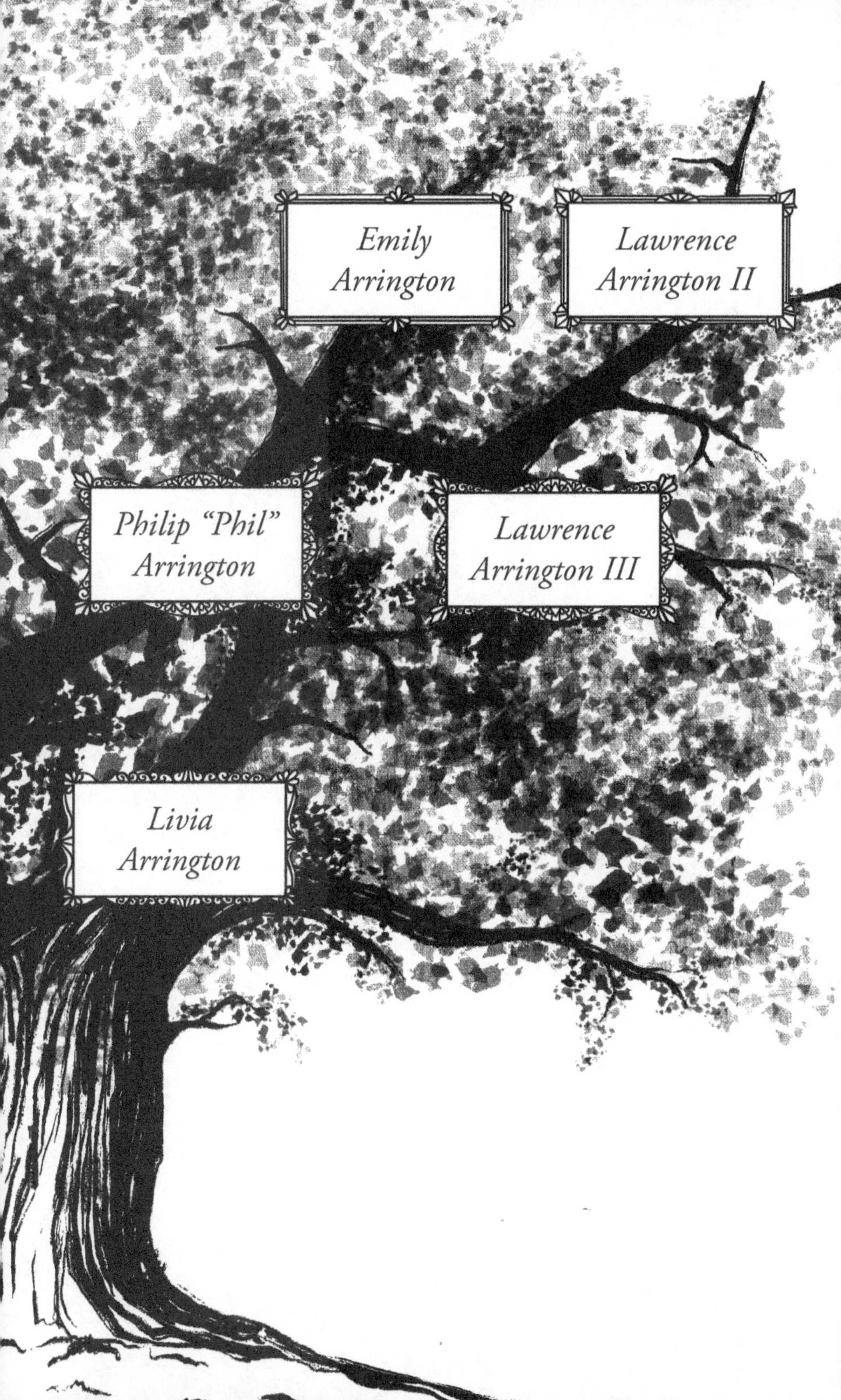
Emily
Arrington
Lawrence
Arrington II
Philip "Phil"
Arrington
Lawrence
Arrington III
Livia
Arrington

Getting There

NEW YORK, EARLY 1960S

Maddie

Before you arrive, you pick your parents. You watch them from the other side.

Velma's skin tone is gold, and she's gorgeous. She wears her hair in a bob and dresses stylishly for her job as a bookkeeper at a Wall Street bank. She's thankful to be living with her folks in a large apartment on Harlem's Sugar Hill because she's saving for the house she'll buy one day.

Velma is unconcerned with being liked. This may explain why, at nearly thirty, she's the only one among her friends yet to marry. She is feisty and takes no mess. Velma believes in a big life where she'll wed nothing less than a handsome professional. Determined to have all the money she needs, she sees herself in a beautiful home, living in luxury. She'll dare to travel to spectacular places where no one in her family has been, like India, Russia, Japan, and Greece.

You choose her for none of these reasons.

She's the one because when you were with Velma in the realm she's in now, you came undone, and somehow you lost her. You left your baby to be fostered by another. It was a grave mistake. You're going back. You're taking responsibility to fix it. You insist on this, though your guides say it doesn't work that way. They tell you that no matter what you did or have yet to do, you can't truly screw things up because all of life eventually moves in the right direction, ascending higher and for the best. They promise that even what feels like a plunge to the pits is really all part of one's rebound and rise, like a dancer's plié before she leaps high, or the way an archer draws the bow of an arrow before letting it go. The goal of all things that unfold on this side *and* that is to elevate souls toward their finest expression.

They suggest you take time for your spirit to rest. But you're eager to wrap real arms around Velma and heal the harm you caused to her heart.

The guides say you'll have no memory of "before" once you get there; no guarantee of repairing what you see as broken. And you remind them they said all things lead toward ascension. How bad could it be?

Your future father, Philip, wasn't your choice, but he's Velma's, and they come as a set. You let him grow on you. Phil's tall and good-looking, and oddly amusing. Wild about school, he holds a BA in psychology, an MA in psychology, an MSEd in clinical psychology, a PhD in clinical psychology, and he's currently enrolled in a diploma-postdoctoral program in psychoanalysis and psychotherapy.

He's a cocky man and can act without prudence and propriety. Phil wants to believe his education makes him superior. He overachieves due to deep insecurity. He lost his father young, and his mother was never kind to her son. These tragedies left wounds. You have empathy for him and his mother as well. You've suffered injuries and caused a few, too.

Velma and Phil's dates take them to stage plays and movies and to hear jazz in smoky bars. Holding hands, they browse antique shops, museums, and bazaars. Hearts touch. Scars are revealed. Each one vows to heal the other.

Phil is in debt and lives in a sparse apartment with a kitchenette near White Plains Road in the Bronx. It's not far from his mother, older brother, sister-in-law, niece, ex-wife, and his daughter, all of whom he once lived with in a house bequeathed by his father. Close to them is a collection of cousins, aunts, uncles, and friends.

Community proximity appeals to you. Life was lonely last time on your own. You're drawn toward this place where you feel you'll belong.

On Valentine's Day, nearly a year into their courtship, you watch Phil and Velma sit on his secondhand sofa after coming in from dinner downtown. Velma is svelte in a tight scoop-neck dress. She opens a black velvet box he presents. It's a set of pearl earrings. Her eyes slowly meet his. There is silence.

"Do you like them?" Phil asks. He takes off his tie.

Her eyes seem to roll, though they haven't left his. "What is *this*?" she demands.

Puzzled, he strokes his chin with his hand. "I thought you *liked* pearls, Vel. You're wearing a string of them."

"They're not *a ring*, Phil." She clenches her teeth. "We're eleven months in! Are you waiting for my carriage to turn into a pumpkin?"

"I don't believe in marriage, Velma. I just got divorced."

She stands and, without further discourse, slips on her André Perugia pumps, grabs her purse and fur coat, and marches her sexy self out of his apartment.

This can't be their end, because you're determined to get there.

While they're not speaking, you drop Velma's name into Phil's dreams. You fill them with scenes of her in his arms and with visions of being beside her, sharing a future. He misses her shapely body and soul.

Weeks later, he phones, as she knows he will. He says, "Velma, this is Phil."

Unenthused, she tsks and answers, "Phil *who*?"

He hoots with laughter at her salty charm. And you beam from your realm, relieved.

They have a small, city hall wedding. Though Velma has savings and could pay for one nicer, her sights are set on property—an asset—not something so fleeting as a party.

Her parents don't offer. They could. They're well-off. But they tell Velma Phil is full of himself.

In her parlor, Phil's mother serves English breakfast tea. She says, "Your Velma's a bit mean and self-centered, isn't she?"

"Mother," Phil says, smoking a cigarette, "the personality types one grows up with are often the same kind one weds."

Gleaning his meaning, she coughs as it goes down the wrong way.

The couple's new place is lush and larger than Phil's previous flat. Velma fills it with plants, mirrors, paintings, and antiques. It's on a street with trees in the Bronx, close to his folks. And Velma's family in Harlem is just a train, bus, or car ride away.

You can hardly wait to be with this tribe.

Phil becomes chief psychologist at a mental health clinic an hour-and-fifteen-minute drive from the Bronx. He takes pride in the job, but the commute becomes crushing.

Through a coworker, he finds a rental in the town of Monroe. The small house is not far from his office in Goshen. It's white with black shutters and sits on a quiet street atop a hill.

When Phil goes to see it, the owner, his coworker's gay uncle, warns him the neighbors won't likely be friendly. He tells Phil he and Velma will be the only ones like them.

Phil believes he's light enough, and Velma's so dazzling the neighbors might not notice or mind. I have a doctorate, he thinks, and a professional job. We've thrived in white *working* environments. We'll be fine.

Velma agrees, and it's settled.

But what about racists? you want to scream.

The mostly homogenous town of Monroe is not what you hope for.

You dream of being in the badass Bronx, where you'll go to your grandma Emily's church. You'll hear soul music coming from car radios as you dance with your cousins on the driveway while your aunties fry chicken and make potato salad, and your uncles play dominoes in the backyard.

When Phil and Velma arrive in Monroe, their water supply has been cut—pipes vandalized. Then bigots chuck eggs at their car and the house. They yell slurs and wave signs with hateful words.

You're destroyed. You sought your guides' blessing and got it. Like it or not, your soul is in prep mode and will soon be deployed.

Velma is ready to fight with her fists, but Phil tries reasoning with the racists and remains dignified. Then a large rock glides through your half-sister Livia's bedroom window, and Phil's respectable Dr. Jekyll morphs into Mr. Hyde. He and his white coworker, a hefty-sized, bearded redhead, march the neighborhood with rifles.

To your surprise, this doesn't end in disaster.

And not everyone in town is so spiteful. Word gets around about how they've been treated. They're invited to attend the Methodist church. A local dentist, thirty years their senior and Black, takes them under his wing. He whisks Phil and Velma to cocktail parties to mingle with the few *liberal* white professionals and their wives. They respect the erudite dentist and soon embrace the new caramel-hued couple, too.

Within a year, Velma quits her job at the bank, and she's pregnant with you, though Phil isn't too big on the idea of more kids. They finally buy in a better neighborhood. Livia visits on weekends and doesn't like to leave. As you get bigger in Velma's belly, Livia's still grieving the loss of her family and all that it will never become.

Phil and Velma are having less fun than they hoped for. Both he *and* she dislike her pregnancy weight. And she hates not working. She misses her job and resents him for enjoying his. And while she finds this town quaint, with its many lakes, rolling hills, and cute old homes, there are next to no Black people in this place. Though she's made a few nice acquaintances, it can't compare to her social life in the city. Her girlfriends back home eschew invitations. They say their husbands find Phil pretentious and can't spend a day with him.

You trust your mother will be so busy she won't be lonely when you get there. She'll adore you, and you'll love her, too. But she's quite miserable now. And when Phil is out, she sits and smokes, and you don't get enough oxygen.

You've got to escape the womb.

The day her water breaks, a month before she's due, Phil is scheduled to play doubles with a few doctors in town. When her pains start quickly, he still believes he can make it. His ex-wife's labor took hours. Velma waits and waits while he showers, brushes his teeth, puts on tennis whites, and gathers a towel, his racket, a sandwich, and balls before finally hauling her to the hospital.

She has a high threshold for pain, and on the way, she bears the contractions without much complaint. Once there, he hurries her in as she carries her overnight bag to the obstetrics wing. Velma's been expected, having called ahead, and she's swiftly led into a delivery room. This leaves Phil, impatient, at the desk, filling out forms. When he's through, he yells to Velma down the hall to tell her he'll be back in a couple of hours.

As he turns toward the exit, a full-figured nurse lurches into the hallway, glowering. "Your wife is seven centimeters dilated!" she shouts.

Phil swivels toward her, his face puffed in a frown.

"The baby is coming. I suggest you *sit down*." She points to the waiting room.

And so, he deflates. No tennis that day.

The other expectant fathers, all of whom are white, eye Phil with expressions of amusement, disdain, and surprise.

Just a few more pushes, and you'll arrive.

Nervous, you realize you won't remember that in this moment "before," you know you're entering a wild mess of a world. You'll have no awareness of your mission to love it back to peace.

You can only hope to succeed. You may not. But you trust that if there are times when you fail and fall into an abyss of despair, this will be a ruse.

You're never alone. Angels' arms will soon catch you. They'll toss you back up and out. And then you'll land somewhere better, even higher than before. And when you open your eyes, you'll see that you're in precisely the place where you were destined to be.

Here goes . . .

Home

MONROE, NEW YORK, 1963

Livia

Livia sat at the red Formica table, leaned down, and dug a forefinger into one of her new shoes. She yanked at the black patent leather. The Mary Janes remained stiff, no give. Her ten-year-old feet were still growing. The shoes would never be a good fit.

At Kiddie Korner, the store in town, they were the last available pair. Livia hadn't said a word to her stepmother about the pain because as soon as she put them on, Velma's typically gloomy face turned sunny, and she'd said, "Oh! Don't they look sharp?" When she asked, "Are they comfortable?" Livia lied.

Now she could almost hear her feet cursing as she eyed them. She sat still as long as she could. Livia wasn't about to mess up her pink Easter dress. It wasn't Easter. Easter had passed, but Velma wanted her in that dress.

She stared at her daddy and Velma's closed door. They always took so long to get ready to go. What were they doing in there?

She didn't mind that she'd be going out with them. Livia enjoyed seeing new things. But she did not like that they'd be looking at a new house. It had taken months to get used to this one and how far this white town was from the Bronx where she lived with her mother.

Her sketchpad and pencil were next to Velma's flouncy fern on top of the oak bookshelf in the living room. She stood, and with each step, the dress shoes bit into the backs of her ankles and chewed on her baby toes like a mean little dog.

She sat back down, pad in lap, to sketch the Formica table. Drawing its simple, clean lines was soothing. This was her favorite piece of furniture here. She'd helped pick it out. Before Velma came along.

Except for the kitchen table, most of the rented cottage was filled with antique furniture Velma had collected. Ugly, in Livia's opinion. Old things with ornate or wavy flourishes felt disorderly to Livia. She preferred crispness. Precision. When she made drawings, they were never of squiggly or sloppy stuff like other kids' doodles at school. Livia drew tidy, even-sided shapes.

Daddy and Velma finally emerged from the bedroom, along with a shroud of stinky smoke. He was puffing a cigarette, and she was putting on pearl studs.

Six months swollen, Velma toddled toward Livia, the heels of her pumps clicking across the yellow-and-white linoleum tiles. She set her Chanel bag on the table. "How do I look?" she asked, posing with a hand on one hip, as if she were something special.

"Nice," Livia said without hesitation.

She was being polite. Her stepmother's golden, fully made-up face did look good. Velma was glamorous, more glamorous than Livia's mother was. The way Velma applied eyeliner, mascara, and lipstick enthralled Livia. She watched her stepmother put her face on whenever she was allowed to. But Velma was unfashionably huge in her maternity dress. She looked off balance, like she could tip over, like she'd swallowed a large pumpkin.

"Well, thanks, Liv. So do you." Velma winked. "We girls have to stick together. Young ladies need compliments." She shot a look at Livia's daddy.

He paid her no mind. Humming Duke Ellington's "Take the 'A' Train," he removed his suit jacket from a chrome chair at the table. "Everyone ready?" he asked, swinging his hips.

Livia stood. "May I bring my sketchpad, Daddy?"

"Yes, you may." He slipped his jacket on and kept dancing.

Velma eyed him, tight-lipped, and blew a gust from her nose. "We're going to look at a house, Phil, not to a museum. What does she need it for?"

"Vel." He stood still now, met her frown, and smiled. "She's creative, honey. It's fine."

Livia looked down at her white ankle socks in the awful black shoes. She turned her lips inward and pressed them together so hard they hurt. If she smiled and Velma saw, there'd be trouble. Wasn't often this woman didn't get her way.

Parked in the middle of the back seat, sketchpad in her lap, Livia could see the country road and leafy trees through the haze of cigarette smoke and between her daddy's head and Velma's. His hair was wet with Vitalis, which didn't work too well to keep his curls slicked back because it was for white people. Daddy didn't have the kinkiest hair, but it wasn't without any kink at all. Velma's hair was pressed and curled. She knew what she was doing.

Their car pulled up and stopped directly behind a metallic-blue Chevy Impala at the bottom of a steep blacktop driveway below a house that sat a few yards above the street.

"Bet that's the agent's car," Velma said.

Livia liked cars. Some were works of art. She recognized the Impala as a 1961 or a '62, not the newest model but pretty close. Her daddy's 1959 Chrysler was older and, in Livia's estimation, a less striking robin's-egg blue. Her daddy could've bought a recent model, if he'd really wanted one. But Velma was especially shrewd with money. She'd worked for a bank before she began growing that gourd in her gut.

"Don't buy a brand-new car, Phil," Livia had heard Velma say. "Cars depreciate. You're better off buying one that's a year or two old. A house—now, *that* appreciates."

Why couldn't they be satisfied with the house they were already living in? Livia had finally stopped having scary dreams when she slept there. Anxiety dreams, Daddy called them. They were nightmares about being left somewhere, alone, and trying to find her way home.

She sketched the Chevy's backside, carefully rendering its straight lines and elegant geometric design. She hoped Daddy would turn and notice how well she was drawing.

He climbed out of the car.

At that moment, Livia looked up. Through the windshield, she saw the real estate agent sitting in the Chevy Impala. He lifted his head to peer into his rearview mirror. Their cars were parked so close that she saw his eyes reflecting back at her. His head whipped around. He stared over his shoulder and through his back window at her daddy as he walked past the front of their Chrysler toward Velma's door.

The real estate man had a widow's peak and a heart-shaped face that reminded Livia of a white valentine she'd made sometime after her daddy moved out, and her mother wouldn't buy any red construction paper. She'd used typing paper. The man was a caricature artist's dream. Caricatures made Livia recoil. Exaggerated details were unbecoming. Still, she watched his valentine-face closely. He squinted at the three of them.

Her daddy was busy helping Velma out of the car. She needed a tug to stand up.

The man threw open his car door and jumped out. "Well, hello, hello," he chirped like a little bird, smiling at Livia's daddy and Velma. "Nice to see you folks." He waved, sticking out an arm in a starched white shirt. "If you'll wait right here just a moment, please, I'm going to pop in and be sure the seller's ready. Just one moment. Be right back."

Livia watched him hike up the bottom part of the especially steep driveway in a few giant steps. The slope of it was practically perpendicular, and the whole thing looked like an *L* that had fallen over clockwise so the horizontal part became vertical. The real estate agent stopped at the top where it leveled out, caught his breath for a moment, and then trotted the last few yards to the front door.

Her daddy and Velma didn't say anything. Livia watched them through the windshield. They stood at the base of the driveway, looking up at the house. Livia couldn't see it too well from inside the car.

Why did they have to live up in the boonies anyway? Before Daddy and Velma moved to this town full of white people last summer, their apartment was right on East 230th Street, just a few blocks from where Livia lived. And sometimes she saw him during the week. Sometimes they had dinner with Grandma Emily. Other times, Daddy took her out for ice cream or for a Coke, even on school nights. When he and Velma moved from the Bronx and rented the small house in this little town, Livia got her own room, which she hadn't had in their apartment. She'd grown to like it, but now she only saw Daddy on weekends twice a month. Why'd he want to live some fifty miles away? Didn't he miss her? If he bought a house, that probably meant he'd never move back to where she lived.

Her heart was thumping in her chest. She took a deep breath and focused on sketching. She studied the chrome bumper. It was so shiny you could've flossed your teeth in it like a mirror. As she filled in its details—three little round lights on both sides and a keyhole—Livia thought a person must really have to love a thing to keep it polished like that.

Her daddy and Velma didn't let her finish the sketch. They made her get out to look at the house. Every step in the awful shoes sawed grooves into her heels and squished her baby toes. She would've worn her Keds, but no, Velma said they had to make a good impression.

Livia climbed the steep driveway slowly. Daddy walked backwards and pulled on Velma's hands to help her to the top. He wore a light blue shirt without a tie under his navy suit. Velma had asked him to wear a tie, but Daddy did what he wanted. Velma sewed her maternity dress herself. It had a matching jacket in the same baby blue as his shirt. She wanted a boy. Daddy said he didn't need another kid. He said he could do without the responsibility, but if they were going to have one, he preferred a boy, too. Livia figured this was the reason for all the blue. Velma made sure the color flattered her skin tone. That woman did everything she could to look good. Her hair, nails, and makeup were always done. Livia suspected she hated being fat with that stupid pumpkin. How could she not, especially after Daddy let it slip that he missed her hourglass figure?

They were seated at the red Formica table when he'd said it during breakfast a few weekends ago. Velma set her fork down and stared at a full plate of pancakes for a long time before she got up and left the kitchen without a word.

"That wasn't nice, Daddy," Livia said. She didn't admit how she honestly felt.

Velma had it coming. She was the one who most often *caused* hurt feelings. Her tongue could slice through stones. Daddy kept eating, as if he hadn't heard what Livia said.

Velma was prettier than Livia's mother *before* the pumpkin. *During* the pumpkin, when Daddy came to get her every other week, he'd stare at Livia's mommy and tell *her* she looked nice. Mommy liked compliments but not from him since he left her. She never said thank you. She rarely even bothered to say goodbye. Sometimes, she'd close the door while he was still speaking. Daddy said she was rude. Livia kept her mouth shut. She wasn't getting dragged into their grown folks' foolishness.

When Velma got to the top of the driveway, she looked at the house, made an *mm* sound, and said, "It's so pretty."

"That's called a colonial style, Liv," Daddy told her. "You like it?" He petted her head like she was a puppy.

Velma had washed and set Livia's hair the night before, and it was smooth. She nodded, but Livia didn't know if she liked it or not. You couldn't know if a home was good or bad just by seeing the outside. That told you nothing about how it felt to live in it. You needed to learn its details. Details mattered. They mattered in art and in real-life things, too.

"See the separate entrance?" Velma pointed to a metal side door. "That's gotta be the room they said you could use as an office."

Daddy lit a cigarette. He inhaled and nodded as he exhaled. "If we were to get it, looks like there's space to add on, too."

Velma lifted her shoulders toward her cheeks and smiled at him with her whole face. She smiled at him as if Livia wasn't even there.

Her heart was beating fast again, and her feet were in agony. She took a big breath in and blew it out slowly. She couldn't stop them from moving. What could she ever do to make her daddy do what she wanted? Not a damn thing.

Livia faced the house. She had to admit the outside was attractive. It was a clean rectangle, two-toned, white over a brick bottom. She lifted her pad and made a rough sketch. There were a lot of bricks, which meant many lines, and none were as interesting as the Chevy Impala's, but she preferred this house's plainness to the larger, older-looking homes on either side. Those had excess flourishes like overhanging roofs and balconies, wraparound porches, and shutters. This one was smaller, simpler, yet it was gigantic compared to where she lived with her mother. She sketched herself in front of the house. Then she added Daddy beside her with his arm around her.

Her mother would seethe if he and Velma bought this house. And Livia would have to listen to it. Daddy never bought her and her mother a house. Velma got to quit her job. Mommy had to work. Livia thought her mother seemed to enjoy teaching, but she still complained about the effort it took to support them. Velma had it easy.

Velma was the one who insisted they needed a bigger house. Her lousy pumpkin was coming, and she wanted Livia's daddy to "stop talking about starting your private practice, and go ahead and start it." But in the house they were renting, Livia's room had billowy white curtains on a sunny window, and she woke to birds singing and no sirens or honking horns. She didn't need any more changes.

At first, the neighbors did not like them being there. They were scary and mean, and they shouted ugly things. She was relieved when they finally stopped egging the house and their car and yelling slurs. One man even came over and told her daddy he was sorry. Other neighbors started being less nasty and left them alone after that.

A high-pitched yelp and laughter turned Livia around. She saw a couple of white girls in sweatshirts and dungarees playing hopscotch up the block. Maple trees with leaves like large hands catching the sun lined the sidewalk. At the other end of the street, on the corner, there was a waterfall. Livia could faintly hear it going *swishhhhhhh.*

"Beautiful, isn't it?" Velma asked, when she saw Livia looking. "Like a fairy tale. A dream."

It was early April and not hot outside, especially with all the shade trees, but Velma was perspiring. Before she started carrying that bump of hers, she wore Chanel No. 5, and she smelled elegant. She couldn't stand perfume while she had that thing in her belly, and without it, her sweat smelled a bit like Grandma Emily's holiday ham.

Velma plucked the cigarette from between Daddy's lips, puffed on it, and then stuck it back.

Livia turned away, back toward the house. She saw a small face appear in the middle window on the top floor. A kid's face. She wasn't sure if it was a boy or a girl. It had dark frizzy hair like a black poodle's, which was similar to her own hair when it wasn't straightened. The face saw her see it and swiftly ducked from the window.

The real estate man came back through the front door, wearing a grim look on his heart-shaped face. "Bad news," he said. He made clicking sounds as he shook his head right, left, right. "Now, we can take a look—you did come all the way here—but I'm sorry to tell you, turns out this house is in escrow."

"What?" Velma sucked her teeth and crossed her arms above her pumpkin.

"But not to worry," the man said. "There's another house available across town."

"I researched *this* house," Velma said. "And this is the one I wanna see. We just spoke this morning." Her voice got louder. "It went into escrow since then?"

"Apparently," the man said. He tugged his ear. "Sorry about that."

Velma lowered her chin and stared him in the eye. "This house better really be in escrow, because we will check."

"And we do have a lawyer," Livia's daddy said. He put a hand on Velma's lower back.

"Uh, you folks—" The man's face went pink. He smiled and winced at the same time. "Now, I think you've got the wrong idea here. *I'm* told the house is in escrow. But, uh, as I said, we can take a look. There's always a chance it could fall *out* of escrow."

Velma's eyes went heavenward and she sighed.

The man pulled at his collar as he cleared his throat.

Livia watched her daddy. He stared straight at the man and smoked.

"Mr. Arrington, you'll have to put your cigarette out before we go in."

"It's *Doctor* Arrington," Daddy said, still staring him right in his eyes.

"That's great. Would you please put your cigarette out?"

"Did you call me over here to look at a house that's *apparently* in escrow?"

The man's color deepened from pink to ruby red. He *really* looked like a valentine now.

"You can wait until I'm finished," Daddy said.

Livia watched the man blink a whole bunch of times. He scratched his widow's peak and then blew air through his lips. He must have blown through his red nose, too, because a booger peeked out and dangled there. Disgusting. No one told him. Velma looked at Livia and squinched up her face. They both smiled. Livia could have sketched that booger-face perfectly, but she didn't draw gross things.

When her daddy finally crushed his cigarette on the driveway with his foot, he stuck the butt into his gold box of Benson & Hedges. The three of them followed the booger-man inside.

Velma wanted to see the room with the separate entrance. It had a checkered floor. Black and white. Shadow and light. Chiaroscuro. Livia learned that in an art book. The room also had built-in bookshelves and a bathroom with a toilet and a sink. A "half bathroom," Velma called it.

"Oh, it's perfect, Phil," she said. "Don't you think? For your office?"

"Would be if it were available," he snapped.

Booger-man stood in the doorway and stared down at his black loafers. Livia's daddy eyed him like he wanted to mush him flat with the bottom of his shoe.

The kitchen, dining room, and living room were up a short staircase on the middle level. A longer staircase led to the bedrooms on the top floor. The dining room and living room shared one grand T-shaped space with an extra-high ceiling. Livia could see the upstairs hallway from there because the hallway was also a balcony that overlooked the dining area.

Velma stared up at the balcony, put a hand on her pumpkin, and said, "Oh. That's lovely."

Two white men in plaid shirts were sitting at a mahogany dining table that faced a large window, with a view of a forsythia bush in the backyard that reminded Livia of buttered popcorn at the movies. The men turned and nodded a greeting. They didn't speak. Velma and Livia's daddy waved as they followed the booger-man through a swinging door into the kitchen. Livia lagged behind.

One man was old and round, with short white hair on his head and a little sticking out of his ears. The other was much younger and skinny, with long dark curls. He had a beard, too. There were crumbs in it. They were drinking coffee and munching on matzo.

The older man turned toward her and smiled. "Well, aren't you a little beauty?" he said. "And don't you look nice today in your pretty pink dress?" His voice was kind. "Would you like a crackah darlink?" The way he said *cracker* and *darling* reminded Livia of Grandma Emily's butcher in the Bronx.

She nodded. "Yes, thank you."

He handed her a big square of matzo. Matzo was like a giant saltine without the salt. She figured he thought she wouldn't know what it was called, but they had matzo in the Bronx.

Velma and Daddy came back through the swinging door as Livia was eating. Velma said to be careful not to get any crumbs on the floor.

The older man glanced down at the Oriental rug, shrugged, and said, "Don't worry about it, dahlink." He raised an arm behind him, toward the balcony. "Please. Go have a look."

As Livia crunched on the matzo, the younger man said his niece was in the middle bedroom but to tap on the door.

When the booger-man started up the stairs, the older man twisted toward him and said, "Why don't you wait here?"

Livia watched the booger-man look back at him. She wanted to turn away because she was still eating, but she also didn't want to miss anything.

“Why trouble yourself?” the old man asked, raising his spotted, wrinkled hand toward the balcony. “If they have questions, we can see them from here.”

They locked eyes for a moment. Booger-man smiled with no teeth and no warmth. Then he said, “If that’s what you want.” He thumped back down the steps.

The old man picked up a paper napkin and held it out. “Please. Your schnoz needs a blow,” he said. “My appetite begs you.”

The skinny man snorted before hiding his face in his coffee cup.

Livia swallowed the last of her matzo and followed her daddy and Velma. The Mary Janes pinched and squeezed as she climbed the stairs. A bathroom was at the top. The medicine cabinet was long and mirrored and had sliding doors. The wall tiles, tub, and toilet were a shiny pink. This detail delighted Livia. The tiles matched her Easter dress perfectly! Was it a sign she belonged there?

“It’s great,” Velma said. “Isn’t it?” She looked at Daddy.

He nodded and turned to Livia. “Plenty of room for all your hair products, huh, Liv?” He chuckled and rubbed her back.

“Plenty of room for *baby* things,” Velma said, like she was correcting him. “That counter has room to change a diaper.”

“Velma, that counter has room to change a grown man’s underwear. There’s space for Livia’s things, too.”

“Mm,” Velma grunted. “I guess.”

Livia wanted to pull one of those shoes off and hurl it at her stepmother. The backs of her ankles were raw. She was sure her toes had blisters. And the space between her ribs began to ache.

The smallest bedroom was closest to the bathroom. All that fit in it was a single bed, a nightstand, and a dresser. Her daddy and Velma didn’t say anything when they looked inside.

The middle room’s door was closed. Velma knocked, and the curly-haired little girl opened it. She was younger than Livia, maybe six or seven years old, and she had a Barbie in her hand. Livia could tell by the smell that it was new. She loved the powdery, plastic smell of a brand-new Barbie. The girl smiled, and a tiny tip of tongue poked through the space of a missing front tooth. Then she sat on the floor with the rest of her dolls. The room had a bed, a desk, a bookcase, a dresser, and a play table with a tea set on it.

"This would be perfect for the baby, Phil," Velma said.

"Yeah. *If* the house were to fall out of escrow," he whispered.

"We'll see about that," Velma said.

"So, that first room would be mine, right?" Livia asked.

"Yes, when you're here, Livia," Velma said. "It would be yours *and* the guest room, just like now, and it'll have the prettiest curtains and nicest bed linens."

What? Her room was the *guest room*? She wanted to look at Daddy to see if this was true, but she couldn't because her eyes welled up, and she didn't want him to know. Would the pumpkin have to share its room with guests, too? Probably not. This wasn't a detail you could see or touch, but it was a kind that mattered even more.

So, she'd have to share her daddy *and* her room? And the pumpkin would get to have Daddy all week, every week, and a bigger room of its own?

Apparently.

She followed them down the hardwood hallway to the last door. The master bedroom was the largest though not that great. Livia's eyes were wet and blurry; she barely bothered to look. She hoped the house would not "fall out of escrow," whatever that meant.

When they all finally went outside and made it down to the bottom of the driveway and their cars, the real estate agent said, "Shall we take a look at the other house?"

Daddy turned to Velma.

She looked at the agent. "We like *this* one."

The man exhaled. "Right. And if it comes back on the market, you'll be first to know. In the meantime, there's a place for sale across town. Here's the address." He handed Daddy a slip of paper. "You know how to get across the Erie Line to Spring Street?"

"Across the tracks?" Daddy asked, like, *Are you kidding me*?

The man crossed his arms. "Look, it's up to you. It's a nice house. You want to see it, make the right on Spring, and keep going about a quarter of a mile," he said. He slipped into his shiny Chevy and drove off.

Livia's daddy opened the car door for Velma. She didn't get in. She looked all around, and then her eyes landed on the waterfall down the street. It poured from a large pond, angled over a straight ledge of rocks, and plunged into a flowing stream.

"Velma, what are you doing?" Daddy asked.

"I'm thinking," she answered.

She was listening, too, and smiling, with her eyes closed now and her head tilted back. Livia had seen that same look of pleasure on her face when she found old furniture she liked at garage sales. Velma was a strange lady.

Livia climbed into the car. She didn't feel like looking at anything or sketching anymore. She didn't want to do anything but take those damned shoes off. Why should she give a crap about any new house? All she'd get was a guest room. She was the weekend kid. Velma's pumpkin could rot. What the hell did it do to deserve its own room and to get to live with her daddy in a big house?

Velma fell into her seat with a thud. Daddy got in and started the car.

Then the young, skinny man with the beard came sprinting out of the house, waving his arms like someone signaling for help. "Wait!" he yelled. "Please, wait!"

Daddy turned the engine off and rolled down the window.

The man ran to the bottom of the driveway, sliding a bit in his sneakers. "Listen," he said, short of breath as he approached the car window. "We didn't want to say anything in front of the agent, but you should know that he came in before you and told us, 'These colored people want to see your house. Legally, I have to show it to them, but I'll tell 'em it's in escrow.' My father wants you to know he's not like that. He remembers when they didn't sell to Jews either. He says if you want to buy this house and you make him a good offer, he'll be happy to sell it to you."

Velma covered her face with her hands.

"Thank you," Livia's daddy said. He looked at Velma and touched her thigh. "Well?"

She plucked a Kleenex from her Chanel bag and dabbed her eyes. "Tell your father we'll take it."

The man nodded. "Would you like to come back in and look around some more?"

"Yes," Velma said, sniffling.

"But the real estate man thinks you'll meet him at the other house," Livia said. She pictured him and his valentine face standing there, waiting.

Velma turned and looked at her. She laughed, even as she was crying.

Daddy smiled. "Don't worry about him, Liv."

Velma blew her nose. She kept crying and laughing as she lifted her swollen self out of the car.

The skinny man began to help Livia's daddy hoist her up the driveway.

"I'll wait here," Livia muttered. She was already unbuckling the straps on her shoes.

"No, baby. You come with us," Daddy said, raising his voice. "Come on, now."

They reached the top of the driveway, and she watched him hold Velma's hand. They were waiting for her.

She didn't want to go. Her feet hurt so much, and it wouldn't be any fun. But if she didn't do as she was told, they'd yell or come get her or maybe even punish her. She had no choice. So, Livia would go. She'd go in, and she would sketch her new room the way she wanted it to be. She'd put herself and all her things inside it. They'd fit perfectly. And it wouldn't be a guest room, ever, even when she wasn't there, because she was *not* a guest! She belonged. She'd draw everything she could think of. Daddy would be there, tucking her into her own bed, with her own linens. There'd be no damned pumpkin. Just her. Livia would draw every detail the way she wished for it to be. And she'd keep drawing and drawing and drawing until it finally felt like home.

Neighbors

MONROE, NEW YORK, 1974

The Megnas

We knew about the Arringtons before they got here.

Irv Silverman tap-tapped on our back door the day the moving truck driver refused to venture up his black diamond–run driveway. Irv asked if the guy could use ours. Of course, we were accommodating. We were good neighbors. Our driveway stretched down from Oakland Avenue in the back, instead of up from Stage Road in the front, and it was a bunny hill compared to his. So the driver came that way, and the truck pulled onto Irv's property from ours. There was never a FOR SALE sign, and Irv waited until that day, when it was obvious, to tell us he was moving.

Now, a neighbor should give you advance notice. We would. That's just common courtesy, but we couldn't be too ticked off. Irv's elder son, Aaron, who, like the Arringtons, was around our age, had died a few months earlier right before Christmas. Not in the house; in the hospital. Pneumonia. And it was very sudden. He'd been living there with Irv, who was a widower, and with his own young daughter, Alice, who was about six.

The rumor 'round town was that the son's wife had run off and left him and the little girl, and there were all kinds of stories whirling around about why. Aaron never mentioned his wife, and we certainly weren't going to ask, because there were plenty of stories dancing in the dust about us, too.

We were sad he passed. Nice guy. Loved kids. He let our boys climb all over his daughter's swing set and all over him, too. We could hear poor Irv next door, sobbing every day for at least a week when Aaron died.

We met Irv's younger son, David, who came to stay and help look after Alice. He was sweet and seemed a bit swishy, but we weren't bothered by that. We thought he told us they had to "sit and shiver," which left us flummoxed. We asked if they wanted to borrow our electric heater. It was quite cold that December. Later, we learned what "sitting shiva" was, and then, oh boy, did we have a good laugh at ourselves about that.

After the moving truck was finally parked in Irv's backyard, that's when he came over a second time. He had something to tell us. We invited him in for coffee, but he didn't want any. He stood on our back porch with a hand braced on the railing and stared over at our son's tricycle because he couldn't look us in the eyes as he said the word *Negroes*. We almost giggled. Not because the term was so funny, but because of the way he said it. He stuttered, and the man didn't have a stammer that we'd ever heard. "Ne-Ne-Ne-groes." And even though he wasn't looking at us, he stuck his leathery neck out defensively, like he was daring us to . . . somethin'. Yell at him? Hit him with a bat? He kept saying what a "nice" family they were. Must have said it four or five times, and he said the husband was well educated, a psychologist who'd graduated from some Jewish university in New York City, Irv was proud to say. And the wife was attractive. She dressed like Jackie Kennedy, and he said she knew about all kinds of antiques and objects of art. She was pregnant, too, and since we were due to have our third that June, our kids would be the same age. This was his sales pitch.

We smiled and nodded and didn't let on that we were offended by his assumption that we'd have a problem with colored people, but we *were* a tad miffed because we'd never been anything but nice to the Silvermans. And they were Jewish. We weren't bigots, and we didn't come from such. Not bad ones, anyway. We went to church in town, and we judged people by their deeds, not by anything else. Now, we might not have known much about Jews, obviously, but we were good neighbors to the Silvermans. We shoveled their sidewalk when we did our own. We shared vegetables from our garden. We took in their mail and watered their yard when they went on vacation, and we always had little Alice over to play with our boys.

Irv didn't know this (that we knew of), but there'd been a neighborhood "meeting" down the hill, where some of the families tried to rile up the neighbors before the Silvermans moved in. It was at the Gores' house, and we thought it was just a barbecue until we got there. We walked in and then walked right back out and took our hot dogs and buns with us when they started spouting that nonsense about horns and tails. We didn't go for that kind of talk.

Audrey, the elderly bohemian lady who lived in the big house on the other side of the Silvermans, rushed out right before us. She had long white hair to her waist that she kept in a braid, and it almost smacked us in the back breeze as she swooped out the door. Her dead husband had been a famous writer in New York City, and they knew plenty of Jews and probably Negroes, too. She wanted no part of the silly meeting, and neither did we.

When the Arringtons moved in that spring, regretfully, we found ourselves at another one of those "meetings." We hadn't meant to be there. We were invited for coffee. Weren't told the occasion.

After word spread about our marital issues, the locals shunned us for a while. (As if they were so squeaky clean.) Not the new neighbors like the Silvermans or old hippie Audrey. The folks *from* here. The ones we went to junior high and high school with.

There was a time when we'd all get together for beers down at Fisherman's Feast. We'd also play checkers or cards or take our babies into town to feed the ducks or go for frozen custard at the Three Bears. And everybody used to bring their little ones to our house the week before Halloween to jump in the leaves and have hot cocoa—that was our thing before we even had kids. But come the fall of '61—after our "summer of straying," if you will—none of the old gang invited us to anything, and no one came when we invited them.

At first, we didn't mind so much. We had our siblings and cousins in other parts of town. But when smiles and waves weren't returned on the sidewalk or at the A&P, and no one wanted to let their babies play with ours, we started to feel the sting. So when we did get that call from Sally (this was summer of 1963), we thought we were being welcomed back.

We walked into the Gores' dining room. It was always dark in there because of all the trees outside, and the house never failed to smell like a stale fridge. We came hand in hand to show them that no, we were not broken, in case the big belly we brought with us, announcing our third munchkin on the way, wasn't proof enough. The belly got a few raised brows. They must have been doing the math in their little minds, figuring out if this was a fraction of us or a whole.

Sally'd made a giant pot of percolator coffee, bitter as she was, and the Ferrells brought their homemade scones, known to be so good the bakery in town used the recipe and sold out of them on Sundays after church. The Jacksons were there, too, and the Zalinskys, the O'Neils, and that irritating Austrian family at the end of the block who didn't talk to anyone, except when they'd have the nerve to say hello as their German shepherd peed on our shrubs while we were standing right on the front porch. They're the ones who should've been run out of the neighborhood. By the time that family moved, our poor hedges were yellow instead of green.

Soon all eyes were on us. What was our plan to make the new colored family unwelcome? It was up to us, they said, to save the property values for the rest of them because of course they knew old Audrey would be no help in that regard. In fact, she was apt to tell them all to take a hike to hell.

That sentiment crossed our minds, too, once we understood we weren't there because they wanted us back as friends. Our hands squeezed tight together, and Lisa kicked inside like she wanted out, same as us.

We told them we respected their right to feel the way they did, but we were not going to make anyone feel unwelcome unless they did something to make us want to, and they hadn't. We'd met the Arringtons by then.

We fell in love with Livia first, because who can resist little girls? She was smart and curious, with cheeks plump as our homegrown beefsteak tomatoes, and that was fun because we missed little Alice next door. Lisa hadn't yet arrived. We only had boys, two and three years old, when the Arringtons moved in on a Saturday in May.

The next day, when we got back from church, Livia strolled over into our yard carrying a sketch pad. She said hello and started drawing our porch. Velma yelled at her to come back and leave us alone, but we waved her over, too. And she sure was striking with her glowing skin, high cheekbones, and chic pixie-cut black hair. Her swollen belly gave us something in common right away. We could offer advice since this was her first, and we'd been around that block twice already.

Phil wandered over, too, in a spotless white T-shirt. He was short-haired, clean-shaven, and the color of butter, so light you could barely tell *what* he was. We had cousins on the Megna side darker than him. We offered ice cream, and Velma waddled back to get some soft cookies. We put 'em together and had ice cream sandwiches at our picnic table on the back porch.

They were personable. Friendly. They liked to have a drink and chat, same as us. Sometimes we did our porch, sometimes theirs. It was pleasant. We'd sit under the stars and watch fireflies sparking in the dark.

One time, though, after both Lisa and Maddie were born, we were sitting around, and Phil told Velma not to talk so much. She was short on sleep, and we'd all had a couple of cocktails—and good God, did she give him a face full of grief about that. "You don't tell me when the fuck I can talk!" Right in front of us, too. Woke the babies and everything.

You'd think we'd be put off by that kind of display. Nope. Didn't mind it, because that meant we didn't have to be so perfect around them all the time either. Our marriage was fine by then, but what couple doesn't squabble once in a while? It was nice to have them right next door for company. Color didn't come up, strange as that may seem. We talked about our families—Phil didn't get along with his mother in the Bronx, and neither did Velma. There were conversations about house maintenance; our roof leaked and their basement flooded when it rained. We discussed decorating, babies, and babysitters. We gossiped. Told everybody's business and a bit about ours, too. You know, just people stuff.

Some of the other families stayed mad at us for not helping them get rid of the Arringtons. Sally Gore, especially. God, she was the worst—nasty as she could be—but as far as we knew, no one did anything meaner than to be unfriendly, and Phil and Velma were tough; they could handle not being smiled at. If anything worse went on, we didn't hear about it.

At first, they didn't seem to socialize with anyone but us and with old Audrey, who liked to talk with Phil about books. Then Phil joined the no-frills tennis club down the street and made friends with a few people, including the coin-collecting Vahanians up on Oakland Avenue, and the Miltons, across the road, who had a boy Maddie and Lisa's age. Our sons were Lisa's best friends, and Maddie felt left out sometimes, so she played with the Milton kid until he took up with the Ferrell kids, who were bullies, and she and Lisa joined the same Brownie troop.

Honestly, we never gave much thought as to what life was like for the Arringtons here in town. Oh, we'd hear neighbors talk about them—they saw the different cars parked on the street and in their driveway, people going in and out to see Phil. They'd speculate there was no way he was seeing patients; he was selling drugs, selling guns, selling *Velma*. We'd just laugh at them.

Now, there was one time, a couple of years ago, when they had a family barbecue. We didn't love that. It was loud—music and talking—and it spilled into their front yard from the back. There were at least fifty colored people standing on the grass outside the house for hours. Picture that. In *this* neighborhood. And the variety of shades they came in! Like a box of assorted chocolates, dark and milk, plus some caramels and peanut brittle to boot. The only white people there were our kids. We were invited, too, but we stayed inside on the phone because it rang all-damn-day-long.

Oh, you should've heard the neighbors. They said things we'd never repeat. And we didn't disagree with all of it. Most of it, yes, but not all. We worried we might've been wrong about the Arringtons. Their yard was full of Negroes. So many. *Too* many. Everyone thought it was the beginning of some kind of invasion, and the locals took it out on us, saying they told us so, and we ruined the neighborhood. And as much as we liked Phil and Velma, we realized we wouldn't be comfortable with a whole bunch of Phils and Velmas. And that was our neighbors' fear—it wasn't the one family; it was more families coming and changing the neighborhood.

The police were called, no surprise there, but the squad car just kept riding up and down Stage Road and didn't even stop, like the cops were scared. People at the barbecue began waving at them. The music was turned down, but the crowd stayed thick as a swarm of bees until it got dark.

We were going to say something about it. We wanted to. But that was tricky because we didn't want to want to ruin the relationship, especially since it really was a good one. So we thought about it. How could we say it delicately? Please don't have *all* your colored people coming here at once. Well, if there's a good way to say that we weren't clever enough to come up with it, so our lips stayed locked.

And then we figured out something about the Arringtons. They didn't want their relatives moving here any more than we wanted them to. They'd moved *away* from them. If they'd wanted to live around a bunch of their own, they could have stayed in the city. And there were actually a couple of colored families in Monroe. Not a lot, and none in our neighborhood. They were mostly on the other side of town. We didn't know them well, but we knew *of* them. They seemed to be fine people. No crimes or anything like that. That kind of thing was a problem in Newburgh and maybe in Middletown, but not here.

Phil and Velma never sought them out. Not as far as we knew. Maddie played with a couple of their kids, two little girls, but Velma didn't invite the colored parents over to visit, at least not that we ever saw, and we would've noticed. We didn't see the Arringtons make any effort to befriend those people at all. Except for one man—Dr. M. G. Beaumont, the Negro dentist. His mother had been the maid of Carlton Winslow, who descended from the family who once owned all the land this town was built on. Dr. Beaumont had a much younger, much lighter sister, and there was speculation that this sister was Winslow's child. The story goes that rich old Winslow was good to both children and to their mother. He paid for Dr. Beaumont's education, college, and dental school. At Columbia University. Well, Dr. Beaumont was at their barbecue. And believe it or not, that distinguished man was the one and only Negro we'd ever heard anything "negative" about around here. Not that there were so many. In fact, there were so few you barely needed a whole hand to count them.

First of all, it ticked people off that Dr. Beaumont went by M. G., and most people didn't know his first name. He wouldn't tell you if you asked. And some people didn't like that. He'd say, with a smile, that he didn't care what people liked; his name was Dr. M. G. Beaumont, and that's all they needed to know. That didn't win him fans, but it wasn't even the *real* negative story, which was a rumor that Dr. Beaumont bought his humongous house on a hill, across from Carlton Winslow's estate, *with cash.* And he paid for it with fifty thousand one-dollar bills. Funny, right? Can you imagine? They had to be counted by hand at the bank in town, where the seller was depositing the money. What we heard was that the same bank wouldn't give Dr. Beaumont a mortgage on another house he wanted, so he saved up and paid in full for this one in small bills, just to mess with them.

We loved that story. Wasn't negative to us. The bigot who told us (guess who)—yes, Sally, of course—thought the colored dentist was disrespectful and should have known his place. We had to bite our tongues to keep from asking what place she thought that was. Sally barely finished high school; her stinking house was falling down around her; mirrors cracked when they saw her coming; and still, she had the nerve to think herself some kind of Scarlett O'Hara of the North. She hated Velma, too—no surprise there—and the two of them went at it, but that's another story.

Dr. M. G. Beaumont was all right with us. We both had a dentist in town we'd seen since we were teenagers, but after we heard about the dollar bills, we made appointments with Dr. Beaumont just to shake the man's hand. And we liked him. He was a good dentist.

Phil and Velma didn't have any more parties on their lawn, and people eventually got over that day. After a while, when other neighbors saw that the Arringtons added onto their home, kept it up nicely, and didn't, in fact, bring crime or squalor or more Negroes to the neighborhood, everyone settled down.

It wasn't until Livia stopped coming on weekends—she went off to college—and Lisa and Maddie were about seven or eight that we realized Maddie wasn't being accepted the way Phil and Velma finally were. Lisa was upset at dinner one night and said that a couple of the mean Ferrell boys from down the hill told her she shouldn't play with the Arrington girl because colored people were trash. Our boys, Matthew and Anthony, were quiet at the table, looking down at their peas and carrots. We knew from the past they didn't like those kids. They'd said they were bullies, and from the way they'd said it, we had a feeling those boys had talked smack about us, too. Their parents gave us crap about our affairs, even though it didn't affect them in any way.

We'd gotten over it. *We* were good. The truth is, there was never any serious problem between us. We'd been "us" since seventh grade. But by our late twenties, we had a mortgage, two screaming babies, and no romance. We agreed we needed *something*. So, we got it. Not right in the neighborhood and not with any locals. Tourists. Up for the summer in the bungalows. We enjoyed ourselves, and then we came back together. That was the plan, all parties knew, and we stuck to it. Sure, there were some complications at the end, but there *was* an end; that was the main thing. Finito.

We asked Lisa what she said to those boys, and she brushed her red bangs back and squinted at us. "I told them to shove it," she said, "and to mind their business because Maddie's my friend, and I can play with whoever I want."

We weren't exactly thanking any angels about her saying "shove it," but she was our girl all right. Lisa was nobody's follower.

The next year—it was October '72—we noticed Maddie seemed down when we had our annual leaping-in-the-leaves party. She'd gone through a depression the year before, but she got better and that day she seemed out of it again. The way she threw herself off the swing into the leaves seemed like an adult jumping off a bridge.

It was strange to see a child act that way. We asked Lisa about her, and that's when she told us that there was a mock election in their fourth-grade class and that Nixon won twenty-one votes to only seven for McGovern. She said Maddie was one of the seven and that one of those bully-boys said only "niggers" and "nigger lovers" liked that pussy McGovern, and he would never win.

Now, that really did stun us. We'd taught our kids to be nice. They'd grown up around Maddie. They knew she was colored, but they'd known her from the time she was born, and we hoped they'd never say something like that. We thought everyone taught their kids to be nice. Even the ones who were prejudiced, because who wants their kids going around saying those kinds of things? It's bad parenting. And what color had to do with McGovern we didn't understand. His thing was getting out of Vietnam, we thought. But there must have been something to it. The kid got it from his parents.

There were people around here who didn't like the idea of Negroes being equal, civil rights, and all that. You couldn't avoid seeing that business on the news, the marching, and bodies being hosed and beaten. Now and then, we'd hear someone get loud, down at Fisherman's Feast or over at the bowling alley, giving their opinion, but we didn't pay all that much attention or think about the Arringtons as having anything to do with that, because it certainly wasn't happening here.

Well, when Lisa told us what happened in their classroom, we wondered if we should say something to Phil and Velma. Let them know that Maddie could count on Lisa. Our family didn't think the way that loud-mouthed kid from down the street did. We mulled it over for days and then we just couldn't. Phil and Velma didn't talk to us about that sort of thing. Maybe it was too uncomfortable—called attention to the fact that they were different. Velma would sometimes mention that she'd gotten into it with Sally, but she would stop short of mentioning anything about color. We knew it was about that, and she knew we knew it was, but she didn't say it. Didn't have to. Everybody knew what Sally's problem was. And Phil never mentioned anything at all. In fact, it wasn't until years after they'd been here that we heard about the way they were treated over in Walton Lake Estates. We were shocked to learn it happened right here in our town. There were no protests that we'd heard about when Dr. Beaumont moved into his house, and that wasn't but a few miles from Walton Lake Estates. We didn't think even Sally would've stooped that low. Well, she might have if other neighbors had been willing, but we weren't like that in our neighborhood. It's one thing not to want a whole bunch of colored people moving in and changing your way of life. It's quite another to throw eggs and rocks and hateful words at them.

The Arringtons didn't come here to change anyone's way of life. That's the thing we realized. They came to live, pretty much the way we live—to be good neighbors, to enjoy the peace and beauty of our small town, and to raise their family in a safe place. It didn't matter what color they were. They were good people. They were our friends. After a while, we really didn't see color anymore.

Pride

MONROE, NEW YORK, 1974

Velma

Livia's graduation from Harvard—excuse me, Harvard-Radcliffe—was really something. What a day. She didn't have to invite me, but she did. So what does that tell you? I was the one who spent the most time with her when she visited on weekends. Phil was off playing tennis half the time or downstairs drinking in his office. I took her shopping and to garage sales, and we both loved the art galleries over in Sugar Loaf. I taught Livia how to dress and do her makeup and how to decorate a room. Showed her a few things about investing and how to stretch a dollar, too. And before she left for Boston, she'd traveled with us to Europe, to the Caribbean, and to the Middle East. So, yeah, I brag about her like she's my own. Why shouldn't I? Our Harvard graduate. Wow.

Livia

Velma whipped me with a belt once when I was eleven. It was in the summer, and the screen door in the back of the house used to slam shut because the pneumatic cylinder was too tight. I didn't know that at the time. I was a child. But it's not a difficult problem to assess. A visit to the hardware store could've demystified it. Daddy didn't mind the slamming. He let it slam, too. But when *I* did it, Velma went berserk. I don't know why she didn't bother to get it fixed or figure out how to fix it herself. She preferred to yell, "Stop slamming that damn door!" And she expected me to take the time to hold the handle and close it manually. What kid, who's eager to run out and play, has the cognitive discipline to carefully close a maladjusted door on an inviting summer day?

Velma

I didn't go to college like Livia did, but since I've been in business, I've taken many courses on art and antiques—some at NYU, some at Cooper-Hewitt. Dealers have to keep learning. I could've gone to college. My father and brother both have degrees. But after high school, I wanted to *make money*. Right away. Got a job as a bookkeeper at a bank, and by the time I left—over ten years later—I'd had three promotions. I was a supervisor with several women working under me. White women, I might add, and this was the fifties into the early sixties.

My last promotion was just before Phil proposed, and when he did, y'know what my boss said when I sashayed into work with my diamond? He wouldn't've moved me into my new position if he'd known I was getting married. That's the kind of nonsense women have to deal with. Phil made me quit the job when I got pregnant with Maddie. Didn't like me having more money than him. Wanted me dependent. Having to ask for my allowance like a damn child. I could've had a killer career if I'd never gotten involved with that selfish son of a bitch.

Livia

I let that door slam one time too many. Velma ran into the yard after me. She grabbed my arm, pulled me back into the house, slipped off her belt, and whipped me, repeatedly, on the backs of my calves, screaming, "I told you to stop slamming that goddamn door! I'm not gonna tell you again, you hear me?"

No one had ever hit me. Not even my own mother, and she had no tolerance for kids. I was traumatized, but I learned my lesson. Velma was crazy, certifiable, like Daddy's patients.

Velma

Phil didn't know anything about money. I was the one who showed him how to invest in stocks. And it was my idea to buy real estate. I had the healthy savings account when we got married. He had debt. And not ten years later, he thought he was gonna divorce me? I gave up a career, my independence, and my figure to marry his philandering ass. Screwed up my body growing his baby. Helped buy the house, raise his kid—and the stepkid, too—and he thought he could toss me aside like an old sweater. Well, guess what? He can't *afford* a divorce from me.

I couldn't believe what he was doing at first. Because who in their right mind would chase after trash like *that* when he had class like *me*? And he's *still* runnin' around looking for trouble. Gonna end up with VD one of these days—you watch. His ding-a-ling's gonna shrivel up and fall off. And I'll be looking at him, like, *Now what, you knuckleheaded, no-dick numbskull?*

Livia

Velma seemed to stay angry. Any little thing unnerved her. If you ate the last cookie. If you accidentally spilled anything—even water. If you didn't make your bed her way. She didn't hit me again after that belting, but there was one time, several years ago, when I knew she wanted to. I was sixteen and visiting for the weekend. Threw my stuff on the bed in the guest room and then pulled the knob on the nightstand drawer, looking for a pen I kept there. I loved its design. The swirling multigreen celluloid was like a spearmint candy stick. The pen once belonged to my father's father, and it had lived in that spot since Daddy moved into the house.

But the drawer was empty, save for the Bible with the white-leather cover Grandma Emily had given me when I finished elementary school. I shook the Bible over the bed, hoping the pen would tumble out. It didn't. My grandfather's 1920s Sheaffer fountain pen was *gone*. I'd just bought a new jar of ink for it, too. It meant something to me to see that little piece of history tucked inside the drawer. His pen was a reminder that I came from somewhere. It was a connection to a man I never knew, who loved my father and who would have loved me, too, had he lived to meet me. Daddy would never let me take the pen home to the Bronx. The rule was it lived in his house, even though he said I could have it, and I didn't get to live in his house.

Velma

Even at Livia's graduation, Phil's eyes were roving. Looking at girls his daughter's age. And I know he's still screwing around at his office in Manhattan. I can't say it doesn't eat at me or that I don't miss the days when he used to look at me like I was a present he couldn't wait to open. But I'm not going to leave and be one of these struggling divorced women, living in a dump and eating sardines from a can. He can go ahead and do what he wants, as long as he keeps the bills paid. I'll survive. *I* won't be the one getting any nasty diseases; I'll tell you *that*.

Livia

Anyone could've taken it since the room wasn't really mine. After Maddie's teenage babysitter tried to kill herself in the bathroom, there'd been a string of Haitian women living with them, one after the other. They cooked and took care of Maddie until, inevitably, each reached an impasse with Velma. Could've been one of them or some other overnight guest.

Velma

We took Livia out to lunch after the graduation, and later, she had some friends over at her boyfriend's apartment for champagne and dessert. I had to use the ladies' room and asked Phil to keep an eye on Madeline. You think he did? He was too busy chatting up some young friend of Livia's. Maddie was restless. She'd been sitting around all day with no kids to play with. She did a handstand or a cartwheel, and she ended up knocking into the table. That was Phil's fault. She was eleven years old. I told him to keep an eye on her. I couldn't watch her every damn second. I came out of the bathroom and saw the chocolate cake—*splat*—on the hardwood floor, looking like something our Great Dane pooped out his butt. Livia was yelling. Maddie was crying. And Phil's useless ass was tucked in a corner with a white girl young enough to be his child.

Livia

I walked out of the guest room, stood on the balcony, and called down to Velma. She was in the kitchen. I asked who'd visited recently. In typical, attitudinal form, she said, "What business is that of yours?" I told her about the pen, and she said, "Well, I don't know what to tell you. Nobody's been here. You must've misplaced it."

Daddy was out. I couldn't ask him. If no one had visited, I figured Miss Madeline pain-in-the-ass pumpkin was the likely thief. She'd developed a habit of poking through people's stuff—pocketbooks, suitcases, drawers, and closets. And spoiled as she was, sometimes she'd pilfer little things she wanted.

I walked to her room, which used to be next to the guest room but was now down the hall—the old master bedroom. Daddy and Velma had a *new* master bedroom on the other side of the house, where they'd added on. Maddie's new room was almost twice the size of the one I slept in, even though, at six years old, she was half the size of me.

I knew where she stashed her trinkets. She collected all manner of baubles: stones, shells, foreign coins, unusual buttons—a mélange of assorted junk—in a Buster Brown shoebox she kept under her bed.

I knelt on the carpet and lifted the purple bed skirt. There were dusty shoes, a beat-up teddy bear, and a pair of orange sunglasses under there. But no box. She'd hid it somewhere else. I let out a noise, something like a growl, and said, "I'm gonna fucking strangle her." When I lowered the bed skirt and turned, Velma was standing in the doorway with her arms folded.

She had a look in her eye like she was about to break my butt. Velma smacked Maddie around and constantly bullied her, but if anybody else so much as threatened the kid, it flipped her switch. I dove past her out of the room. And thank God I was wearing tennis shoes. She was on my heels as I flew down the hallway, jumped all seven steps, made it into the kitchen and out the back door, which, now that I think about it, might have slammed.

I ran down to the waterfall. There was a little island in the stream beneath it that I'd usually get to by climbing down the grassy hill opposite the sidewalk, then stepping across a few chunky rocks to the middle of the stream onto a lone patch of land. You had to step carefully if you didn't want your feet to get wet. Velma would never take that chance. I'd be safe there until Daddy got home.

There was a birch tree on the island with a low branch that created a small nook to sit on. For years, I'd park myself there with my sketch pad when I needed to get away.

But that day, when I ran toward the waterfall, before I even reached the corner, I saw Madeline across the street with two little Black girls, sisters, browner than she was, from a family who lived on the other side of the underpass in town. It was rare to see any Black people in Monroe, so three of them together must have startled passersby. They were wearing two ponytails each, looking like fraternal triplets. They stood on the sidewalk near the silver railing above the stream, their silhouettes contrasting with the white water thundering down behind them in sheets. I would've drawn them if I'd had my supplies.

Then I saw that Maddie had our father's old shoeshine kit on the sidewalk in front of her with one sneaker up on the cast-iron footrest. Like the missing pen, the kit had belonged to our grandfather.

All three girls were waving to cars stopped at the light on the corner. It looked like they were trying to flag customers.

The nice thing about Monroe was that it was safe enough for small kids to be out by themselves. And the bad thing about it was that, because it was safe, people weren't always watching what their dim-witted offspring were doing. I knew nothing of the other kids' financial situation, but they looked healthy, well-dressed, and well-groomed enough to conclude that they didn't need to earn their own living just yet. What I did know for sure was that our father hadn't earned a doctorate to see his daughter stand on the corner and shine anybody's shoes, especially here in Monroe.

I ran across the street and grabbed the shoeshine box with one hand and my simpleminded sister with the other. I pulled her away from her friends, back toward the house. I wasn't scared of Velma at that moment, because Maddie's transgressions—going into Daddy's closet, taking the shoeshine kit without permission, removing it from the house, and crossing Route 17M without an adult—were way worse than what I'd done.

On the way home she whined and wriggled out of my grasp and into the middle of Stage Road. I caught her by the wrist and yanked her the rest of the way up the street and then finally pulled her up the steep driveway. She must have lost her footing. By the time we got to the top, she was on the ground, and I saw that her knees were scraped raw—pink and white, like a sliced grapefruit. Blood oozed down her shins.

She was screaming as we went inside. Velma gave me a steely-eyed look that meant she'd deal with me later. I told her the mischief Maddie had been up to.

Maddie said, "She hurt me. She pushed me down and dragged me up the driveway!"

I looked at Velma. "I did not. She must've scraped herself on the sidewalk."

Velma eyed Maddie and shook her head. "You are one clumsy kid."

Maddie wailed like a siren.

Without another word, Velma carried her up to the bathroom. She didn't seem angry about the shoeshine kit. I stood in the doorway as she sat Maddie on the pink tile counter, took off her bloody sneakers, and washed her legs in the sink. Then she dabbed Mercurochrome on the scrapes. Maddie sniffled, squinted, and gave me the most malicious look she could. Velma covered the scrapes with wide-sized Band-Aids.

Finally, I asked Maddie, "Did you take my pen out of the guest room?"

"Is that what you were looking for?" Velma asked.

Velma

When Livia saw that splattered cake, she started shrieking about how Maddie always ruined everything. Maddie pulled up her pant legs and showed the scars on her knees that Livia had given her when she was six. And then Livia brought up that damn pen and how no one respected her things. Jesus, both those girls could hold a grudge like a tug-of-war death match. That situation was Phil's fault. He never mentioned anything about an heirloom. The only thing in *drawers* that man was ever concerned about was white women's private parts. I sold that pen in my shop. *I* found it in *my* house; it was collectible, and I sold it. So what? It's not like it was rare. Those pens were mass-produced.

And no, I didn't admit it. What difference would it have made? Livia was gonna blame Maddie whether she knew what happened to it or not. In her mind, Maddie had the thing she really wanted.

I don't believe Livia gave a nib tip about that pen. What she cared about was that it had been given to *her* and not to Maddie. I bought her another one.

Livia

The next time I visited, Velma told me she found the pen in Daddy's office. That wasn't true. My grandfather's initials were engraved on the gold-plated clip. The engraving was worn down, barely perceptible, but I paid attention to details like that. I didn't let on that I knew she was lying. If you knew her, you'd understand it was better to let it go.

A couple of years ago, our dog Brutus ate one of Maddie's miniature turtles, and it was Velma's fault. While Maddie was at school, Velma had gone into her room, where the turtles were, to read her diary. Maddie was ten, so I don't know what she thought she'd discover. She left the door open. Brutus trotted in there and helped himself to a snack from the terrarium. Velma drove down to Grants. I was visiting from Boston and went with her. She bought Maddie another turtle.

"She'll never know the difference," she said.

"You sure about that?" I asked.

And she said, "Livia, please." She set the turtle in its place without saying anything.

When Maddie came home, her response was immediate. "That's not Archie. You tried to trick me, Mommy!"

Velma slapped her across the face and called her ungrateful.

Velma

I always did my best to make Livia feel included. Tried to do things with the girls together. Once, I took them to the pediatrician in town to get their ears pierced. Maddie was four. Livia was fourteen. She went in first and screamed bloody murder just to mess with Maddie.

Of course, Maddie did *not* get her ears pierced that day, which was Livia's plan. Couldn't blame her. I could understand her wanting to have something just for herself. And to be honest, the way she carried on in the doctor's office, like it was excruciating, made me laugh. We could hear her in the waiting room. Maddie's eyes were as big as tennis balls, and her mouth hung open. I asked if she still wanted to get her ears pierced, and she shook her head, looking at me like my cake wasn't baked.

Livia

Velma was . . . difficult. It wasn't just my opinion. There was a consensus. For a while, I wondered why, because from my perspective, she had a house and people to help her with it, nice things, and her own business; her life seemed better than my mother's. And though my mother wasn't exactly nice to me, she wasn't mean like Velma either.

Then, a few years ago, we went to visit Velma's parents in Harlem. I'd just turned seventeen, and it was during Easter vacation. Velma's mother could *cook*. Our family didn't come from people who made magic in the kitchen like that—Grandma Emily loved me to bits, and she tried, but she boiled everything. Even hamburgers. She left Bermuda to come to the States at eighteen, and I guess no one taught her.

But dinner at Velma's parents' house? Her mother grew up in South Carolina, and her father was from Jamaica, and oh, the flavors danced across my palate like a culinary tour de force. I was mostly preoccupied with eating, though I did notice that Velma kept calling her mother by her first name. Althea. I'd met her parents before, though only briefly. I hadn't spent time with them. Velma would never let Maddie call her by her first name. She insisted on "respect." I was curious why she wouldn't give her mother what she demanded for herself. On the drive back to Monroe, I asked, "Why do you call your mother Althea instead of Mom?"

You would have thought I asked what year she was born, how much she weighed, when she lost her virginity, and if she had boils on her butt.

"You need to mind your goddamn business," she shouted. "You don't know better than to ask personal questions like that? What the hell is wrong with you?"

She went on ranting. I tuned it out. Maddie hugged herself like she was scared.

Daddy finally said, "That's enough, Velma."

I knew the woman was out of her mind so I shrugged it off, though I was no less curious.

That night, after Velma and Maddie had gone to bed, I was still awake and heard Daddy playing jazz on the hi-fi downstairs. I went to his office and found him at his desk, scribbling on a yellow legal pad and sipping scotch, with Brutus splayed out at his feet like a rug. I curled into the patients' recliner across from him.

He filled a pipe with tobacco, lit up, and sat back in his chair. "Sorry about the way Velma spoke to you today, kiddo. She can be pretty touchy."

"Why couldn't she tell me why she calls her mother Althea? What's the big deal?"

He looked off for a while and pinched the bridge of his nose, as if his sinuses were bothering him. Then he leaned toward me, rested his forearms on his thighs, and said, "It's a secret, Liv. She doesn't want anyone to know."

"If she doesn't want anyone to know why she calls her mother by her first name, maybe she shouldn't call her mother by her first name."

He sucked on the pipe and then exhaled, smiling. "Velma does plenty of things that don't make sense." The smoke bore a hint of vanilla.

"You're going to tell me, right?" I asked. "You know I can keep a secret."

He scratched his cheek. "You should ask her yourself."

"After the way she chewed my face off and spit it at me?"

"Livia, it's *her* business. Let her tell you." He sipped his scotch.

"Fine. You know what?" I stood. "Why do I even bother to come here?"

"What are you talking about? I'm here, honey."

I walked out of the room and headed toward the stairs. He stood up, and I heard him take a step. Then a stomp. It sounded like he'd stumbled. I turned around, and he was still on his feet but with his arms out, as if catching his balance. Drunk.

I moved toward him. "Are you all right?"

Brutus was looking up at us from the floor.

Daddy fell back into his chair. "She's . . . *adopted*," he said slowly.

I didn't move for a moment. My brain was recalibrating. How did I not know this?

Now he spoke as if his mouth were moving through something viscous. "She doesn't want people to think less of her."

I leaned against the doorframe. "Why would they think less of her?"

His next words came out like a long sigh. "Iiii can't tell you that, Livia." There was a pause as some inner thought made him shake his head. "But . . . some of Velma's . . . behavioral idiosyncrasies stem from things that happened to her."

"Oh. Really?"

He nodded. "Childhood trauma."

I went back to the chair and perched on the edge. "So that's why she's so mean?"

He set the pipe into an ashtray on his desk. Then he picked up his glass and swirled it in a circle. "She doesn't always empathize with others' feelings," he said, still slurring a bit, his tone occasionally ascending and then descending like notes on a scale. "And I think she's sometimes unaware of her own feelings. As a child, she had to suppress them. If she'd felt everything when she was abandoned, she couldn't have survived. So, my sweet," he said with a sad smile, "don't take everything she does to heart."

"How old was she when she was separated from her parents?"

"Four? Five?" he said, shrugging. "That's what she told me."

"Why does she call her father *Dad* and her mother *Althea*?"

He breathed in and out and stared in front of him at nothing. He was thinking, probably about whether he should say any more. He ran a hand from his forehead over his curly hair. "His mother was caring for Velma through the foster care system before he was married. She already knew him as a father figure by the time he met Althea."

Interesting. And the p-i-t-a pumpkin knew none of this. Daddy said she wasn't going to know until she went to college.

If she went to college, I thought.

I remembered how devastating it was when *one* parent left me. I pictured a tiny Velma, left by two. Maybe she never got over it. I could understand that.

Velma

I know both girls think I'm nuts. That's their father's doing. I could've punched him when he told Livia my business. He did not need to do that. It's *my* past. It's got nothing to do with either of those girls. Phil thinks every damn thing is because of your childhood. That's stupid. My childhood wasn't easy, but I'm fine. And my discipline hasn't hurt Livia. She graduated from Harvard, for Christ's sake. It hasn't harmed Maddie either. It's taught them both how to behave. I hit Livia *one* time. Not because of my childhood. But because my one-year-old kept me up all fucking night, and she'd gone down for a nap when Livia slammed that goddamn screen door and woke her up. Excuse the hell outta me for being tired and losing my temper. They can criticize and analyze all they want. I've done damn well. Got myself out of Harlem. Traveled the world. I love my work. And I'm a doctor's wife with an Ivy League–educated daughter. So what does that tell you? I must be doing something right.

Far Away from Here

MONROE, NEW YORK, 1971

Maddie

Maddie wears pink tights, pink slippers, and a black leotard. Her hair frizzes out of careless braids. With thighs like sausages in a crowd of Slim Jim legs, she's the only honey-colored girl piqué-turning across the floor among her mostly blonde third-grade friends.

She's been home from vacation in West Africa for nearly two months. And still, she hasn't told her parents that she was sucked, licked, prodded, and probed against her will for hours when they left her with a babysitter at Hotel Ivoire in Abidjan so they could attend a party at the American ambassador's house. She tries to forget, to wish it away.

Finished with spinning from one side of the room to the other, Maddie now stands in the center of the studio, in the second row with the other girls.

Mrs. Kannel, the teacher, dances a combination as she faces the wall-length mirror. The girls follow behind. Kannel demonstrates the choreography multiple times. Maddie forgets some of the routine, as she has done before. This doesn't bother her. She likes learning the steps and being around the other kids. She follows along as best she can and enjoys the music—classical piano.

Kannel pivots to face the class and watches, keen-eyed, as the girls execute the moves she's just demonstrated. Maddie smiles and follows the bodies in front of her. She's having a good time.

Kannel, in a black V-neck, long-sleeved leotard and skirt, studies Maddie like prey.

Maddie notices Mrs. Kannel's dark bangs, dark-brown irises, and red lips, and it seems she's staring at her for longer than usual. And she's not smiling. Mrs. Kannel is nice on the days Maddie's mother drives for the carpool. Today, Kimmy's mom has driven.

When the combination ends and the piano stops, Kannel orders Maddie to step forward into the front row. Maddie obeys, though she trembles now because she knows she needs to watch someone in front of her to follow the steps. She changes places with Kimmy, who's elegant and tall, even at their age. Maddie feels schlubby in comparison.

Kannel tells the piano player to start, and then she commands Maddie—*only* Maddie—to do it again.

Maddie dances the first few steps she can remember. Soon, she stops and stands there. Still. Mrs. Kannel crosses her graceful arms. Her bright blood-colored lips tighten as she frowns. Maddie smiles timidly, with the hope of cajoling the woman out of her dour demeanor. It's not that she doesn't care about ballet or that she's intentionally being disruptive. Maddie's been depressed and going through a hard time. Trauma has rewired her brain, and she's different since the event. Her ability to focus is impaired. She's tried to pretend it wasn't real, but what happened *was* real; a man touched all her private parts, and she doesn't know what to do with this reality. *Processing* it isn't yet in her vocabulary, nor is the term *sexual assault*. Maddie's afraid to tell, because her mother has explicitly stated that she's not allowed to let anyone touch her private parts. Maddie's afraid Velma will hit her if she finds out. She worries she'll be blamed, as she's typically blamed for everything that makes her mother mad.

Kannel knows nothing of Maddie's troubles. She only knows Maddie is messing up in her class. She glowers. Then she steps forward, leans into Maddie's face, and in an exceedingly scornful tone says, "Duuuh-*uuuuh*."

This hits Maddie like a blow to the chest. She winces, stunned by this grown woman implying she's a "retard" in front of her friends. Maddie doesn't use that word, and Mrs. Kannel doesn't say it, but she knows what her teacher means because bullies taunt the slow kids at school in the same way.

She blinks at Kannel and feels her face grow warm, a crushing shame squeezing her heart. Her forehead begins to sweat.

Maddie is too young to understand the "low expectations" some educators have of children of color. She worries that everyone thinks she's dumb. Standing on the hardwood floor, she stares up into her teacher's inhospitable face. She doesn't cry. She numbs herself and then turns and walks across the floor, through smells of sweat and hairspray and across tiny rocks of resin, as she makes her escape.

When the empty dressing room embraces her and the grace of solitude sets in, Maddie lands on the floor in a small ball, knees pressed into her eyes, hugging her arms around her legs, elbows in her hands. She stays like this until the urge to sob passes. Soon, she grabs her Danskin pants from the cubby and pulls them on over her tights. She changes her shoes and sits back on the floor, cross-legged now, surrounded by dance bags as she listens to the piano in the next room and to the distressing sound of Kannel's voice until class is over and she's free to leave.

On the ride home, Kimmy's mother drives her Ford station wagon with the wood-paneled exterior, and Kimmy, who's kind, pats Maddie's thigh and sits beside her in the back, sharing her silence, though she could speak with Bunny, who's in the front seat bragging about how she'll be going on pointe soon. Bunny, who has silky hair like Kimmy's, is perpetually good at everything.

Kimmy's attractive mother, with the coiffed platinum hair, eyes Maddie in the rearview mirror occasionally and says nothing. Maddie likes Kimmy's mother, despite finding her puzzling.

Intriguing. The woman regularly gives the impression she's thinking a multitude of things while revealing none of them.

When Maddie gets home from ballet, she sits at the round oak table in the kitchen in front of the sliding glass doors and stares out into the backyard. There are a lot of trees, and the leaves are turning yellow and orange, some beginning to fall. Brutus is stretched out, snoring a few feet away. Velma drops a Swanson's TV dinner on the table. Maddie's mother feeds her these when her father stays at his Manhattan office. Maddie hopes her beautiful mommy is going to sit down and eat with her. She doesn't. Velma strides across the room in a ruby-red blouse that makes her skin glow and goes to the desk where mail lives in messy bunches beneath the wall phone.

Maddie doesn't hate Swanson's. The fried chicken is dry, yet crispy and salty, and it's good to her young taste buds. But she manages only a few bites. She would like her mother to ask about her day. She's heard other mothers ask their daughters about their days.

Her mother slits open an envelope with what looks like a dagger. Her long-lashed eyes find Maddie's peering back at her. "Something wrong with the TV dinner? You usually love them."

"I'm not hungry, Mommy." She has her attention. Maybe she'll hear it in Maddie's voice. Maybe she'll ask.

The phone rings.

Velma's face dims. "Now, you know we don't waste food around here. Sit there till you finish it, please." She picks up the receiver and carries it on the long cord out through the swinging door and into the dining room.

Maddie quickly scoops some mashed potatoes into her hand and tiptoes to where Brutus is lying on his thin bed. He's also leashed to the black metal banister of the stairs that lead up to her parents' bedroom. The dog slowly lifts his big head and licks the white mush off her fingers.

Maddie feels sorry for Brutus. Her mother chains him up in the house like a prisoner when her father isn't home. And when he's naughty—for instance, if he growls at her mother or eats something off the table when he's free—she punishes the dog by chaining him to a tree in the backyard and throwing stones at him. Her mother says dogs don't have feelings. Maddie thinks grown-ups know everything, but she's convinced Brutus *does* have feelings. He must. She's heard him cry when he's sad.

Velma returns to the kitchen through the swinging door, still on the phone.

Maddie swiftly glissades back to the table and sits, unsure if Velma has seen her or not. She takes a bite of chicken.

"Oh, Caitlin, honey," Velma says, "thank you so much for calling, dear." Her voice is full of kind concern. "I'm gonna miss you, too, sweetie . . . You sure you'll be okay? . . . All right, then. Be sure to write me and let me know how you're doing. Stay safe, now. Bye-bye." Velma hangs up, sniffles and, without looking at Maddie, walks past her and Brutus and up the stairs into her bedroom. She closes the door.

Her mother rarely uses the warm, kind voice she just used with Caitlin when she speaks to Maddie. Maddie doesn't think that's fair. She gets up and plops her plate, along with the silver TV dinner tray, onto the kitchen counter.

Caitlin was Maddie's babysitter when she was little. She had long, pretty hair, like Maddie wished *she* had, and she used to make Maddie go to bed before her bedtime. Then she'd bring her boyfriend into the house. Maddie spied on them from the balcony outside her bedroom door when they kissed on the couch in the living room. She told her mother, and her mother said, "Y'know, nobody likes a tattletale."

Maddie heads to the stairway that leads down to her daddy's home-office waiting room. The stairs are covered in new mustard-colored carpet that feels cozy on her butt, like someone's lap. She often sits in this spot in the center of the house, alone with her thoughts. As she sees it, Mrs. Kannel hates her, and everyone thinks she's an idiot. They already believe they're better than her and feel sorry for her because she's Black, and being Black is like being poor or handicapped or whatever's the worst thing you can be when you live in Monroe.

"What's going on? What are you doing here?"

Maddie turns to look up at her mother. Her mouth feels dry.

Velma folds her arms and eyes her questioningly. When Maddie doesn't answer, Velma frowns.

Maddie's eyes move to Velma's stocking feet, where a corn on her left baby toe is visible through the sheer fabric. She clears her throat. "I don't want to go to ballet anymore," she says.

Velma exhales loudly. "Huh. So, you're a *quitter*? You know, quitters don't amount to anything."

Maddie turns away from her and stares at the black-and-white tiles on the floor at the base of the carpeted stairs. She doesn't cry. She's trained herself to zone out. Expressing emotions leads to punishment. And her mother's harsh reply is merely one of an incalculable number of cruelties she's sent Maddie's way, not only with words but with walls she's slammed her into, open palms, blunt objects, and long silences.

Years later, Maddie will wish her mother had asked what happened. Velma *doesn't* ask. She never will. And when, in adulthood, Maddie finally shares what Kannel did to her that day, Velma will laugh and laugh.

Maddie sits, hunch-shouldered, on the carpeted step and feels her mother's eyes sear into her back.

"All right," Velma says. "*Don't* amount to anything. You think I care? Fine."

She's tried her best to be a good girl. But that day, a voice whispers to her from somewhere within, and Maddie turns, faces her mother, and tells her exactly what the voice says. "You're a mean lady. And if you're not nicer to me, when you get old, I'm gonna stick you in the home and leave you there."

Maddie's not exactly sure what "the home" means or where it is. But she's pleased with the courage she's somehow had to utter these words.

Velma's lips part, but she's speechless as she gapes at Maddie. Her eyes darken from brown to black. Her jaw clenches. She lunges, swinging a hand, and socking Maddie in the head so hard the little girl's ear stings, and she sees stars pirouetting through her mind's eye.

The front door is down the steps. Maddie stumbles toward it and doesn't look back. Dazed, she cannot run, but she walks out and makes her way slowly to the driveway and then onto the sidewalk. Maybe she's running away.

She has no jacket, and it's getting cold. The sun is setting. Holding her sore ear, Maddie heads down the hill toward the waterfall at the corner. When halfway there, in front of the brick house two doors down, she sees her redheaded next-door neighbor Lisa Megna a few yards away, heading up the sidewalk. Lisa is wearing a bright yellow sweater, and she's with her older brother, Matthew, who's in gray sweats. Matthew jiggles change in his sweatpants pocket with one hand, and with the other, he carries a paper bag from Palen's Drugstore, probably full of Hershey bars, his favorite. Lisa's candied yam–colored hair flops against her shoulders as she skips toward Maddie.

When they meet, Lisa is smiling wide, her two front teeth only half grown in, and Maddie is moved to be greeted by someone who's happy to see her. As they hug, Maddie's tears let loose, waterfalling down her face.

Lisa leans back, eyes big and round as quarters. "What happened?"

"I wish I had a different mom. Mine hates me!"

Lisa embraces her again. "Oh, don't say that, Maddie. Don't say that. Your mother's your best friend." Without letting go, Lisa twists her neck toward Matthew, as if to ask for confirmation.

Matthew Megna is tall, dark-haired, and cute, in Maddie's opinion. He's eleven and has never been a chatty boy. He smiles at Maddie a bit sadly and without teeth, and then he shrugs in a way that says, *Maybe. Maybe not.*

Maddie knows Lisa means well, but Lisa's mom is normal. She can't understand. "I'm going to the island," Maddie says.

Matthew takes off his sweatshirt and hands it to her.

"That's nice of you. I'll give it back," she promises, taking it. She puts it on and lets its sleeves cover her chilly hands. Then she trots down the street. She covers her throbbing ear with her hand. It's warm. Her cheek aches, too.

At the traffic light, a cobalt-blue VW Bug beeps at Maddie. The driver waves. Maddie squints to get a better look. It's a teenage girl with long dark hair. Maddie scoffs. She isn't up to waving back at Caitlin, the one her mother talks to like she's a treasure. She crosses 17M and descends the grassy hill to the bank of the stream. She navigates over the rocks in the water to a spot of land in the center where there's a birch tree. She leans on a branch and stares up at the waterfall, letting its gushing sounds soothe her like a lullaby.

Maddie won't know this as she rests against the tree, but Caitlin has just turned eighteen and bought that car, and she's leaving Monroe to escape her abusive father.

The first star blinks on in the sky. Maddie stares up and marvels at how far away it must be. She wishes for the day she can be every bit as far away from here.

Far Away from There

NEW YORK CITY, 2022

Maddie

As Maddie rereads the message on her laptop, a flush of heat rises within her. It expands to her barely lined fifty-nine-year-old cheeks and long neck, which, not as blessed as her cheeks, is beginning to sag. She blows air through slightly parted full lips and begins to perspire, the flying monkey's note riling her considerably. She pulls a drape of graying curls off her back with both hands and loops it into a thick knot that stays put. She turns from the standing desk toward a window that stretches the length of her apartment and faces urban treetops clinging to their last days of green, a mourning dove perched in one.

It's not yet nine in the morning. Traffic rumbles down Lexington Avenue. Maddie's still wearing the rumpled black sweats she slept in and sipping coffee with collagen from a white mug. She hasn't worked out or showered, which puts her behind schedule. There are multiple tunes to review for a show that night. Fortunately, her partner is at their weekend house in Connecticut, giving her space to rehearse.

> Maddie,
>
> I saw your mother at her shop yesterday.
>
> She was stunning, as usual. Fully made up, tailored gray slacks, a white silk shirt, and heels. Stylish as ever.
>
> And thanks to you, she was sad. Shame on you.
>
> She mentioned your letter again and that you're still not speaking to her.

Velma's getting older, Maddie. She won't be around much longer, and then how will you feel?

She's your mother. She misses you. If you could find it in your heart and time in your busy schedule to call her, that would be so nice.

Caitlyn

Caitlyn needs to mind her fucking business. As Maddie's forehead creases into a frown, she stops it with two fingers pressed between her brows. Face yoga. Turning back to the Facebook message, she hisses, "Of all people, *you* should know that when an adult isn't in touch with a parent, they've tried everything possible to get along with them. When said parent can't control their toxic behavior, no contact is the last option. It's either cut them off or be undermined, riddled with anxiety, and unable to function."

What a day for this bullshit. She needs to focus on tonight's gig. Headlining at the Blue Note is a big deal. She paces the parquet floor. Maddie doesn't have the bandwidth to deal with Caitlyn or Velma or self-doubt today. As she eyes her pedicured feet, her heartbeat drums in her ears. The mere idea of being in touch with Velma again induces panic in her thumping heart and jittery stomach, yet she can't kick the propensity to defend herself.

"Flying monkey" is a term spawned by *The Wizard of Oz*. It refers to the creatures that swooped in to do the dirty work of the Wicked Witch. These days, it's used to describe creatures like Caitlyn, who do the dirty work of a narcissist, like Velma.

It can be challenging to explain cutting off an elderly parent.

As Maddie finishes her coffee, she walks to the retro kitchen with its red appliances and festive mint-green walls. She sets her mug in the sink and thinks of the many musical events the birth-giver made about herself when she once-in-a-million-moons showed up. She remembers the times Velma didn't bother to come—there were plenty of those—and she watched and waited and hoped. Sometimes Velma got there as Maddie's set was ending so everyone could witness her grand entrance. She'd swoop in, harried and histrionic, not ask how it went, and then prattle on about the unreliability of New Jersey Transit. Later, she'd call and, without a trace of irony, ask, "Who said I was pretty?"

The woman cut Maddie down over and over. So why can't she stop feeling guilty?

When Caitlyn Gore was fourteen, the story goes, she attempted suicide in the Arringtons' bathroom one night while she was supposed to be watching Maddie, who was four at the time. Velma repeatedly tells "Monroe tales," in which she's the hero. This is one of them. Paraphrased. She came home and found lanky, long-haired Caitlyn, whom she adored, unconscious on the pink-tiled bathroom floor. She got the child to the ER in time for them to pump her stomach of the full bottle of sleeping pills she'd scarfed down. She saved Caitlyn's life.

"Yeah, yeah. Yay, Velma. Never a concern about how she left me with you, Caitlyn," Maddie says, reentering the large living room filled with standing and hanging plants. "*You* were irresponsible. And if I had been you, I'd be dead. She would've been pissed off that I took her sleeping pills. She probably would have slapped me and given me a speech about how lucky I was and how ungrateful and then left me on the floor to die after telling me I looked fat and how much thinner she was at my age. Later, at my funeral—if she even *gave* me a funeral—she'd shrug and say it served me right. She'd never wonder *why* I killed myself. She wouldn't care because everything in Velma's world is about Velma. 'Your mother was stunning.' Fuck you, Caitlyn. I've had to hear about how fucking beautiful Velma is from every-damn-body, including Velma, for almost sixty years. She's a mean, ninety-something monster who still drives, works, shops, cooks, and goes up and down stairs because she doesn't want to go into a nursing home and because she's outlived almost everyone, and the only one left who wants to deal with her is you."

As Velma tells it, Sally Gore, Caitlyn's racist mother, found it humiliating that Caitlyn was working for the Arringtons, which she and her husband had, unbeknownst to Velma, forbidden. Even more embarrassing was that Velma, an uppity "N-word" (their description, per Caitlyn), was privy to their family's problems. When they pumped Caitlyn's stomach, the teenager told the doctor she felt unloved and unwanted, and she'd like to die. The doctor then articulated this to the Gores in the ER waiting room—in front of Velma, which she repeatedly recounts with glee when she speaks of how she witnessed Sally and her runt husband being lambasted by the doctor.

Unloved and unwanted? When Maddie was still talking to Velma, she had the nerve to tell her this story over and over with her imperious judgment and lack of self-awareness, as if she had ever made Maddie feel loved or wanted.

"When I was eight, I told her if she wasn't nicer to me, I was gonna stick her in the home and leave her there. Did she tell you that, Caitlyn? The woman barely remembers my childhood, gives zero fucks about it. Gave me back all the photos I'm in—didn't want them—can't remember anything I went through, but she remembers I said *that*."

Sometime after Caitlyn's suicide attempt, Sally threatened to slap Velma when Brutus, their Great Dane, defecated on the edge of the Gores' property. Velma claims she didn't know it was their property. She thought it was the woods. Maddie wouldn't be surprised if she did it on purpose because Sally was so hateful, she wanted the Arringtons, the only Black family in the neighborhood, to leave. The word was, she tried to get other neighbors to help her. She failed, but Velma found out. The dog was large, and his excrement was considerable. Velma claims she quickly cursed Sally out and disabused the woman of any notion that her whiteness would protect her from a swift slap *back*. Velma thought Sally was low class. She said the woman expected her to be deferential, like Black maids in the movies, but Velma was no one's maid; she *had* a maid, Gertie, who was white. Velma was a doctor's wife who shopped at Saks Fifth Avenue and vacationed on other continents. Sally wore flip-flops and curlers to the grocery store, and neighbors said her house smelled like something had died in it.

Caitlyn moved back to Monroe following the death of her abusive father. He was an old, racist relic, in Maddie's opinion. In 2006, she went home for her friend Lisa's mother's funeral, and Mr. Gore was still slinging slurs like Monroe was a Cracker Barrel Confederate state, and he was the grand wizard of the KKK. When Sally finally croaked, hopped a broom, and flew her ass home to Satan last year, Caitlyn began visiting Velma at her antique shop. Velma can be as nasty as Sally was. Maddie guesses that's what Caitlyn likes about her.

Sally called Maddie the N-word on Oakland Avenue when she was in sixth grade. She was bundled up and climbing off the school bus in her snow boots complaining to Lisa that Ricky, Sally's scraggly haired, snaggletoothed son, called her that, and Sally, who happened to be there to pick Ricky up, said in her gruff, throat-full-of-smoke voice, "You *are* a nigger. You *are*." While it was not the first time Maddie had been called the slur in that neighborhood, it was the first time she'd been called one to her face by an adult. The way Sally said it was like she was telling Maddie she was less than human. And Maddie was too young not to feel the sting. She told her mother, and Velma's response was, "Oh, so what? That fleabag bitch threatened to slap me once."

"People like Velma and Sally want to tell you they did their 'best.' But did they, Caitlyn? Did they really? If I had a husband or wife who treated me the way my mother does, people would be supportive of my ending the relationship. They'd tell me I was a fool not to have done it sooner. But when it's *your mother*—oh, then, never mind.

'C'mon,' you say, 'she's an old lady. You only get one mother.' *Yes.* And only one life."

Maddie's fingers click across the keys as she blocks Caitlyn on Facebook. She takes a few deep, centering breaths and pushes through her anxiety. She's been programmed to prioritize her mother's feelings and to feel guilty when she doesn't.

She does stretches, a core workout, and curls and flies with a set of ten-pound weights. She showers and changes into yoga pants and a T-shirt. Then, for over an hour, she works at her upright piano, reviewing songs. While practicing one of the more complicated jazz compositions, her fingers feel heavy and move too slowly for the tempo. She hums rather than sings the vocals, preserving her voice.

When her iPhone buzzes and she sees the text that's come in, her body tightens.

SUZY

Hey. Don't trip, but I just got off the phone with my mother, and she just spoke to your mother, who told her she has tickets to your show tonight.

"Caitlyn's" taking her? Who dat? And WTF? Hasn't it been like a decade since Aunt Velma showed up at your shows?

She's suddenly willing to let someone take her almost-hundred-year-old ass into the city? O-kay . . .

Thought I'd give you a heads-up.

Maddie sits at the piano and stares at the text for a long while. She blinks at it several times. When she finally sets the phone down, she clenches the wood at the edge of the keys. Velma is fucking with her. Maddie's first instinct is to be enraged. But that's what Velma wants. A reaction. Maddie won't fall for it. She doesn't have time.

She eyes the keys, plays, and picks up the tempo, the music sprightly now, despite the heaviness weighing on her.

Last year, just before Thanksgiving and while the pandemic was still worrisome, Maddie had been writing a semi-autobiographical musical for a theatre in Brooklyn. One piece dealt with the sexual assault she endured when her parents left her with a hotel babysitter the summer she turned eight. The musical's producer, a colleague who regularly hired her on jingles, said Maddie needed to dig deeper.

Maddie had never understood her parents' thought process the night they left her in that room alone with a man. The producer was confused by it, too, and said Maddie must work harder to help an audience believe these parents would leave their young daughter with some guy they didn't know.

Typically, when Maddie used to call her mother, Velma couldn't keep quiet long enough to listen to anything Maddie tried to say. On *this* day, she could picture Velma in the store, smartly dressed, and with her short hair perfectly styled and dyed, sitting beside the glass jewelry showcase in her oak rocker with the seat she'd caned herself. Velma used to stand from eleven to five behind the showcase, leaning on its countertop, from the time she was in her late thirties up until her late eighties. More recently, she reduced her hours, and she sat down. Sometimes she napped. That day, there were no customers, and she was in an irascible mood when she picked up the phone.

Maddie prefaced the conversation with how important it was that she ask her something; her work hinged on it, she explained.

They got into it, and Velma raised her voice. "When we came back to that hotel room you were *fine*. You were sitting up, smiling—there was *nothing* wrong with you. Nothing at all. Your father would tell you the same damn thing, but he can't because he's dead!"

And Maddie felt her blood pressure rising. The woman pulled lies out of her ass whenever it suited her. "I was *not* fine," she said. "I was a little girl, and I was assaulted."

And Velma said, "Well, if you *were*, then why the hell didn't you *say anything*? You should've said something!" She screamed this, throwing the fault at Maddie and the responsibility away from herself.

Maddie hung up.

She doesn't remember the entirety of the assault. But she remembers how it started with the man peeling off her pajama top and licking her prepubescent nipples. And she remembers crying and asking him to stop and not being able to get away. The rest of what she recalls appears in fragments, like a dream she can barely grasp the diaphanous edge of before it flies away.

Maddie wrote Velma, saying she wouldn't talk with her about the assault again. She added that Velma had never taken responsibility for any mistakes or sincerely apologized for anything. Velma did not respond. Maddie sent a Christmas gift that went unacknowledged and unreciprocated. Her mother did not call, nor did she ever write back.

The silent treatment is on Velma. It's been in her playbook since Maddie was a toddler. She stops speaking to manipulate Maddie into reaching out. Velma expects her daughter to apologize for calling her on her toxic behavior.

When Maddie realized that Velma was, once again, punishing her with silence, it was as if a spell had broken. All desire to reconnect vanished. If she ever owed her mother some debt as a daughter, it was now paid off.

Seated at her upright piano, Maddie looks out the window at the trees. The dove she saw earlier has flown off. Leaves turning from green to yellow flutter in the breeze. As she takes them in, an odd *whoosh* sensation comes over her, and somehow, she and her piano are pulled into the memory of the day she told Velma she'd stick her in the home after Velma said she was a quitter and wouldn't amount to anything. She's at the waterfall on the island beneath the trees, and she finds herself staring sideways at her younger version: little Maddie, cheek swollen from Velma's slap, leaning on the birch branch, wearing an oversized gray sweatshirt. The splashing water makes music. And the metallic smell of wet rocks and the musty-leafy odor of algae fills her nose. The two Maddies eye one another, open-mouthed and with raised brows. Grown Maddie soon smiles at her younger self, who, in turn, beams back shyly from a tear-stained face.

A look of knowing passes between them. And a look of love. As they silently regard one another, an unspoken awareness floods their minds. The Maddies realize that all of time is happening *now*. And then. And it's also yet to come.

Perhaps they both stood up to Velma that day.

Grown Maddie plays for young Maddie, who's delighted by the music and whose heart is soothed to see that she *will*, in fact, amount to something one day. She begins to dance, arms in arabesque as she smiles up at the only star in the sky.

Maddie's apartment slowly rematerializes around her. As the past fades from view, the light of the star is the last thing to disappear. Shreds of guilt peel away like birch bark. With eyes and hands on the keys and music in her ears, Maddie understands why she kept trying with her mother for as many years as she did. Trained, like a beaten dog, she was terrified to quit.

If Velma shows up tonight, or if she doesn't, Maddie is determined to thrive. Her show will shine no matter what fresh hell the night may bring because surviving her mother has been like strength training for a soul that's growing as strong as all the fucks that have never been given to darkness because they're too busy sparkling, swirling, and sharing their light where it's wanted and loved.

To the Moon

MONROE, NEW YORK, 1978

Phil

After my last patient of the night, I zip over to Lucca's, the Italian restaurant by the edge of Walton Lake. I sit solo at the bar and watch through the window as the full moon rises over the water. Marvelous. I've long admired this lake and the way it's nestled by dense canopies of trees, puffy and thick as Afros. First thing I fell in love with in Monroe. Before the hillbillies made themselves known.

Lucca's is a decent spot for a country town like this. The patrons don't bother me with the double looks I receive elsewhere around here. Some locals can't get used to seeing a Black man who carries himself like he knows he's somebody because he *is*.

When Maddie's not at the house, the new one—we just moved last month—this is where I've been coming to avoid Velma. I have my scotch and talk to the bartender. Maddie *is* home tonight, but because of Velma's vindictive ass, blabbing about my girlfriend, the kid's avoiding me.

My regular bartender is Nino. Gino. One of those. Tonight, he's not here. This new guy is young. Barely twenty-one, I'd guess. Shag-cut strawberry blond hair that looks like it would glow in the dark. He's wearing a black silk shirt, open, no tie, and a mood ring on his forefinger. It's blue. That's supposed to mean he's copacetic right now. He's got a wedding ring on his other hand. Christ. So young. I've been there. I *had* to do it. In the fifties, if you got someone pregnant, you were obligated. Up here, it's not unusual for kids to marry right out of high school. Willingly. I'd *never* marry if I could go back in time.

"I'll have a Dewar's dry Rob Roy," I tell the bartender. "That's with *dry* vermouth."

My regular guy knows how I like it, but most of these Monroe folks don't get it right if you don't tell them. I loosen my tie and light a cigarette while I wait. I wish my regular bartender were here. Good listener, that Nino. He respects me because one of his friends was my patient years ago, and he says I helped the fella through a tough time. I don't remember it, but it's nice that Nino knows a bit about me. My reputation. He lets me talk without interrupting. He's generous with the drinks and keeps his opinions to himself.

It's a Thursday. After eight. The place is quiet. There's an old couple, wide and white-haired, holding hands. And a group of middle-aged women all dressed up. Most of them are overweight, stuffed like cannoli into tight summer dresses. They're drinking champagne and celebrating something but not so loud that it gets on my nerves.

The room smells pleasant. Inviting. Like garlic bread baking. The walls are peppered with pictures of Florence, Siena, and Lucca. I don't think most of the patrons know they're looking at Tuscany. I took Velma to Florence, back when I could tolerate her.

Louis Prima is playing "Sing, Sing, Sing." I resisted Prima, but he is damn good. Dom, the owner, spins the same white jazz guys all the time. Frank Sinatra, Tony Bennett, Mario Lanza, Louis Prima, and that's about it. I wish he'd play some of the guys my father liked. I've teased him. *Hey, Dom, how about some Louis Armstrong, Cab Calloway, Nat King Cole?* Dom laughs. Says nothing. And I don't push it. I'm not looking for a fight. He can do what he wants. In my waiting room, I play the music I like, too. If you can't do what you want in your own place, what's the point?

Velma's always trying to set her goddamn rules at the house. Wants to tell me I can't have certain people over. I finally bought a place with a pool and a tennis court, something I've dreamed of since childhood, and she thinks she's going to tell me I can't have people playing tennis and swimming there? Bullshit. I'll do what I damn well want.

There are a few loud men at the other end of the bar. They're midforties, I'd guess. Around my age. They look like the type I don't normally see in here. T-shirts and blue jeans, drinking beer on tap. Laughing. Crass. I've run into people like them who've never been out of this town. The kind whose kids make fun of my kid's hair and call her names.

Dom insists on a quiet dining environment. The bartender asks them to keep it down.

One of them turns toward *me* as if *I've* complained. He has a crew cut, and he stares the way this type often does, like they're trying to suss out what a guy my color with an Afro and an earring is doing in tailored clothes and driving a sports car. I ignore him. Stub out my cigarette.

Strawberry Blond has his back to me, and I can't see what he's putting in the drink. When he turns around again, he asks, "What's goin' on, Doc? Things all right with you?"

Huh. I'm surprised he knows who I am. Don't remember seeing him before. But it's hard to miss *me* in this town. And I must be more bothered than I realized because that's all it takes to get me running my mouth about Maddie not talking to me. I haven't even started drinking yet.

I shouldn't, but I tell him, "My wife and I haven't worked as a couple for years, but we bought a new place because I'm trying to have the best life I can with what I'm stuck with. God knows it's not easy to get divorced in this state. For her, being married is about me financing her lifestyle while I get nothing out of it."

The guys down the bar start singing along to Louis Prima's "I Ain't Got Nobody." I wish they'd shut up. I'd rather hear Prima's voice than theirs, and they're drowning him out.

Strawberry Blond says, "Guys, please." Sounds like he's pleading.

They take it down a notch. One gets up and heads toward the bathroom.

Strawberry Blond pours in red vermouth. "So, you're like her sugar daddy?" he asks.

"Something like that," I say. The lollipop comes to mind. "She's made me a sucker. But not one that gets licked."

He snorts, adds ice cubes, and then hands me the glass.

I know the drink is wrong before I taste it, and when I do, I tamp down the urge to snap at the kid. He's been decent. And I'm not trying to make myself unwelcome. I remind him, "Say, uh, I asked for a *dry* Rob Roy. *Dry.*"

"Shoot," he says. He takes it back and raises a finger. *One moment.* He refills the beers for the singing townies. Then I watch him remake my drink with the right vermouth. But he gets its portion and the scotch's mixed up.

I'm annoyed now. Still, I don't complain. He gives it to me. I drink it and light another cigarette. I'll catch him before he makes the next one.

"Since my wife wouldn't agree to split up," I go on, "I travel without her when I can. Keep an apartment in the city where I have my other office. I bought the best house I could. You've probably seen it, down where Lakes Road meets Laroe. Big stone wall? The estate?"

The kid shrugs.

"My father would've been astounded to see how far I've come. He died when I was ten. Right after he retired. Before I was born, he was a Pullman porter. You know what that is?"

"Mm. Don't think so," Strawberry Blond says.

"Of course you don't," I say. "Why would you? Pullman porters were men, *Black* men, who worked on trains to serve guests. Like butlers. They carried bags, cleaned the sleeper cars, shined shoes, that kind of thing."

He scrunches his nose, and skin wrinkles around his blue eyes in a wince of disgust.

"Yeah, sounds bad, but that was a good job in my father's time. This was the turn of the century. He was fifty-seven—twenty years older than my mother when they met. Second marriage. In his day, Pullman porter was a job a lot of men wanted. But my father didn't like being a servant."

"I can relate," Strawberry Blond says, smiling with tiny, corn-on-the-cob–like teeth. Then he puts on a formal voice. "May I get you another one, sir?"

I'm not done with the first so I know he's joking. I draw on the cigarette and exhale. Tap my ashes. He dumps the glass ashtray and then sets it back in front of me.

"And being called 'George,'" I continue. "My father hated that, too. His name was Lawrence, but passengers called all the Pullman porters George. Or boy." I shake my head. "He detested that."

"Why'd they call them George?"

I look at this strawberry blond kid with microdontia who's crossed his arms, staring at me, and I think, *Why am I telling him all this*? What does he care? If *I'd* been born when my father was, this kid would probably be calling *me* George. My daughter is who I should be talking to. She doesn't know any of this. Nonetheless, I go on. "George Pullman founded the Pullman Company," I say. "Calling all the porters George was a way to dehumanize them."

The kid's mouth horseshoes, curving down at the corners, which seems to evince that this is interesting to him, yet he's skeptical.

"He was a classy, dignified man. Always well dressed. Tall. Impeccable posture. He quit being a porter and did a year of college but left to stay home with his first wife when she was dying. Then he got a job as a customs inspector in Manhattan. Did that for years. Worked all through the Depression. Saved his money. Paid off his house, and when he retired at seventy, he dropped dead.

Almost immediately. That's why I'll never retire." I stare into my glass at the melting ice cubes and realize my eyes are moist. "I still miss him," I say. "His relentless kindness toward me. He was fun, too. Used to play games with us and tease my mother. He wasn't a believer and she was, and he'd poke fun at the fantastical stories in the Bible and ask her to explain how they worked: 'Now, tell me *how* did Jesus turn water into wine, Emily? Let's figure *that* trick out and we'll be rich.' And he'd wink at my brother and me when she'd get flustered. He was gentle. Encouraging. Didn't raise his voice or criticize, like my mother did. I wonder how things would've been different had he lived another ten years. He would've raised me. All *she* ever did was tell me what was wrong with me." I drain my glass.

The bartender grabs it and starts making another Rob Roy. "Wait, wait, wait," I say, bobbing two fingers in the air. "Now listen. The way Nino makes the dry Rob Roy is three ounces of scotch," I show him three fingers. "And two ounces of dry vermouth." I've got two fingers up now. "You got it?"

He looks at me askance. "Nino?"

"The other bartender."

He snorts. "His name's *Gennaro*. Sorry, but I'm only supposed to do two and a half ounces of scotch, not three. That's what Dom says." He turns around and pours.

Gennaro? No. He must mean *Gino*. And I won't quibble about half ounces. My cigarette is smoldering in the ashtray. I press it out. "Yeah, my father did well for himself, but I don't think he could've imagined a lifestyle like *mine*. My own practice. A big house on multiple acres. In this idyllic town, far from family, where I'm practically a pioneer. Now, my mother, on the other hand, she hasn't said a positive thing about me, ever, that I can remember."

The bartender adds ice and a twist of lemon peel and sets the drink in front of me.

I taste it. Smoky. Citrusy. Mm. I bring my fingertips to my lips and then kiss and spread them. "I brought her to the house. My mother could see it was beyond anything she could've dreamed; nicer than anywhere she'd ever *been*. Her papery eyes looked all around. But did she say anything nice? No one in our family has anything close to what I've achieved, but not one kind word out of her mouth. She told Velma, 'It'll be hard to keep clean, won't it?' As if Velma cleans her own house. You know why she's like that? Because when I told my mother and brother, years ago, that I planned to be a psychologist, *they* said I was an idiot. My brother called me a fool. To my face. And *she* said no white people would go to me. Well. They were wrong, wrong, wrong. I treat plenty of people. Of *all* colors. And she's annoyed by it. My brother was interested in psychology. He thought a career in it couldn't be done. Maybe *he* couldn't do it. He's a civil servant like our father was. I work for myself. But are they proud? Do I get *any* credit? From *anyone* in my family?"

The good ol' boys down the bar shoot me slit-eyed looks, and Strawberry Blond puts the mood-ringed finger to his lips, shushing me. Maybe I *have* been speaking in elevated tones. His ring is green now and getting lighter. That's supposed to mean he's less relaxed than he was. *If* you believe in those things, which I don't.

Through the window, I see the white-haired couple waddling like penguins to their wood-paneled station wagon. A patch of moonlight shines on them as the old man opens the door for the woman and guides her in.

I continue, mindful not to be too loud. "You'd think my wife and daughter would be appreciative," I say, "and not have so many goddamn complaints. Right?" I turn my head one way and then the other. "Last Sunday, Velma's down at her shop, and my daughter tells me she wants a ride over to her friend's house who's having a pool party. I say *no*. We have a pool. We *have* a pool, dammit, and *I'm* having friends over to play tennis. I don't feel like driving her. She can swim at our place. She's not running things around here. She'll stay home because my girlfriend is bringing her kid, and I need *my* kid to keep hers occupied while she and I play doubles with my buddy Morton and his wife, Muriel."

Strawberry Blond pats at the air in three downward notches, telling me I'm too loud.

I toss back the rest of my drink.

He takes the glass. Starts making another. "You have a wife *and* a girlfriend?" he asks. "Lemme guess—your daughter was upset. That why she's not speakin' to you?"

"She didn't know about the girlfriend at that point. Most weekends, I bend over backward to accommodate that kid. She has a Saturday afternoon voice lesson in the city. Do you know, I drive all the way up here from my Manhattan apartment, where I spend Friday nights with another woman I date, and I pick Maddie up and turn around and drive her right back into the city for her lesson. I wait for her and then after, I take her shopping or to a museum and later to dinner and sometimes a movie, or a play, or to hear jazz. She loves New York. I spend a lot of time and money on that kid, so she can miss a party to do something for her father, don't you think?"

He raises his eyebrows and bites on his bottom lip with his tiny teeth. Hands me the drink. I taste it. It's good.

"Maddie likes little kids. And she does play with my girlfriend's daughter, who's four."

"Wait. This woman has a little kid? So, she's divorced?"

"Oh, her husband's an *ass*. Years ago, the joker tried to tell me I couldn't get a Great Dane. *People like you don't have dogs like that.* I thought to myself, *You watch me, motherf—*. I got the Dane, of course. I got something else I bet he thought I couldn't get, too."

The bartender covers his mouth with his hand. The ring is yellow now. Maddie says that means anxious, but that's nonsense. He's visibly appalled. Fuck him. Is it my fault these condescending men's wives fancy *someone like me*?

The women in tight dresses leave the restaurant. Now it's just the good ol' boys down the bar. They're snapping their fingers and humming along with Sinatra's "Fly Me to the Moon." I almost want to join them. The tune swings with joy. But the lyrics don't hit that way today. Frank sings of longing for someone. Worshipping them. And I think of my father. His warm, encouraging eyes. If I stay quiet, I'll cry.

"From what I can tell, Maddie has a good time with the chubby little girl. If she suspects anything during the day, she doesn't let on. Me and my girlfriend play doubles with the other two. We swim, have a bite to eat. Maddie's fine."

"Hm," the bartender grunts. "What's the girlfriend like?"

I look Strawberry Blond in his blue eyes. I think I know what he's asking. "Creamy skin," I tell him. "Slim. Straight silky hair. Very pretty."

He glances toward the guys at the end of the bar and then looks at me again. Doesn't smile. "I'm closing out soon. You gonna want another one?"

"I'm good," I say. "After the girlfriend leaves, Maddie is unusually quiet. Sullen. Remember, she doesn't know the nature of my relationship at this point. Maybe she sensed it—I don't know. But something's bothering her. I ask if she had a good time with the kid, and she says she would've had a better time at the party she wanted to go to. Fair enough. I offer to take her to dinner. She wants her fucking mother to come. Velma's still at work, and I sure don't want to be bothered with her dumb ass, but if it makes my kid happy, fine. So, we meet her mother down at a restaurant across the street from her shop. I hate the place; it's for tourists. It's got the crowd from the Renaissance Fair, and it's like a giant barn. The food is animal feed. But I go. For Maddie."

"Why didn't you come here?"

"Ha. Good question. This is *my* spot. And thank God I didn't. Velma shows up wearing too much makeup, as usual, and too much perfume. She kisses me on the lips and smiles like it's a date. Now, this behavior is bullshit. We can't stand each other. We barely talk. Barely sleep together. We're only married because she won't agree to a divorce. She's trying to keep up appearances for Maddie, I guess, and make her think there's something left between us, which there isn't. Velma used to be an attractive woman. Not anymore. She stopped smoking, started stuffing her face without exercising, and she's matronly now. The restaurant has a salad bar, which I order as my main course because, unlike Velma, I watch my weight. The two of them, Velma and Maddie, sit at the table while I get my salad, and when I come back—I haven't been gone two minutes—Maddie's in tears, and Velma looks like John McEnroe right after he's screamed at an umpire. I think they've had a fight. Velma's always picking on Maddie. Maddie looks at me, and for a second, I see my mother. The way she eyes me with contempt. Velma jumps up. Points in my face and says, 'You are nothing but a n-i-g-g—.' We're the *only* Bit-O-Honeys in this room full of marshmallows, and the crazy nut says the actual word. Makes a scene. A complete fool of herself. She keeps yelling. Cursing."

"Well, I mean—"

"In the middle of the restaurant. Unbelievable. Who would want to be married to a lunatic like that? No manners. No class. You can take her out of Harlem, but I guess you can't take the ghetto out of the girl."

"Wow," Strawberry Blond says. He blinks and lets out a breath.

"So, the two of them leave, and I'm left there with my salad like some loser. I support both of them. I pay for *everything*. I don't know what the hell Velma does with her money. She sure doesn't pay a goddamn bill, yet I have to put up with being disrespected in public."

Strawberry Blond squints like he's trying to get a better look at something on my face. He tilts his head. "You made your daughter babysit for the child of another woman you brought to your house while your wife was at work, and you're complaining because she flipped out?"

"I *told* you we're not a real couple."

His eyes widen. "That's *your* story. Does she live there?"

I bite an ice cube and look at him. "I *will* take another drink."

He exhales. "Gimme a second."

He walks down the bar to the blue-collar guys. He refills their glasses. Gives them their bill.

I light a cigarette. If Nino were here, he'd see it my way. When I'm paying for drinks, I can do without the judgment. Anyway, *I* know there's no reason for Velma to care if I have a girlfriend. And nothing happened that day. We played tennis and swam. The issue is my kid, and Velma poisoning her against me.

The bartender comes back. Starts making another dry Rob Roy. "How do you think your wife *should* have acted?" he asks.

"Well, first of all, Velma didn't need to tell Maddie anything. She could have waited until we were at home to talk to me." I blow smoke. Tap off ashes.

He laughs. "I gotta say, if *my* dad did that shit, brought one of his strays to our house, man. My mom's from Naples. He'd be immediatamente morto. Dead." He drags one finger across his neck.

"But are your parents still in love?"

"What difference does that make? It's her house. You don't bring it home with you, man. Did you never learn that? Before I got married, my father made *sure* I knew." He sets the drink in front of me.

"Maybe it depends on the home. Mine has amenities. It's the kind you *want* your girlfriend to see."

"You're wild." He walks away, shaking his head. Closes out the beer drinkers' tab.

I sip. It's flawless. A mellowed-out calm comes over me. I don't care what this kid thinks. I don't give a fuck what Velma thinks, either. I *do* care what Maddie's thinking.

The guy with the crew cut lurches toward me. Drunk. "Hey. Where you from?"

"Here," I say. "*Why*?"

"*Before* that," he spits, combative.

I exhale loudly. "The Bronx. *Why*?"

The guy's teetering on limp spaghetti legs. "No, before that?" he says. "What *are* you?"

Ugh, I think. *Here we go.*

"He's from *here*, Jerry." The bartender is back. "Pay up and go home, please. Bye."

The drunk has an alcoholic's red-veined nose, and his nostrils flare. "You're *colored*, aren't you? I've seen you." He points shakily at me. "You're that fuckin' colored bastard who tried to live in Walton Lake Estates back in the day."

I stay seated. Calm. I don't *want* to fight this motherfucker, but I'm not afraid to. I *can*.

"So what if I am, cracker?"

"Dominick," the bartender yells toward the back. "Dad. C'mere!"

"We egged your shit." The guy laughs in a strange staccato—"Eh eh eh eh eh eh eh eh." He sways and stumbles. "Chased your monkey asses out."

His buddies come toward us now. One of them has a beer gut poking out from his T-shirt. He rolls his eyes and seems more exasperated than aggressive. "Jer, c'mon. What the hell? What're you doing?"

"F-f-f-fuckin' with this coon."

"All right, enough," Beer Belly says. "Shut your dumbass up before Dom comes in here, and you get us banned."

The bartender's got a hand on his forehead. The mood ring is black, the color of stress. He says to the friend, "Please. Get him outta here. *Now*."

"I'm *tryin*."

The third friend, who's skinny and bald with a thick ginger beard, begins to laugh hysterically.

Strawberry Blond shakes his hands in the air and shrieks, "This isn't the place for this crap!" He's really unnerved.

The drunk goon pitches toward him precariously. "Oh, you wanna throw *me* out? What about this baboon you got here?"

Strawberry Blond's face is red as wine now. He leans over the bar, cupping his hands around his mouth. "*Where are you, Dad?*"

I put my fingers in my ears; he's so loud. Christ. I didn't know he was Dom's son. "It's going to be okay," I tell him.

He says, "You should go."

I'm thinking, *I* should go? I don't *think* so.

The friend with the beard is still laughing as if he can't stop.

The drunk bozo collapses on the bar and then slides like a soggy noodle to the floor.

His buddies try to pull him up and stand him on his feet. The effort fails. He ends up laid out on his back. The bearded friend, whom I suspect has pseudobulbar affect, is laughing so hard I think he's wet himself. There's a spot on his crotch. I'm smiling, because these ofays are a mess. Must be the full moon.

Dom, who's in his late fifties with slicked-back hair, strides toward the bar quickly and with purpose in a crisp, dark suit.

His bartender son sputters, "It's outta control."

Dom can see who and what the problem is, but he's distracted by Ginger Beard's laughter. "Hey piss-pants, think you're at a comedy club? Shut up."

"It's, it's a condition I have, Dom. Sorry. I—I can't help it. I'll go."

"*Good*," Dom says. He gestures toward the door.

Ginger steps outside, leaving the beer-bellied buddy alone with the drunk flat on the floor.

Dom peers down at him. There's a beat of silence. When he finally speaks, his voice is so quiet it's a strain to hear it. "Misbehave in my restaurant again, I'll take a bat to your head, stuff rocks in your pockets, and throw you in that lake out there." Then he smiles. "Get home safely. Have a nice night."

It gives me a chill.

The drunk is silent. He might be unconscious. Beer Belly drags him toward the door.

Strawberry Blond rubs his eyes. "Guess I gave him too much to drink. Sorry."

Dom caresses his cheek. "Not your fault. It's a bar. Drunks happen." He turns to me. "Pleasure to see you, Doc. Your last drink is on me."

"I appreciate it," I say.

He walks back from whence he came.

I watch through the window as they pour the inebriated imbecile into the cab of a pickup.

I don't feel bothered by anything he said. I never cared what bigots said or thought about me. What I care about is when they try to set limits on what I can do or be or have. I'll stand against anyone, Black or white, who tries to stop me from living freely, like a man.

Strawberry Blond puts money in the register and comes back to stand in front of me.

"He didn't chase me anywhere," I say.

"*What?*"

"I stayed in that neighborhood for almost a year before I bought my first house. I didn't *let* anybody chase me out."

His wide eyes seem astonished. "Are you—? I'm *done* for the night. Okay?"

"Yeah, yeah, fine." I stand and have a little trouble taking out my wallet.

He writes up my tab and hands it to me. He's charged me for three drinks, and I've had four.

"I don't mean to be rude," he says. "I'm tired. Good luck with your daughter. I'm sure she'll get over it."

"I hope so. But I treat people every day who still aren't over things. It's how I make my living." Swaying a little, I hand him the money.

Before I leave, I stop to use the restroom. When I come out, I wave to the kid.

He's wiping down the bar. "Get home safely," he says. "Have a nice night."

I fumble with my keys in the lot. The only other car is Dom's Coupe DeVille. When I finally unlock the door to my two-seater and climb in, I sit without starting the engine. I might be too drunk to drive. Maybe I don't want to leave.

For a long while, I watch the moonlight shimmering on Walton Lake. I feel my father's presence. I know it's not real, but I see him in the corner of my eye; the dark skin of his neck and cheek gleaming against the white collar of his dress shirt. The sweet scent of his hair pomade wafts toward me. If I turned, he'd be there in the passenger seat beside me.

"I wish you could have seen all the years I spent studying, training, and working to build this life, Daddy. I've been around the world. I have a good career. Bought the house of my dreams. Would you have been proud of me?"

"My sweet son," I hear him say. "I've always been proud of you, darling. But pride isn't happiness. Is it? Yes, you have your beautiful house, and yet, where are you *now*? Sitting here, drunk, with me." He touches my hand. "Your greatest achievement, son, will be when you build a life where you can shine in the world *and* still be eager, always, to get back home."

But Where's Home?

A NOVELLA

1.

Monroe, New York, 1980

Suzy

So, one day my mom tells me Aunt Velma told her that Zeke Odom finally asked Maddie out. We're excited for her, but Aunt Velma read it in Maddie's diary, so we can't say Snickers 'til Maddie asks Aunt Velma if she can go, which is like a whole week later, and then we all have to act surprised. I *do* act surprised; then I feel bad and tell Maddie her mother told my mother, but I tell her she can't confront her mother because then my mother will know I told, and Aunt Velma will know my mother told, and that would be a mucked-up mess.

According to Aunt Velma, Maddie's been writing in her diary about nobody but Zeke Odom since she was in the seventh grade. I'd die if I had only *one* cute brother to choose from all these years. Dag. If Maddie lived around me, she'd've dated a few cute boys by now.

What Aunt Velma doesn't seem to know is that there's another dude Maddie kind of likes, but he's white. Like *snow* white. Like a Viking. That's what Maddie calls him. Guess she didn't mention the Viking in her diary, or maybe Aunt Velma doesn't want to tell my mom that Maddie liked a white boy.

Anyway, when Zeke Odom picks Maddie up to take her to the movies, according to Aunt Velma, he just toots the horn outside. Now, in the boy's defense, Maddie and her parents moved to a big-ass "estate" in a neighborhood across town (this white town) from where they used to live, and the main house has an insanely long driveway. My mom says it's not that impressive 'cause it's not like Monroe is Greenwich, Connecticut; it's nothin' but a hick town filled with average white folks. According to my mom. Maybe so, but it's easy to see how it could be intimidating because you can't tell which entrance is the front. The only door you can see from the street side leads to an enormous glass porch that kinda looks like a greenhouse, and it doesn't have a "front door" look. The real front door is up a stone stairway around the back that leads to a patio that overlooks a red-bean–shaped pool, and down a hill behind that, there's a tennis court. And there're two cottages. The small one is close to the main house, and the bigger one is like an acre away and sits above the tennis court at the opposite end of the property and has its own driveway. I mean, hick town or not, maybe Zeke Odom was like, what kind of palatial craziness? The place looks like a small village. Maybe he didn't know where the hell to go.

Maddie tries to run out the "front" door, which is, as I said, in the back, but Aunt Velma grabs her, rubs some rouge off her face, and says in that gritted-teeth Aunt Velma growl, "You're not going any-damn-where. That kid needs to get his ass outta his car and come to the door like a gentleman."

He beeps again, and Maddie sasses off to Aunt Velma, "You're crazy. Let me go!" And when Aunt Velma doesn't, Maddie, *risking her life*, says, "You're just jealous, 'cause no one likes *you*."

And then Aunt Velma pops Maddie in the mouth.

I'm hearing this on the extension while Aunt Velma is telling my mom, as if slapping Maddie is as normal as making dinner or walking the dog. My mom doesn't say it to Aunt Velma, but later she kisses her teeth—*tsssk*—and tells me, "Ya auntie vex wid dat arrogant man she neva should 'ave marry and takin' it out 'pon Maddie."

I've been telling my mother about this stuff for years. She didn't believe me. Since we were small, I've been seeing Aunt Velma pop

Maddie. Sometimes for little things, like eating the last snack cake or leaving a towel on the floor. And just a few months ago, I was at the house when redheaded, freckled, Peppermint Patty–looking Lisa Megna, who used to be their next-door neighbor before they moved, called Maddie and asked to borrow a pair of crutches that were in their basement. They weren't even Aunt Velma's. The previous owner left them there. Maddie brought them upstairs and asked if Lisa could take them. Lisa was still on the line, and I saw Aunt Velma morph into a maniac.

Her eyes flashed wild, and she chased Maddie around the dining room table, holding up one of those crutches, screaming, "What've I told you about putting me on the spot?" Finally, she caught Maddie and beat her to the ground with that crutch.

I was shaking. Didn't know if I should be scared, sad, or call the cops. We went into Maddie's room after, and she cried.

When I told my mother, she said, "Gyal. Stop dem tales 'bout yuh auntie." Then she waved me away like I was a funky smell. But I did try.

So, Zeke beeps a third time, and Maddie starts crying.

According to Aunt Velma, she's crying because she thinks Zeke's gonna leave (not because she just got hit in the face), and when he beeps a fourth time, Maddie rips her arm away and runs off. The boy never does get out of the car, not even to open the door for Maddie. Aunt Velma says Zeke has no damn class, and on that point, I concur.

Maddie tells me later that while he's driving, they stop at a red light. Zeke kisses her and puts his thick tongue way deep in her mouth and almost down her throat. She isn't expecting all that; it's very fast, she says, and out of nowhere, and it doesn't feel one bit romantic. I'm listening to her tell the story, and what it sounds like to me is that Zeke Odom was hoping to not even get to the damn movies. Sounds like he was angling to park somewhere and get Maddie into the back seat. The thing is, Maddie has no experience messin' with boys. She's not fast like that. Sounds like he thinks she is, though. And I'm wondering *why*? What's his rush? Why's he tonguin' her down soon as she gets in his car? This is what I think: Zeke's around nothin' but white boys, and they think Black girls are easy. It's in their genetic memory. Any enslaved woman was theirs if they wanted her. Now, they see Black chicks in movies playing long-legged hoes in hot pants. They hear Donna Summer singing "Love to Love You Baby" and Labelle's "Voulez-Vous Coucher Avec Moi," and 'cause they don't know any *real* Black girls, they think *all* of 'em are ready to spread their legs. And here Zeke is, this lone brother around all these clueless jocks, so I bet that's where he's getting his misinformation.

Poor Maddie. Even though she thought she liked Zeke because she pretended he was something special, she didn't know his ass from Adam or Eve. And she made up what she wished he'd be: a dude who'd really dig her and think she was special, too. She is, but how would he know that?

They do end up at the movies that night, but they don't really watch. They mostly make out the whole time, and he feels her up, and she tells me she doesn't really like it. I ask her, "Why'd you keep making out with him, then?

And Maddie says, "What? I thought I had to. Isn't that what I was supposed to do?"

I'm like, "Uh . . . no, Maddie. If you don't wanna do something with some stupid-ass boy, you don't do it. You tell him to take you home."

She says, "Then he won't like me, Suzy."

And I say, "So what?"

And she goes quiet.

I feel bad for her. I don't even tell her about my new boyfriend (who's fine as hell and really nice) and what a great time we're having, because Marcel is my third boyfriend, and she's never even had one.

The next time we talk, she brings up Ron, the Viking. He's in her choral singing class, and he's started leaving nice notes in her locker. He folds them up and slips them in through the cracks, and they say things like, "You look really pretty today," and "You sounded amazing in your solo!"

They cut class one afternoon, and Ron the Viking drives her to a diner and tells her he likes her. Maddie doesn't say how she feels.

She told me she wasn't really sure, but the next day, he holds her hand when they walk down the hallway. She likes it at first. No one had ever held her hand at school before. But then, the whole time they're walking together, people are staring as if it's some kinda shock and horror that this white boy's holding her hand.

She said some people seemed mad and others scrunched their faces in disgust. Some girl had the nerve to rush right through them and rip their hands apart. Maddie won't hold his hand again because of that day and also because even though he didn't seem to care what she is, she's afraid his family will have a problem with her. She wasn't worried about our family. I don't know about my mother, but I think I'd have a problem with it. Because Maddie needs to have at least one Black boyfriend before she has a white one. She needs to know that not all Black dudes act like Zeke Odom did. Too bad Maddie's going to NYU instead of an HBCU like Howard, where I'm going, because I don't know if she's gonna have many options at NYU. I really hope she comes to visit me. I know there's gonna be so *many* fine brothers at Howard, and even though I already have a boyfriend, I cannot wait!

After the Viking and the terrible date with Zeke Odom, Maddie said she was giving up on boys. She didn't even want to talk to them. Said she needed to get out of Monroe, go to college, and *then* start dating.

Last weekend, I'm visiting her and we go to a party at her hazel-eyed friend Julia's house, where I'm sitting there watching all these no-rhythm–havin' kids dancing to God knows what 'cause it damn sure wasn't the beat, and Zeke shows up. Now, I'm not gonna lie; the boy looks tas-*ty*. I see him, and I'm thinkin', day-um. This dude's pretty, like Muhammad Ali. Smooth, peanut butter–colored skin. Thick eyebrows. Big boulder-like shoulders. Zeke Odom's as fine as Maddie's been saying he is. I can see why she pined for him all these years. And turns out I was right about what he was hoping for on that date.

This is what went down: We're all sitting on Julia's basement stairs. He's up top, heads our way, and when he sees Maddie, he plops himself on the stair above us, meets me, makes chitchat, and then I move down a step, like I'm a-talk to Peppermint Patty–looking Lisa and Julia, who're sitting there, but we all listen and hear him say to Maddie, "Can I ask you a personal question and you won't get mad?"

I'm thinking, Aw shit. Somethin' foul's 'bout to come out his fine-ass lips.

He doesn't wait for her to answer before he says, "You ever been fucked?"

Julia looks at me, eyes bugged out like a bumblebee's—like she can't believe what she's hearing. Peppermint Patty/Lisa slaps a palm to her forehead, and all I can do is try not to laugh.

Maddie's mouth falls open, but nothing comes out.

And he says, "Well, do you wanna be?"

I see Maddie's tongue lying limp in her mouth. She looks catatonic, staring at him, like one of those damn near-dead people you see in the old-folks' home.

He says, "'Cause every other girl I ever went out with, I always fucked 'em on the first date."

Maddie's eyes, cheeks, and lips droop down her sad face like a wilting flower. And then tears start falling, and she's palming them off her cheeks, embarrassed.

And then something interesting happens. I see this look splash over Zeke Odom, like a cold glass of water landed in his face. I would say the brother's having an *oh shit* moment, like he realizes he got it completely wrong about my cousin. And he says, "Aw, man. Did I—? I thought you—I mean, I heard you wanted to—"

"What?" Maddie demands, like she's fussing at a dog who's wet the floor. "What did you hear? You heard stuff about *me*?" She wipes tears away again, but she seems more angry than sad.

And he sighs, and in a different-sounding voice, a softer, sweeter one, he says, "Damn. I'm sorry. You're probably scared of me now. Are you? I don't want you to be scared of me." He's looking at her, trying to get her eyes to meet his, and now she won't look at him.

She stares at the carpeted step below her. His hefty shoulders slump forward, and he hangs his head as if he feels bad for real. Then he sighs, stands, and big as he is, he somehow looks small when he climbs back up the stairs.

Whew. Patty/Lisa got up and hugged Maddie. Me and Julia didn't move for a minute. I saw something in Zeke—something almost *nice*—that I didn't see when he was talking that shit about *every other girl on the first date*. I told Maddie I thought he figured out he made a mistake. Maddie said she didn't care. He didn't act nice at all when they went out. She said he treated her like trash.

So. So much for that. Too bad. Maddie's pretty sure things'll be better when she gets out of Monroe. I hope so. Hope they'll be better for Zeke Odom when he gets out of there, too.

2.

New York, New York, 1980

Phil

Phil glanced at Maddie in the passenger seat as he rounded a curve and his RX-7 hugged its way down the West Side Highway. They'd just come off the George Washington Bridge, and her curly head was turned, straining to look back at the Little Red Lighthouse. She did this without fail when he drove her into the city. She'd been doing it since she read the book in kindergarten.

Phil smiled, remembering how she'd crane her neck and shout, "I see it, Daddy! I see the Little Red Lighthouse. It's the bridge's best friend."

He watched her clinging to this last shred of childhood, still delighted by the sight, though she was no longer little. They were heading to her new residence at NYU, and then he'd be off to meet his new love, Muriel, who was waiting at his office, which was barely two blocks from Maddie's Fifth Avenue dorm.

There'd be no "empty nest" because she wasn't leaving the nest. Not really. He'd see her all the time. They'd go to dinner and movies and to the jazz clubs in the Village, like they'd been doing since she was thirteen. Sure, it might be somewhat different, because he was soon to be free and because Muriel would undoubtedly take some of his time. But they'd stay close.

He'd remained in the house, one toe stuck in his miserable marriage for Maddie's sake. Now he could finally move on. Fuck Velma and her cruel and inhuman treatment. He was ready to sue her for financial abuse. *She* was at fault—holding him hostage, running up bills, berating everything he did. He *had* to move out.

They weren't speaking, hadn't been for months, since their blowout in May. He'd brought Velma and Maddie to a tennis resort in Vermont during Memorial Day weekend. On the second night, Velma went ballistic when he offered Maddie some grass, which she was undoubtedly already smoking with her friends. That woman could make the biggest unnecessary fuss over the smallest things.

At least they managed to attend Maddie's graduation together. They put on a front for his mother and her parents, but their lives were separate. He'd been sleeping in his home office cottage. Phil was glad he'd bought the place so there was a separate living arrangement. It would've been lonely if not for Maddie. And she'd needed his support, so he'd stayed.

She performed in a Beatles tribute—a singer's showcase on the Upper East Side organized by her voice coach. Velma refused to attend. She could've gone separately. She could've at least pretended to take an interest—it was Maddie's first professional appearance in the city—but Velma didn't think about anyone else's feelings.

Just a few weeks ago, Maddie called him at his Manhattan office. She was sobbing as she told him she'd left home. She was staying in their old neighborhood at Lisa Megna's house because Velma had attacked her in the middle of the night. Maddie said she'd knocked over a lamp by accident while Velma was out at an auction, and she woke up to her mother hitting her in the face with the lampshade. Her bottom lip was split open. Maddie asked for money to stay somewhere else. But this was early August. Phil had his share of her tuition to pay, *and* he'd hired a divorce lawyer.

"You'll be leaving for school soon," he told her. "Can you stick it out a few more weeks? Stay in the cottage when I'm gone." He also gave Maddie the keys to his Manhattan office so she could go there when he was in Monroe.

All Velma gave Maddie was the silent treatment for embarrassing her by involving the Megnas. Velma's lucky that's all Maddie did. She could have called the police. She could've fought back.

Even with all Velma's abusive nonsense, Maddie still craved her approval. It pained Phil knowing how much she wanted her mother to see her perform. During the showcase, he could see Maddie's eyes darting wildly around the audience from the stage. And when she couldn't find Velma, disappointment spread across her face like a curtain. But *he* was there. He wouldn't've missed it. She sang "Yesterday" with great emotion, and boy, did she carry a tune. Phil looks forward to the day she graces the stage of Madison Square Garden, and his friends and colleagues can see what a sensation she is. Because of him. Not the talent—he can't sing, and Velma's tone deaf—but because of the lessons he paid for and drove her to. The time and attention he invested. That's why she's great.

After her Beatles showcase, he took her to celebrate at Bradley's, a jazz spot near his office. Maddie didn't bring up Velma's absence. It's been that way for years. The two of them hanging out, he and Maddie against that difficult woman. His daughter was the one beacon that shined through these last dark years.

He pulled up and double-parked in front of the green awning of Rubin Residence Hall. Maddie had only one box with her bedding and a large duffel bag with her clothes. He couldn't fit any more in the RX-7's hatch. He'd bring the rest of her things down over the next couple of weeks. As far as he knew, Velma hadn't offered to help.

He got out, opened the car's back door, and handed Maddie her bag.

"Aren't you coming in?" she asked.

He shook his head. "Can't. I'm rushing. Go find your room. I'll leave the box in the lobby near the security desk.

Maddie sighed and slung the huge bag over her shoulder. "Bye, Dad. Thanks for the ride."

"Oh, don't look so glum," he said. "I'll see you soon." He kissed her cheek.

She tottered into the revolving door, holding the bag vertically to fit inside. Phil watched through the glass as she entered the lobby and weaved through the throng of parents and kids toward the elevator. He lifted her box from the back of the car and felt his lower back tweak into a spasm. Dammit. Middle age and its goddamned indignities. The fucking thing wasn't even heavy. Wincing, he carried the box inside and dropped it, with a thud, near the guard's station opposite the revolving door. Her name was on it. She'd find it. It took him what felt like a full minute to straighten up again.

There were parents everywhere doting on grown kids: hugging, crying, helping. Jesus, you'd think this was nursery school the way they were babying young adults. Phil couldn't stay. Muriel was waiting. He left and then eased carefully back into the driver's seat.

As he headed around the block and toward the garage on Twelfth Street, Phil smiled. Even with his aching back, he was exhilarated by thoughts of romance and sex and hopefully a massage. He was ravenous for adult company, for the new life he was sailing into just as the kid was entering hers. He would escape his miserable marriage, and Maddie was getting out of Monroe. They could both be happy now. And even if the divorce got bumpy, which it likely would, knowing Velma, at least he and Maddie had each other. Any rough waves ahead would certainly be smoother than where they'd been. They could ride them out together.

3.
New York, New York, 1980
Maddie

Madeline Arrington
Writing Workshop
Professor Williams
Journal Assignment
Fall 1980

Dear Professor,

I have to begin by letting you know this assignment makes me anxious. I recently gave up keeping a journal after my privacy was violated. I'd hoped the days of my clandestine thoughts being read by others were over. I realize this class requires it and so I'll try my best. Since this isn't "private" either, events may be altered, and names may be changed to protect the innocent. Or left as is to punish the guilty.

September 14, 1980
Maddie
I love my dorm. It's an elegant building in the coolest location on lower Fifth Avenue, but at the moment, my room is h-e-double-L! My blue-haired punk rocker roommate—I'll call her "Jennifer"—who's a junior, put up a divider today. What for? So she can "do the nasty" while I'm in the room. (!)

"You can do it, too," she tells me. "Everyone has to have sex." I'm standing there, probably looking like Shirley Temple seeing Bill Bojangles's jigglies because then she goes, "Ooh. I see. You're a virgin." She tilts her head, like, *poor thing*, and says, "That's adorable."

She seems entirely unbothered that I'm not white, but she is concerned that I might be the only virgin in the entire dorm. That's how obvious I am. You can tell just by looking at me.

I may not be one. Technically. There was an incident with a grown man when I was eight, but I'll set that aside. It shouldn't count. Hopefully, virginity's still mine to lose.

I'll understand if you consider me a loser because no one would have me. Some days I feel the same way. What you may not know is that I skipped eleventh grade. To get away from home. I'm seventeen, younger than most freshmen. Also, my town had limited options for girls like me. From what I've seen so far, that may be the case here as well. There are only a few Black guys in the theatre program and their interest in girls is dubious, but I already like it here better than where I was because at least I see some other Black students in the dorm, even if they're not in my program. And my classmates don't seem to have that hysteria about what I am—or what I'm not. I get the feeling these theatre kids, even the white ones, may not have fit in where they're from either. I think this is the right place for me.

October 12, 1980

Maddie

Life's been a flowing stream of goodness! Greenwich Village is everything I wanted. My academic classes are near Washington Square Park, which is amazing—so many cool people hanging out there every day—all colors, classes, sizes, and sexual orientations. My academic classes are this one (Writing), beginning French, and History of Performance. My acting, singing, and movement classes are at the Lee Strasberg Theatre Institute near Union Square, which is walking distance from my dorm. And I'm still taking private piano and voice lessons in the Theater District with the coach I've been with since I was thirteen.

The roommate situation has improved as well. Jennifer took me to a midnight screening of *The Rocky Horror Picture Show*, and she dressed up as Dr. Frank-N-Furter and knew all the songs. I knew none of them, and it was still so fun! When we were walking back from the 8th Street Playhouse in the middle of the night, I asked when she thought she'd start having guys over.

She turned to me and smiled. "Could be girls, too. I don't discriminate."

It wasn't the answer I was looking for, though I'd prefer girls, actually. I'd be much more comfortable in my underwear, frizzy hair, and with no makeup on around another girl.

My dad's office is just a couple of blocks up the street. Since I've been here, we've gone out eat, to a Fellini movie (awkward—it was all about sex), and to hear jazz at the clubs on University Place. The other night we started out at Bradley's and saw Betty Carter. Then we went across the street to the Cookery to see Alberta Hunter. She's so cute with her bun-head and her big smile. She's in her eighties, and she sings this song called "Handyman" that's entirely innuendo about her man performing sexual favors. Coming from someone her age, it's hilarious, except for the fact that even this little old lady is getting busy and I'm not. Also, listening to a song of that nature with my father is weird. I act like it doesn't bother me. It does. But I can't afford to go to these places myself, and I'm curious, so I go.

In acting class, I got paired for scene study with a gorgeous guy from Washington Heights called "Gustavo." I don't know if he's straight, but as the French say, ooo-la-la! He has the yummiest-looking full lips and glowing-bronze skin. He was sitting in front of me when our teacher, who used to be a movie star in the old days, paired us because, of course, the only two brown people should work together. (Okay, I'm Black, actually, and more beige than brown, but you get what I'm saying.) Gustavo turned to me, tipped his tan suede Kangol, and flashed his perfect you-can-tell-he-wore-braces teeth. I think I might've gaped at him. Since we really are the only two people in the class who aren't white, the pairing seems presumptuous, possibly even condescending. Can't complain, though. Gustavo's hardly hard on the eyes.

October 19, 1980

Maddie

My life sucks. Gustavo and I walked to my father's office tonight to rehearse our scene. He gave me the key a while ago and said I could use the place when he's not around. I've already been a couple of times on the weekends, and he wasn't there. It's supposed to be empty on Sundays. He's supposed to be home, in Monroe, where our house is. And so, I brought Gustavo, and on the way, I'm kind of bragging about how cool it is that I'm allowed to use the apartment.

We get there, I unlock the door, and it only opens a couple of inches. The security chain is latched. I go, "Dad?"

His noisy parrot starts squawking, and I hear a woman go, "Phil! Maddie's here!"

And I smell cigarette smoke and cologne and, well, bodies. Then through the crack, I see this naked white lady zoom by. It's fast, but I recognize Muriel's voice. She's from Monroe. She and her husband, Morty, who just died a few weeks ago (!), used to play tennis at our house with my father. They got married in the living room of our first house when I was seven. I remember because it was before Miss Dowd (our housekeeper) was with us, and my mother cleaned the whole house for their wedding, and I had to help.

My father comes running toward the door, his whatchacallit all out. I squeeze my eyes shut, and he goes, "I'm busy here, Maddie!" Then, boom. The door slams in my face like a slap. And I still hear his annoying parrot going, "Reeeeeeeeiiik, reeeeeeiiik!"

Gustavo's standing next to me. I don't know how much he saw, but I know he heard everything. He goes, "No problem. We can rehearse in my room." And he buttons his suede jacket.

I stand there, staring at the door.

"C'mon, chica," he goes. "We got work to do. Vamanos."

"He's still married to my mother."

"Damn, that's wack. You a'ight?"

I wasn't. He understood when I told him I needed a drink. Then I got carded at Ponchitos when I tried to order a margarita.

He pretended to joke about it. "What? You forgot how old you are?"

He kept his cool, but I could tell he was irritated. I wasted his time.

We ended up back in his dorm room, where he wanted to rehearse in the first place. There was no alcohol. I knew he was ready to get to work, but I couldn't stop thinking of my father and Muriel. Together. I was pacing and babbling, and I wanted to scream. My father's always been a cheat. And I really didn't appreciate seeing it up close. Why'd he give me that key? Couldn't he have called and told me not to come there today? I have a phone in my dorm room.

Gustavo sat on the gray rug beside his bed and opened the Samuel French booklet. "¿Estás lista?" He stared at me.

Finally, I stopped pacing and plunked down next to him. I landed close. Too close, I guess. My thigh was touching his, and he slid a couple of inches away as if I were contagious. I couldn't help it; I started to cry and said, "My dad's a douchebag."

Gustavo held a fist to his mouth and looked at the ceiling. Then he sighed, and it sounded like a huff. "Okay. Put it into the work." He was mimicking our acting teacher. He was trying to be polite, I think, but he wasn't trying to hear about my problems. That's fair. Why should he?

We read through the scene three times. I cried through every line. This irked him. I could tell by the way he gritted his flawless teeth when he said, "Yo. You gotta give it some nuance, nena. Know'm sayin'?"

I was thinking, *Who's Nena?* I guessed it's something like niña? The Spanish word for girl? His accent is super New York, slightly Spanish, and—I've got to say—*so* sexy.

"It's okay," he said, "if you wanna use yourself and put what you're feeling into the play, but you also gotta make sense, y'know? Emotion, that's cool and all. Too much, though? That's like over-salting your beans." Then he added, "Can you be off book by tomorrow?"

He gave me a hug before I left. I wanted to latch onto him like a tick and press my hips into his. I would have if the feeling seemed mutual. He patted my back as if burping a baby. Not mutual. It was the kind of no-oomph hug my sister gives me. The kind reserved for people you're not that fond of.

Since our acting teacher wants us to practice putting our real-life emotions into our work, which didn't go well with the scene, I thought I'd try putting my tsunami of feelings to use in another way.

The music room on the second floor of Rubin Hall is a closet with a mirrored wall and an upright piano. I played and watched myself perform "Out Here on My Own" from *Fame*. I sang through tears, staring into my red-rimmed eyes, and wondered why the fuck my father didn't tell me not to come to the apartment. He told me to use those keys . . . I kept singing, trying and failing to keep my voice steady and on pitch. It cracked as rage roiled inside me until it exploded. Then I was banging the keys, singing and hitting more bad notes than good. My lack of control scared me, but I couldn't stop. I pummeled the piano the way my mother often hit me when she'd lost her mind, and the way I could've clobbered my father, over and over and over, until my fingers were sore.

4.
Monroe, New York, October 31, 1980
Maddie
I'm back in Monroe. Merde. I did not want to be here. Earlier this evening, I got a call from my grandfather, who told me he was on his way to pick me up because my mother drove head-on into a tree. Seriously.

I was worried when I heard, but her station wagon was the size of a yacht, and though it won't recover, as it turns out, she will.

It's been a colossally crummy week. On Wednesday, "Victor," the acting teacher formerly known as a movie star, watched the scene with Gustavo. When he asked how I thought it went, I stood on the black-box stage and stuttered like a dumb shit, "Uh, uh, uh, I, I, dunno." I mean, it was obvious the question was a trap. And it didn't help that Victor, though quite short, is exceptionally hot, which makes me nervous. He's got that ethnic, New York, dark hair, dark eyes, Al Pacino-esque, actor-y look.

"Then, I'll tell you," he seemed pleased to say. "It wasn't good. Your character's been through difficult times to end up where she is. Which is an *asylum*, for crying out loud. She's lived real pain. Find something within you that conveys that. Your job on stage is to create emotional honesty, Maddie, not melodrama. Make me believe you."

It's not like I haven't been trying. I used my imploding family. That's painful. How are my real tears dishonest? I think Victor just doesn't like me.

Monday, my father left a handwritten note at the front desk where I get my mail, telling me that he served my mother with divorce papers. Why I needed to be apprised of this, I don't know. He's living out of his Monroe office, Manhattan office, and now also his mousy girlfriend Muriel's house. And my mother's lost her last good marble. Hence: the car crash.

After class, when I got back to the dorm, I was trying to enjoy my college life. My roommate, Jennifer, and her girlfriends were planted in the middle of our carpeted floor, listening to Devo on her boom box. They wore Halloween costumes, except for matchstick-skinny Jen, who was in her usual chunky lace-up boots and all-black ensemble—jeans, a long-sleeve T, with her short electric-blue hair and eyes framed by round, wire-rimmed John Lennon glasses. I joined them while we waited for the Halloween parade to pass by our Fifth Avenue window.

They smoked clove cigarettes, sipped Budweisers, and kibitzed (Jennifer's word) about the men in our dorm. They're having no more luck finding a boyfriend than I am. According to them, too many of the guys in the School of the Arts are more into bulges than boobs. Even Mia, Jen's jaw-droppingly gorgeous Japanese and Jewish friend, is having it rough. That girl's *so* pretty, *I'd* date her, and I'm not even into girls. She looked amazing dressed as *I Dream of Jeannie*. She told me her mom begged her to go to college to find a husband.

"Begged," Mia said. "On her knees. And I can't get any action. Mr. Stop-Your-Heart-Handsome in the room below mine is polite, kind, Jewish, and pre-med"—she made checkmarks in the air with her finger. "My family would gobble him up like Godiva chocolate.

I thought maybe I could, too. Decided to pay him a visit, only to find that he and his hunk of a roommate share the same bed. That smashed the wedding cake against the wall." She looked at me. "My mom took me to get a diaphragm before I left home, and I haven't used it once."

I said, "Your mother let you get a diaphragm? I've never even seen—" Then I clapped a hand over my mouth like a dork.

They laughed but not in a mean way.

Jennifer said, "No problem. We all had to learn." She hopped over to her bag, pulled out a pink plastic case, flipped it open, and showed me her sperm blocker. It was like a miniature Silly Putty–colored kiddie pool. Jennifer squeezed its edges, and then let go as she yelled, "*Diaphwammie*!"

The thing sprang across the room toward my unmade bed.

Then Mia and their other friend, Racine, a bombshell brunette in a forties-style femme fatale costume, took their diaphragms—they carry them around!—from their respective bags and let them go springing across the room, too. It was a game to see who could fling theirs the farthest. Femme folles! That means crazy women, so I learned in French class, and in this moment, that's exactly what I thought they were. But they were so fun and nice that I kind of fell in love with "folle."

Jennifer picked hers up and explained how to put the spermicide jelly inside and around the edges, and she showed me how you squeeze to insert it. I tried not to let on how much I valued the instruction. Not that I need a diaphragm, but I hope to one day.

The parade started, and we watched the kooky, colorful people streaming down Fifth Avenue in all their bawdy glory. Medieval getups, devils, angels, drag queens, cops who looked like male strippers, and dozens of S&M outfits. I was able to enjoy it for about ten minutes. Then the phone in our room rang. Grandpa, saying my mom's in the hospital.

When my grandparents got to the dorm, I ducked into the back seat of my grandfather's gold, midseventies Cadillac Seville as fast as I could. The "pimpmobile," as I call it, has flashy spindle hubcaps, and the car is so ostentatious it could star in a blaxploitation film. I'm embarrassed to be seen in it outside of Harlem. I crouched down out of view and asked, "Is she okay? Anything broken?"

Grandpa's voice was curt. "I cahn't ahnswa with any cer-tain-ty," he said in his haughty accent. It's Jamaican but not the cool patois kind. His is cultured, like a Rastafarian who went to college *and* finishing school. "We shall see when we get there, Madeline Ann." He loves using my middle name, which no one else does, ever.

His car smelled of leather, cigars, and men's musky cologne. I stared at the back of his plaid cap. Beside him, Grandma Althea's blue-gray hair was coiffed, and her fists were stuck to her chubby cheeks, as she trembled and whimpered in her South Carolinian honeyed tone, "Have mercy, Lord. Please, have mercy."

This made me start to tremble, too.

When we walked into the florescent-lit hospital room, my mother's nose was swollen and purple, and her eyes were black and blue. I didn't want to cry, but tears threatened to seep out. I'd never seen her like this.

White gauze bandages were wrapped around her head, and there were reddish-brown spots of dried blood on them. A nurse told us the fractures were minor. Still, my mother looked broken—and not just her bones. I was afraid to touch her.

We haven't been getting along. Not that we've *ever* gotten along that well, but she used to have a good side sometimes. This past year, not so much. She still thinks it's okay to hit me if I do something that annoys her. It's always been her go-to punishment, even when I was little, too little to not make mistakes. It needs to stop.

I stood at the foot of her bed and didn't move. Grandma and Grandpa pulled chairs up on either side of her. They stuck their wrinkled hands through the silver railing to hold hers.

"I have nothing to live for," my mother said.

And that's when I knew she *meant* to crash into that tree. She glared at me, eyes speckled with scarlet blotches like they were bleeding. "He left me," she said. "My life is over." Her voice smoldered with accusation. I think she *wanted* to say, *You happy now?* My mother has accused me of "dating" my father, because of the way he'd take me into the city to plays or movies or to hear music. For me, the trips were a chance to get out of Monroe, which I've always been glad to do. And she's accused my father of treating me like "the wife." He says he's educating me. Exposing me to music, theatre, cinema, and great artists.

It's not my fault he left her.

I said, "There are other things in your life besides him, Mom." I had the urge to call her Velma. "Mom" didn't feel right.

"I'm all alone. I don't know what I'm gonna do," she yelled, like a catastrophist. "How'm I gonna live?"

I was thinking, *You're asking me? I can't even order a drink at a bar.* I shrank back, hugged my arms, and squeezed air from the puffs of my ski jacket. "You'll be all right," I said. "You have your antique shop. And you had a life before your marriage. You'll have one after it, too."

It occurred to me that *I* was the only one who didn't have a life before their marriage.

My grandparents sat there and said nothing.

"What'll I do?" Velma wailed. She seemed lost, babbling on like a baby. "What'll I do? What'll I do? What'll I do?" It sounded like she was drugged.

My grandfather squeezed her hand. "Don't you worry; we're with you, love. You're not alone."

There was no place to sit, and I was exhausted. It'd been such a long week. After a few minutes, I finally stepped away from the bottom of her bed, kissed her cheek, and told her I'd be back tomorrow.

My grandfather's voice boomed. "No," he commanded. "You will stay right here. Sit down, Madeline Ann." He removed his cap as if he might fling it at me like a Frisbee.

Grandma's muddy-brown eyes puddled, and she was trembling again.

"Where?" I asked, looking around. "There are no chairs."

"On the bed," he snapped, pointing as if it were obvious. Then he steepled his fingers and leaned toward me. "You'll stay here and comfort your motha."

Bless his old-school heart, thinking he can tell everybody what to do. I'm seventeen, not seven. Guess my mother hasn't told him that we aren't close like that. I've tried to be. But when I'd come home from school, where I was miserable, and try to hug or cuddle her, she'd push me away and tell me to leave her alone.

"She has you and Grandma to comfort her," I said.

Velma sucked in a gasp that sounded almost like a scream, as if I'd done something truly egregious. She bent toward me, and I could see from the way she winced that this caused pain. "Apologize," she said. "Right now."

"Have mercy, Lord," Grandma chanted. "Please, have mercy."

What was I supposed to be sorry for? She *did* have them, and she and I both knew she didn't want me. Still, I said, "I'm sorry, Grandpa." Then I added, "But you're *her* father, not mine."

"Now you listen," he said.

"She's lucky to have parents who comfort her. You're a good dad," I said and left.

Since she and my father officially split, my mother hasn't once asked me how I'm feeling. Nor have my grandparents, even though it's my broken family, too.

In the taxi to the house, I wondered why Velma would want to hurt herself over my father. It makes no sense. He's been unfaithful for years. She couldn't love him anymore. Could she? I don't see how, but my grandmother still has starry eyes for my grandfather, even though everyone knows he has a younger mistress and two kids with her. I've never made sense of that either.

When I got home, I roamed the living room, looking at all my parents' stuff: antiques, paintings, Turkish rugs, and artifacts from places we've visited around the world. Phil and Velma are collectors of beautiful things. "Things" shouldn't be the sum of our family's experience, but that's what it feels like it's been about for them—acquiring stuff, and houses, and vacations, and status. For show. To prove how far they've come. If there was a time when we were building love and happiness, I don't remember it. And still, standing in our stylish house that sits on acres of manicured land, looking at the collection of lovely things, the moment felt elegiac, even if I couldn't and still can't pinpoint why. Maybe because it's really over—the way it feels when you go through a loved one's belongings after they die. Those things were part of their aliveness, and they're a tangible reminder that all you get to do now is remember what's intangible and gone. Even though we weren't a happy family, we were what I had.

I sat at my piano and played melancholy chords.

Immediately, I thought of the fallen movie star and how he'd probably roll his eyes and call my performance overly dramatic. And he'd be right, but what-the-fuck ever. My mother did just crash into a tree, and everything's a mess, and so I allowed myself all the drama I wanted.

Someone banged on the door.

The aggressive force of the *boom, boom, boom* annoyed me. It was after ten, too late for trick-or-treaters, in my opinion. I ignored it. Then my father's voice was hurling toward me like an oncoming storm.

Ugh, I thought and kept playing. As the creaky door whined open in the foyer, I tried to drown it and him out. C minor, A minor, E-flat minor, F-sharp minor.

"Didn't you hear me calling you?" He stomped into the living room, sloping forward with a hand on his back, like it ached. Then he yanked a pack of cigarettes from his tweed coat. His hair was different. He'd cut it short. Super-short. So short there was nary a kink to be seen. My father's high yellow, like me, and with this new hairstyle, he could almost be white. Did he do this on purpose? To match Muriel? If so, I didn't want to know.

"Mom almost died," I said.

"So I heard." He struck a match and lit up. "Your mother had no intention of dying. She's trying to play the victim because she thinks that'll get her more money." Smoke shot out of his nose.

I kept playing my somber chords and said, "You're a dick, Dad."

"Look," he said before taking a ferocious drag and then blowing the smoke out, "I realize this is upsetting, but I'm still your father, and you will not talk to me that way."

"And do you 'realize' you're always flinging that I'm-your-father shit in my face, like it entitles you to respect? Did you respect our family? Getting your knob polished every time you were around white women? Bringing them to our house?"

Blood rushed to his face. "That's what your mother wants you to believe."

"I believe it because I was *there*! You made me stay here and babysit one of their kids."

"Well, it's more complicated than that. Y'know, your mother and I weren't sleeping together anymore."

"Stop." I plugged my ears with my fingers.

He took another drag.

"And quit smoking around me," I said. "I'm sick of breathing your polluted air all the time." I tried to wave the cloud away with my hands. "Why'd you give me those keys?"

A vein throbbed on his temple. "Because your mother hit you. Did you forget about that? Why didn't you call first? It's my apartment, not yours. And your mother didn't care who I slept with. She moved out of the goddamn bedroom."

"Because you kept cheating on her."

"Your mother cares about herself and money," he shouted. "And that's it."

"We have no family because of you." I slammed the piano keys. An ugly clang echoed in the room.

He walked past me, and with his hand on his lower back, he stooped forward through the milky haze of smoke. It hovered around us like an eavesdropping ghost.

He picked up a soapstone vase from an end table next to the sofa, cradled it in the crook of his arm, and then came back in my direction. "I'm not abandoning *you*, Maddie." He stopped still and looked me in the eyes. His face was ashen, as if this fight were burning him out. "Our relationship hasn't changed," he said. "Okay?" His voice softened. "I was dying in the marriage. Couldn't you see that?"

I don't know if he expected an answer. He didn't get one. He claims Velma's "playing" the victim, but he did treat her like shit. And she took it out on me. And no, I did not see him "dying" in the marriage. He did whatever the hell he wanted. He's always spent at least two nights a week at his apartment in the city, sometimes more. Since I can remember, he's taken yearly ski trips to France or Switzerland without my mother. For all I know, he could have a mistress and other kids somewhere, like my grandfather does.

I stared at the piano keys.

He crossed to the carved wood-and-marble foo dog side table and leaned over to stub his cigarette out. "Ah!" he shrieked and braced his back again. He froze there for a few seconds. Then he picked up a Waterford candy dish that was next to the etched brass ashtray he'd just used, and slowly he raised his torso back to the sloped posture he'd come into the room with. He held the items, one in each arm, moved toward me again, and barked, "I tried to make this as painless for you as possible." Then he plodded into the kitchen like an old man, though he's only forty-seven. "That's why I waited until you left."

I leaned back from the piano to watch him wrap the vase and dish in paper bags. I said, "Oh, you think having to deal with all this stuff while I'm in school is better? You think you did me some kind of favor? I'm *here*, because you and Mom have more drama going on than I do, and I'm the one who's studying drama!"

He kept talking to me as he packed the soapstone vase and the glass dish, but he soon ripped open some of the Halloween candy on the counter and stuffed his face, and with his mouth full, I couldn't understand what he was muttering.

I wanted to ask where he was taking the vase and dish. I knew he wouldn't do that if my mother were here. Instead, I got up and went down the hall to my room. I locked the door and didn't come out to say goodbye when he was leaving.

I'm ashamed to admit that when he was gone, I went into the kitchen and devoured a ton of Reese's Peanut Butter Cups. I couldn't stop once I started. I hate when this happens, but it's been happening off and on for years, mostly when I'm not in a good place. Afterward, I stick my finger down my throat and try to get rid of as much of it as I can because I hate being fat even more than I hate that I sometimes can't stop bingeing.

5.

Monroe, New York, 1996

Velma

Sixteen years later, Velma sits at her round oak kitchen table. It's lived in the same spot since the seventies. Her constant companion, Elodie, a French poodle, died earlier in the week, and without her, the house is quiet. Silence elicits anxiety, so Velma keeps the TV on in her second-floor bedroom, even when she isn't up there. The noise filtering down is company. It's cold, though that she doesn't mind. Heating oil is one expense Phil can't be forced to pay because what does he care how low the temperature goes in a house he doesn't live in? But the mortgage remains in both names, and he still uses the ivy-covered cottage adjacent to the house, and with it, the water and electricity, too, and she enjoys his annoyance at subsidizing these expenses.

Velma's been staring at a crate full of Maddie's old stuff since she got home from her shop. It's mostly files, sheet music, photos, and correspondence. There are also a few composition notebooks from her freshman year at NYU. She knows good and well her daughter doesn't like her reading them, but Maddie's been using this house as a damn storage unit at no charge. If her daughter doesn't want her going through her shit, she needs to come and get it.

She flips through the pages until her eye catches those with "my mother" and "Velma" on them repeatedly. And as she begins to read, she feels her pressure rising and a growing urge to tell the kid what she thinks. But they aren't speaking at the moment due to disagreements about Maddie's upcoming wedding, namely, the guest list. Velma wants to invite more of her friends. And also, this business of "jumping the broom." Why would anyone want to mimic something from slavery? And, as far as Velma's concerned, she has as much right to walk Maddie down the aisle as Phil does. Why should he get all the perks? And he wants to bring that bow-wow Abby Goldberg. If that cunt is gonna be there, Velma certainly won't be.

She reads a few more pages, and finally, she can't continue until she's written some thoughts of her own.

Maddie,

I've been hoping you'd come and get these goddamn boxes out of my basement. But I don't know when or if you're gonna make it back East, now that you've decided to stay out there in California so far away. I've been sorting through your stuff and getting rid of what looks like trash. The rest, I guess I'll pack up and send to LA unless you make arrangements for it. Which I'm sure you won't.

So listen, I've been reading your little notebooks again. I'd forgotten what a bitch you made me out to be. That may have been your impression, but I was not as awful as you describe. It was a terrible time, and I was in a fight for my life. Your father, with his fancy lawyer, said he was going to beat my ass in court. You recall that? But he sure didn't, did he? It's that SOB's fault this house hasn't sold. The place needs a ton of work, and you know he's tighter than a nun's hoo-ha. He'll sit in that cottage and let it crumble to the ground around him before he'll put a dime into fixing a damn thing.

I set a good example for you and Livia. Didn't want you girls to think a woman had to give up and take any old BS from a man. Now, I know you think you're in love, and I wish you well in your marriage, I do, but always stand up for yourself. Challenge everything. Do not accept things you don't like just to get along. Because once you do, trust me, there'll soon be another thing, and then another, and another, and it's never worth it. Remember that. I'll be sending this crap out to you when I finish sorting through it.

Mom

6.

November 1, 1980

Maddie

I took a cab back to the hospital earlier today. When I got there, I was Velma's only visitor. Though the bloody gauze around her head had been changed, it still made me cringe to see her face all banged up. At least there was a seat beside the bed this time. I took it and braced myself for the inevitable barrage of complaints about my father. Turned out I was her target, not Phil.

"You know, Grandpa was very hurt by the way you spoke to him." She squinted her bruised eyes at me, and I could discern a frown, despite how swollen her face was.

"He shouldn't be bossing me around." My head began to pound and I rubbed my temples.

"You just be nicer to him. He's done a lot for me."

That's irrelevant, I thought, though I didn't say it.

"I've been meaning to tell you something," she said. "It's time you knew."

Oh God, I thought. *What now?* I didn't say that either.

"Althea and Dad are . . ." Her exhale went on so long she could have put out a fire.

"What?" I asked. "They're what?"

She touched her nose and flinched in pain. "They're not my real parents." She lowered her chin, avoiding my eyes.

It felt like something had shoved me in the chest. And then my stomach had that sensation of an elevator descending. After that, a whoosh went through my head like a shock wave. I had to plant my feet flat and hold on to the edge of the hospital chair because the earth had moved in a strange way.

My grandparents weren't my grandparents? How could that be?

I stared at her.

She was looking down at the frosted cinnamon-colored polish on her nails. Her hair, poking out of the bandages, was matted, blood still in it. Her face remained purple in places. Eyes spotted with red. The hospital gown seemed tight around her neck.

"My birth mother was a maid," she said, staring at her fingers. She picked at the polish. "A *live-in* maid. And she couldn't keep me with her where she worked. She was from Jamaica. I stayed with what I thought were different babysitters. Some were Jamaican immigrants like her. Later, I found out they weren't *babysitters*. They were foster families. Sometimes she'd visit me at these people's homes. I was four when I was placed with your grandfather and his mother. She didn't have any girls, and she liked dressing me up like a doll and doing girly things with me. She said my mother couldn't take care of me, but that I didn't have to worry, because she'd be my grandmother. She'd always look after me. After I'd been staying with them for a few months, my mother visited. She was upset by the way I behaved around them. She said I was too comfortable, like I belonged there and not with her. She pulled me out of their house and said I wasn't going back; she'd find someone else to look after me. But I liked them. I felt safe there. I wasn't safe with my mother. She didn't have a real home for me. She kept her own place but lived at work, and the reason I ended up in foster care is that she left me alone in the apartment for days when I was just a toddler. I barely remember it, but when I saw the court papers, they said I was removed from the home due to 'neglect.'"

Hearing this made me feel anxious. Guilty even, though I don't know why.

"I ran away from her on the street that day," she continued. "I was screaming, and someone must have called the police, because they showed up, and when they did, I gave them the address my foster grandmother had made me memorize. They brought me back, and she and her son, your grandpa, eventually won legal custody."

My head was heavy on my neck. I dug a few fingers into the mess of thick curls and propped them against my scalp to hold up my skull. "What happened to your mother?" I asked.

Velma lifted her eyes to mine briefly before returning to polish-picking. "She visited. Every few months. Until I was about eleven. Maybe twelve. She refused to step foot in the house. My grandmother said she and Dad invited her in, but my mother resented them for taking me, and she would only stand at the door. I stood there too. She never stayed more than ten or fifteen minutes, and she'd always say the same thing as she stared at me: 'Mi just want ta see ya.'"

The look on Velma's face and the soft, desperate sound when she spoke as her mother stunned me. It was Caribbean sun and steel drums—lighter, warmer, and more loving than my mother's voice. And it was as if I were there, seeing my real grandmother standing in that doorway, facing the little girl she'd lost and longing for things to be different. It was somehow familiar, like my own memory.

Tears slipped into my voice as I asked, "Where is she now?"

Velma folded her arms and the image was gone. "*Why*?" she asked tersely.

"Maybe you could find her?"

"Maddie," she scoffed. "I'm sure she ended up a bag lady. She's probably dead. And anyway, I'm not interested. I have a family. I lived with my grandmother for years. But as I got older, she began doing kooky things. She heard voices and thought she had to ward off evil spirits. She wasn't right in the head. I ended up with another foster family for a while, during high school, but Dad stayed in touch. I always saw him as my father. My grandmother ended up hospitalized, and once she was better, we reconnected. Dad married Althea. He wanted me to live with them. Eventually, they legally adopted me. *They're* my family. Why would I want to find her? For what?"

"Because . . . she's *your mother*." I couldn't believe this needed explaining.

"She didn't have the means to take care of me, Maddie," Velma said, raising her voice. "That's how I ended up a ward of the state. At times, she was on the street. She's *not* my mother. *Althea* is my mother. And what're *you* crying about? This has nothing to do with you!" She was shouting now.

I wiped my face with the sleeve of my jacket. "She's my real grandmother. Maybe I'd like to find her."

"Oh, for Christ's sake, this is why I didn't want to tell you." She touched a bruised spot between her eyebrows and winced as if it hurt. "I wanted you to hear it from me and not your father. You're old enough to know that *I* had a tough childhood. *Me*. And my father, who you mouthed off to yesterday, took me in and gave me a life. And I want you to treat him with respect. You understand me? If I wasn't in so much pain yesterday I would've smacked the sour outta you and any sweet left, too."

My chest tightened and my teeth clenched. I leaned toward her mangled face. "No, you wouldn't have. Because you are *not* hitting me anymore."

She tilted her head and said, "Humph."

"I'm too old for you to be putting your hands on me."

She sat straighter. "Then, you better watch your mouth and not give me a reason to."

I stared her dead in the eyes, thinking, *You better not give me a reason to fight back.*

She didn't flinch.

My mother feels more like an enemy than a mother a lot of the time. It would be nice to have a mom who enjoyed being my mom instead of always fighting me. I leaned away from her. "Where's your real father?"

Velma relaxed into her pillow. "Oh, Jesus, who knows? I barely remember the man. She took me to visit him once when I was maybe three years old. No memories of him other than that. He must've acknowledged me, though. His name was on my birth certificate—Liberov."

"Liberov?" I heard my own skepticism. "And he was Jamaican?"

She shook her head. "Russian. He was a Russian Jew."

Now I was astonished. "He was *white*? So, you're *mixed*?"

"Oh, please, what does that even mean?" She squinched her face and spat the words at me like they tasted spoiled. "In *this* country, if you're Black, you're *Black*. Period. I don't consider myself mixed. Althea and Dad are Black, and so am I. So are you."

My mother is considered "light-skinned," though she's browner than I am, and her hair is kinkier. My father and I look more mixed race than she does. I never would have guessed.

I couldn't process any more. I was reeling, trying to understand who she is. Who *I* am. I'm *still* trying to understand it.

Not only is our family broken, but she's lied to me my whole life.

7.

Monroe, New York, 1996

Velma

As Velma thought over what she'd been reading, it occurred to her how rarely she'd let herself think about those people who didn't raise her. Aside from the house visits, her memories were too dim to bring into focus. What had stuck was the brutal fear of being left alone and not knowing if or when her mother was coming back. That panic lived somewhere inside, and it could rise like an unexpected flood and overwhelm her. It *did* sometimes when she contemplated being alone in this big house without a soul who wanted to keep her company.

Philip took her to Puerto Rico once, early in their marriage. Maddie was eight months old, and they left her with his mother and cousin May for a long weekend. When they got back, Maddie wouldn't come to her; she refused to even look at her. Velma lifted the baby out of the playpen. Her little eyes were dark and shiny as polished stones. They glared. Her fat cheeks reddened and puffed with rage. That baby smacked Velma right in the nose with her pudgy baby palm. It hurt, too. Enough that Velma might've socked her little ass back if Phil and Emily hadn't been there. She'd never seen Maddie hit anyone or anything before. But she recognized that rage. She saw herself in it. If someone who's supposed to look after you leaves you helpless and not knowing what's going to happen, they have something coming to them, and it's not a kiss.

Velma's birth mother stopped wanting "just to see" her, as it turned out. Her foster grandmother moved them around a bit, but they were listed. Her mother could've found them. If she wanted to.

Maybe she went back to Jamaica. Maybe she died or just stopped caring. As for her father, if there was a hell, Velma hoped he was burning there, as he should be. That man wasn't poor. Her mother was his hired help. He never gave Velma a damn thing but his name. She'd been more than happy to give that shit back.

8.

November 9, 1980

Maddie

I got a card from my cousin Suzy. Guess my mother told her mother that she told me she was adopted. Suzy wrote to say that we're still cousins and always will be. She also said she'd run into a guy from Monroe I liked for years, Zeke Odom.

Turns out he plays football for Hampton University, and he'd gone up to Howard with his teammates, where Suzy and her boyfriend saw him at a party on campus.

Suzy said Zeke was nothing but nice. And she said he spoke highly of me and that he wished things had gone differently between us. Whatever. He was never my boyfriend because he didn't want to be. But he was cute and one of the only Black guys around where I'm from. I'd dreamed of being a couple from the time I was twelve years old, and I saw him play Pop Warner football.

This morning, I was having breakfast in the dining hall with Jen and Gustavo when Gustavo announced that he had a girlfriend. *Had*, meaning past tense. They broke up the day before yesterday.

"I'm sorry, Gustavo," I said. "Breakups are really hard." I hoped my condolences sounded convincing. I was acting, and according to my teacher, I suck, so . . . Meanwhile, my heart was turning cartwheels.

In all the time Gustavo and I have spent together—in class, rehearsing, hiking back to the dorm, and in the dining hall—he never mentioned the girlfriend. He's always been nice but never flirty—not with me or *any* girls that I've noticed. I thought he might be gay. Or asexual. But no. He's just been someone's loyal boyfriend. And now I swooned.

I was wearing a red dress and heels, because I got suckered into going out with my father and the former family friend he's now fucking. Since Halloween, he's been leaving messages that I've never returned. Then Muriel called me two days ago and apologized for "isolating with Phil while we established our new relationship."

Ew. She said she realized he needed the connection with me, and so "they" were ready to include me in "their" life. She makes me want to barf. I never said I had any interest in being included in "their" life. I might appreciate hanging out with my father once in a while but not with her. Ugh. And yet, there I was, about to see them.

"Ooh, mami," Gustavo said, his eyes sweeping over my body. "You been hiding those nice legs. You're always in sweat pants and jazz shoes. You should dress up more, chica." He batted his eyes at me.

My cheeks felt like flames had lit up inside them. "Merci," I said, immediately regretting it. I'm taking French, which I wanted to practice, but I also wanted to sound cool, which I did not.

Jennifer grinned at Gustavo and fingered her blue hair. "So what happened with your girlfriend? Why'd you break up?"

Before he could tell us, Frannie, a girl from Monroe who goes to school here, appeared at our table. I figured she would gloat about Reagan's recent landslide and how she got to vote for him. I was envious. I wasn't old enough to vote for Carter. Suzy got to vote for him. She said most people at Howard did. Most people from Monroe are conservative working-class Republicans. They hate Carter. Most of Monroe can't stand anyone who supports civil rights. I graduated a year early to get away from the "Frannies." It's unfortunate that this one's here. She used to have super-short hair, like a boy. Now it's long and wavy and the color of wheat. Contact lenses have replaced her Coke-bottle glasses, which isn't fair of me to say because contacts have replaced mine, too. And I have to admit her blue eyes are pretty. She's almost attractive. At least she still has acne scars. And she's big. But solid. A thick chick. Like, could-beat-my-ass thick. As she hovered over the table, she was almost as tall and imposing as the dining hall's refrigerator.

Frannie and I were cheerleaders when I was in seventh grade and she was in eighth. These days, she's built more like a linebacker than a pom-pom girl. Not that I think my body's any better. Since I've been here, a layer of baby fat has spread across my butt, thighs, and belly like butter, even though Jennifer taught me how to improve my binge game. The trick is to puke ice cream. Why? Because it's almost as good coming up as it is going down.

Frannie tried to sit with us, and Jennifer stretched an arm across the chair, faked a smile, and said, "Saving this seat for a friend. Sorry." She knows I don't like the girl. Jen's the coolest.

In high school, a couple of years after a debacle at my slumber party—where Frannie got into it with my cousin Suzy and later told the football team (including Zeke Odom) that my cousin was violent and in a gang, which was not true at all—she and I talked it out in the hallway after gym class, and it seemed like we might be friends again. She invited me to her house.

The day I was supposed to go, she showed up at my locker and said, "My dad didn't know you were Black. When I told him he said, 'We moved out of the city to get away from the niggers and the spics, and now you wanna bring one to our house?'" Her eyes went to her shoes, and she told me she was sorry.

Even though her apology seemed sincere, I couldn't look at Frannie after that. She reminds me of other so-called friends from home who think they're better than anyone who isn't white.

Today, Miss Linebacker was dressed for church and looked uncomfortable in a skirt suit with a frilly Elizabethan-style high-necked shirt. She said, "I heard about your father. My mother says everyone's talking about the scandal. I feel so badly for you, Maddie. It must be terrible. You handling it okay?" She raised her eyebrows, and tense grooves appeared on her pockmarked forehead.

I wanted to spit my coffee at her. "Je suis bien, Frances," I said. "Thanks for your concern."

"What's with the French?" she sneered.

"What's the scandal?" Jen asked. Her voice had an edge, and her eyes went skinny—the way they do when she's about to sledgehammer someone's feelings.

"Oh. Maddie didn't tell you?" Frannie's face brightened. "Her father's committing adultery with a woman in our hometown."

Jennifer squinted through her round glasses as if Frannie were out of focus. "That's a scandal? Every minute of every day, somebody somewhere is cheating."

"Well . . . uh . . ." Frannie pitched forward, looking at Jennifer like she was stupid. "Her father's *Black*."

Jen gasped and, with a hand to her chest, said, "Heavens to Murgatroyd!" Then she threw Frannie's condescending expression back in her face. "Your little town sounds provincial. And so do you. Black people have dicks and pussies like white people. And people with dicks and pussies have sex. We're the same species, in case you weren't aware, dumbass."

I could've kissed Jennifer.

Gustavo's laugh was long and melodic, almost like he was scat singing. He-eee-eee—ai-ai-ai-eee-eee-eee-ai-ai.

I held my lips together, but oh my God, I felt my mouth curl up at the corners and didn't dare look at anyone because I'd bust out giggling. As much as I do not like the girl, I wouldn't laugh in her face like that.

As Frannie marched away, Jennifer taunted, "Be gone, bigot."

I thanked her and stood up to leave.

"Come by after, nena," Gustavo said. "Lemme know how it goes."

His accent is so cute and seductive. For example, "goes" becomes goce. *Lemme know how it goce.* There's no "z" sound at the end of words like throws, blows, or nose; it's throce, bloce, and noce.

He winked, and my heart banged in my ribs like it wanted to break out and fly into his arms.

Jennifer hugged me, and when she did, she bumped into my coffee and knocked it over onto my camel-hair coat. I felt a sudden surge of terror. At home, I was apt to get popped for spilling something on expensive clothes. Then I remembered: Velma isn't *here*. She doesn't have to know. Whew.

Gustavo shoved a wad of napkins at Jen and me, and we tried to sop it up, but it was time to go, and off I went, dripping out of the dining hall with a big brown stain shaped like the state of Florida covering my thigh.

I couldn't be mad at Jennifer. It was an accident, and she's the best. When I shared what Velma said about her birth parents and the way she told me she didn't care where her mother was, Jennifer smiled sadly, nodded, and said that was probably a defense mechanism. That never even occurred to me. And I'm the one whose father's a shrink. She made me realize I should try to have more compassion for Velma.

When I spotted my father in the lobby, he was wearing a bespoke dark-wool suit that I remembered because I'd been with him when he was fitted for it by a flamboyant tailor whose shop was just a few blocks from here. Today, he had his arm around Muriel, who couldn't be bothered to dress up. She was in designer jeans, fuck-me pumps, and a white ski jacket. My father held her waist as if he couldn't bear to let her go.

I have no memories of him ever holding my mother that way—like he adored her. Muriel is a mousy, thin-haired, dirty blonde. I'll be the first to admit my mother's not easy to deal with, but she's definitely more attractive than Muriel.

And yes, I realize looks are not all there is to attraction, but why is it, every time I've known my father to be into a woman—at least three different people in the last couple of years—it's been a plain, skinny white lady? It's not that I have anything against white women. It's that my father's repeated choices feel like an intentional rejection of Black women. How am I supposed to feel about that?

Muriel's long-haired little girl was with them, too. Nine-year-old Amy. She's cute. Probably because she takes after her daddy. He introduced me as if I didn't know the two of them. I've known them for years. I've been to their house, and they've been to ours.

Amy welded her face to her mother's belly and refused to say hi. Who could blame her? The poor kid's father died less than two months ago, and now my father is with her mother and spending nights at their house. And she has no choice but to roll with it. I'd probably refuse to speak, too.

As we exited through the revolving door onto the sidewalk and passed under the green awning, he said we were going to his friend's art opening in Soho. And instead of a cab, he was taking his Mazda RX-7—the two-seater—which meant Amy and I would have to stow ourselves in the rear hatch like luggage. He headed toward the corner.

I hesitated. "Dad. I'm wearing a dress. Can't we take a taxi?"

"Don't start with me," he said without looking back.

"I can take the train and meet you there."

He turned and shouted, "Get in the goddamn car!"

On the drive downtown, Amy and I had to crunch into a trunk with a glass cover. Unsafe and probably illegal. I've ridden back there before, during high school, but I'm too big and too old for it now. My father is an eccentric and careless idiot. And what the hell is wrong with Muriel? Who lets their little girl ride in a glass trunk?

Amy's dirty little Frye boots were on my fancy wet coat, which she said had a "penis stain" on it, once she finally decided to speak. When the car hit bumps, my head bounced up and occasionally tapped the glass. And when it fell back, it hit a brown paper bag full of knickknacks my father had apparently taken from our house.

At the art show, Phil left me alone and introduced Muriel and Amy to the other attendees. When he finally introduced me to the artist, he called me Livia, my sister's name. I felt like he'd spat in my face.

The artist, a spiky-haired woman in her forties who wore a man's three-piece suit, smiled and said, "Thanks for coming, Livia."

I cleared my throat. "Actually, I'm his other daughter," I said and told her my name.

And my father frowned at me as if *I* were the one who'd done something offensive.

He turned back to the androgynous painter and the work, which was etchings in black and white of naked women in groups, their bodies draped around each other like shawls. The pieces were pretty and kind of dreamy. The women barely had faces, almost abstract, though you could clearly make out their entwined bodies, seemingly happy, in a matriarchal bubble. I watched my father and his new family for a moment. I knew he wouldn't miss me if I left. I stood straight and tall in my heels and walked out.

Back at the dorm, I took my shoes off in the elevator and rode it to Gustavo's floor. The hallway smelled like popcorn and pot. He cracked the door open just wide enough to show his face. And that blinding smile.

"Hola, chica," he said quietly, standing on the threshold so I couldn't see inside.

A female voice yelled from behind, "Who the hell's that, Tavo?"

He heaved a sigh and closed his eyes. "Sorry," he whispered. "I'm a have to talk to you later." The door snapped shut.

For several seconds, I stood there without moving, dazed, like someone had knocked me in the head.

He told me to come by. He flirted with me.

Students passed, going to and from rooms, and I was aware that I looked conspicuous loitering there, like a strumpet in my hot-pepper red dress and my ridiculous stained coat, holding my high-heeled pumps. I turned and carried them over my shoulder, one finger in each shoe, as I padded down the carpeted hallway toward the stairwell in my stocking feet.

A budding lyric to the tune of Michael Jackson's "Ben" came to me. I entertained myself by singing as I made it up. "What's the reason not to hate my liiife? No-thing ever seems to wooork ooout riiight. Men are rotten to the bone. I should have stayed at home. This bullshit makes me mad. Wanna do something ba-a-ad . . ."

Back in my room, I shoveled a whole pint of ice cream down my throat and brought it up again. I guess this habit is kind of like a drug, a stress reliever. Better this than alcohol or shooting up, right?

9.

Los Angeles, California, 1996

Maddie

When Maddie opens a box from Velma and reads the included note, she has to pour herself a full glass of wine. Her mother is still as angry as ever and acts as if the divorce happened yesterday.

Maddie is thirty-three years old. In a few weeks, she'll be getting married. Since she got to L.A. a couple of years ago, Velma has been trying to draw her back into the drama. The most recent catastrophe was when Phil had been staying at his cottage at the estate, and he and Abby Goldberg (whom he's been seeing on and off since the seventies) decided to go away for the weekend. They left Abby's car in the parking spot near the street, far from the house, at the base of Velma's considerably long driveway.

The car didn't impede Velma's ability to enter or exit the property. It was so far from the house that she didn't have to look at it if she didn't want to. The mere fact that it was there drove her to berserkville.

She called Maddie. Why? Excellent question. No. Good. Reason. That's why. It's just the way she is. If Velma's upset, she dumps it on Maddie. When Maddie's upset, however, Velma's catchphrase is, "Well, I don't know what to tell you." Then she changes the subject to herself and talks nonstop until she's ready to hang up.

Maddie told her, "Mom. It's been sixteen years since you separated. Why do you care what he does?"

"I will not be disrespected," Velma roared.

Maddie had to hold the phone away from her ear.

"This is my house. That bitch is trying to stake her territory. I'm gonna smash her windows and slash her fucking tires."

While her reaction was over the top, Maddie took into consideration that when she was nearing the end of high school and Phil was still living in the house, he did have sex with Abby Goldberg in the master bedroom while Velma was at work. According to her mother, they left the room disgusting, disheveled, and stinking of sex. The woman's purse had spilled onto the bedding, and it included a receipt for art supplies, as well as a note from her daughter Flora, who had once been Maddie's friend.

Velma surmised that leaving clues meant they wanted her to know. She claimed they were purposely rubbing their affair in her face. She moved into the guest room that night, but she did not *leave the house*, which, according to Velma, had been Phil's goal. Velma made it her mission to make sure Phil would never, *ever* get the house for himself (and whatever whore he thought he was gonna have living with him).

Maddie worried her mother might face vandalism charges if she damaged the vehicle. So, from Los Angeles, she called around and found a tow service in Monroe to get the car off her mother's driveway and moved onto the street.

Now she's in the midst of planning her wedding, and neither of her parents can stop their endless acrimony. They're fighting over the walk down the aisle; Phil claims that if Maddie allows her mother to share the duty with him, which Velma insists upon, it will suggest that he's been half a father. And if she doesn't let Velma do it, her mother has not only threatened to withhold her less than 2 percent contribution to the party that Maddie's financing almost entirely herself, but she also says she won't come. There's no way to win.

Maddie's accepted that both Phil and Velma are immature and out of their minds. Unfortunately, acceptance doesn't necessarily lead to peace of mind if she's forced to interact with them.

Sometimes, she avoids Phil's calls for weeks. And when Velma treats her to extended bouts of silence (which she often does, after saying something horrible, provoking Maddie to lose her temper, leading Velma to ignore Maddie, claiming she's the actual victim), it's a relief.

Maddie stares at the package Velma sent. She gulps her wine. She should absolutely not look through it. It will only uncover old wounds. It will be torture.

But isn't that exactly what she's wired for? They built her. Her crazy fucking parents constructed a repository for masochism that is her mind, and they live there. Maddie has tried and tried and tried again to evict them—to finally be free. Yet they refuse to leave.

10.

November 16, 1980

Maddie

A week later I've still had "pas de sexe"—none—while Jennifer's been sleeping with some grown-ass rock musician and others in his apartment a few nights a week. I hoped to have popped my sweet berry with Gustavo by now, but apparently, his novia told him, "I ain't goin' nowhere."

I think he's afraid of the girlfriend. I believe him when he says he's getting out of the relationship, even though Jennifer says he's almost certainly lying.

"Learn this while you're young," she told me. (She's only two years older than I am.) "Men lie. All the time. Especially about women. They don't even think of it as lying. They think it's one of their patriarchal inalienable rights."

This is no great revelation. Of course men lie. Everyone lies. Still, I want to believe him.

I'm doing well in singing class. Our teacher is Black, she's been on Broadway, and I'm her favorite. She always lets me sing longer than everybody else. But acting class has been about as fun as having my nails plucked with pliers.

I did an improvisation that I thought was going well. In the scene, my classmate Tina was trying to get me to go to a party, and I was trying to get her to stay with me because my mother was visiting, and I didn't want to be alone with Velma since all she does is bitch about Phil.

The ex-movie star stopped the scene. "What keeps you there, Tina? Listening to Maddie's whining?"

I winced like he'd just slammed my finger in a door.

Tina's from Canarsie. She didn't like his attitude and gave him hers. "Empathy, Vic-tah," she said with Brooklyn moxie. "And my parents are spendin' a fortune to send me to this school. What? Am I supposed to walk off the stage?"

Victor's scowling face whiplashed as if she'd smacked him. "If you're just going to sit there," he said, louder, "try coming up with some behavior that makes someone want to watch you. Otherwise, you're wasting your parents' money. You can't learn to act by doing the same whiny scene about Maddie every week." Then his eyes departed Tina's and moved to mine. "*Enough* with your parents' divorce."

I slithered off stage, wishing I were invisible.

Why can't Victor ever say anything good about me? Maybe if I told him I'm part Russian, he'd be more impressed. I could be a descendant of Stanislavsky for all he knows.

When I sat down, Gustavo squeezed my knee like he felt sorry for me. I didn't want his pity. I wanted him to fan my fiddle and cool my heat. To poke the needle and grind my wheat, like the singer Alberta Hunter's "Handy Man."

After class, Gustavo walked back to Fifth Avenue with me. As we cut past Union Square and around the dope addicts, a throng of pigeons rose around us. Wind blew in our faces, and he told me he wanted to transfer out of our section because of Victor.

He said, "That Long Island girl, Sassy—dios mío, she cries every week about being a slut. And Jack always does the same improvisay-tion about losin' a sibling. Victor doesn't complain about them. But he doesn't wanna hear about me trying to be independent of my family or you struggling with yours. Why? 'Cos he relates to them, chica, and not to us."

I nodded as if I could see that. But coming from Monroe, where one teacher slapped me and another let a kid call me a nigger every day and told me to ignore it, if Victor was biased, he was still nowhere near as bad as what I'd experienced elsewhere. I guess if you've grown up in the city and you're used to having teachers and kids of different races around, your expectations are higher.

It's obvious Victor doesn't like me, though I can't be sure that's because of my color. It seems to be because he thinks I can't act, and he might be right. And even if it is because I'm Black, I'll only have him for an academic year. I can deal with it.

I licked my lips and tossed Gustavo a small smile. I've been using a touch of Ultra Sheen to tame my frizzy curls. And I've been trying to watch what I eat and do sit-ups. I was wearing jeans and leather boots—no more sweats and jazz shoes. I hoped he noticed.

"Nothing wrong witchu acting out your situation to sort through your emotions, Maddita. Maybe it's not perfect 'art' yet, but don't listen to him. You're real. That's what's great about you. It's beautiful. And Victor should be trying to help you refine that quality instead of shutting you down." Gustavo took off his cool suede hat and placed it on my head. "You've gotten better, chica. You didn't push, and I believed you. It was good work."

I thanked him and tried not to squeal or grin too widely.

Gustavo's a really good actor. He's been studying since he was a kid, and he's already been in a couple of movies and on TV. The fact that he saw something worthwhile in my work made me feel high. I was practically floating!

He wanted to take me to dinner.

"Like, on a date?" I asked.

He didn't confirm, but we stopped at Beefsteak Charlie's near the dorm and sat in a booth. He said, "I'm done with my girlfriend. But it's complicated, see, 'cos she's super aggressive, and she goes to Purchase, so sometimes she just hops a bus and shows up at my room." He sighed anxiously. "We were high school sweethearts at Performing Arts. I care about her a lot, I do, but I've been trying to move on for a while."

I was still wearing his tan derby. I touched its rim to be sure I hadn't imagined it.

"Why can't you just be firm and break it off?" I asked. "It's not like you're married."

He set his fork down and shoved his fingers into the curly wilderness atop his head. "But she's practically like family. Her mami works at my papi's restaurant." He stared at his plate in thought as he tugged at his hair like he was punishing it.

I learned that Gustavo and the girlfriend have been together since ninth grade. She was his "first." It's a lot to compete with, and I'm not sure I can—or want to.

He paid for my salad and walked me back to my room.

When he went to kiss me, I leaned away. "Not if you're still with your girlfriend. That would make you a cheater."

He took his hat back, batted his lashes, and asked if I'd give him a minute to untangle his situation. Without replying, I went inside wondering what the hell that meant. I still don't know. Does it mean wait, while he finishes messing with his girlfriend? How long is "a minute"? Does it mean, don't date anyone else? There isn't anyone else, but damn, he has some massive cajones to ask.

11.
New York, New York, 1980
Velma

Velma met Maddie at City Center for the ballet. She'd been feeling better since her dad and Althea had given her money for a lawyer and a bit extra to live on. She loved the auditorium. It was magnificent, Moorish, with an arabesque ceiling and mosaic tiles.

So much was still up in the air, but on the plus side, the swelling on her face had subsided, and she had her looks back, thank God. Makeup covered the bruises and the fading scars. She'd treated herself to a stylish haircut, and there'd been lots of compliments. And since Phil left, she'd lost fifteen pounds. From stress, but so what? She was a size six. Velma hadn't been a size six since before she got pregnant. And in her tan Sasson pantsuit, in good-quality suede, she caught more men's heads turning to look at her than at her daughter. Maddie was chunky in an ugly down jacket that Phil must've bought her. That bulgy thing wasn't flattering at all.

The two of them sat and listened to the orchestra warming up—strings pinging and symbols clanging. Maddie glanced around and complained that there were no other Black people in the audience. This girl always focused on the negative. No *you look good, Mom.* Or *thanks for the tickets, Mom.*

"What goddamn difference does it make?" Velma said as she removed her jacket. "*We're* here. And we came to see the dancing, not the audience. Can't you do anything but complain? Maybe try asking me how I am. How 'bout that?" She watched Maddie stare at the back of the seat in front of her.

The kid hissed out a long exhale. "How *are* you?" she finally said, enunciating her words like she was chewing them.

"I'm *fighting*. That's how I am. Your smug, son-of-a-bitch father thinks he's so damn clever. Thinks he's gonna beat me, take everything, and put my ass in the street. The fucking idiot is too stupid to know how much I know about what he's hiding. And don't you tell him either." She scratched a piece of dry skin off of her lip.

"What's he hiding?" Maddie asked.

Velma turned and squinted at her. "*Money*. What do think this fight is *about*? Listen, if you're ever in a situation with a man you don't trust, you look at his mail and you go through his trash. Remember that," she said, punctuating her advice with a pointed finger.

Maddie rested her head against the rim of the seat and said, "He's making me take out a federal loan for next semester's tuition. And he says I might have to move out of the dorm, because you stopped paying your half of the bills on the house, and you won't contribute what you promised for my expenses."

Velma's face went hot. She growled out a breath. "Your father was the one who chose to do this, *now*, as you started school." She sat up straighter. "He makes three times what I make, Maddie. Trust me, that bastard has your tuition, and he can afford the dorm. He's just cheap. Trying to conceal his income, because he thinks he'll get away with giving me less. You know all those skiing trips he's taken to Switzerland over the years? Did you know he's been depositing money over there?"

Maddie didn't answer.

"Yeah, there's a whole lot you don't know," Velma said. "The more you stir the shit, the worse it stinks."

Maddie turned to her. "There's a lot I didn't know about *you* either. Stuff I *should* have known." She covered her ears. "Stop telling me all this. You stress me out, and it makes me eat."

"Oh, please. What do *you* have to be stressed about? *I'm* the old lady going through hell *and* menopause at the same damn time, and *I* look fantastic."

Maddie scoffed. "You're not that old, Mom. You could even remarry one day."

"Ha," Velma said, staring straight ahead. "I've got less than no desire to go traipsing through any more tragedies." She shook her head. "Marriage is one damn disaster after another. Any of that syrupy, romantic happiness is behind me now. I'm just trying to survive." When Velma turned to Maddie, she was greeted with the same condescending sneer that Phil used to give her, like she was some dumbbell. "Who the hell do you think you're looking at like that?"

"You sound silly," Maddie said. "Things won't be unhappy *forever*. If you have dreams and plans, there're always things to look forward to."

"Yeah, you think that, because you're twenty-some years younger than me. Wait 'til you're my age."

"I'm thirty-some years younger than you."

"Don't be a smart-ass. Life doesn't work that way, Maddie. Dreams are baloney. You get what you get. It's not always happy, and it's never what you hoped for."

Strings plucked and horns whined from the pit.

Maddie crossed her arms in her puffy coat. "I don't think that's true. I think we *make* what we get by believing in dreams and pursuing them."

Just then, a gaggle of six little Black girls in shabby-looking school uniforms plopped down directly in front of them.

Velma's jaw tightened. "Yeah? And what dreams do you have, Miss Madeline?" She rolled her eyes. "That you're gonna be a star someday?"

Maddie stared at her for what seemed like a long while. "You don't even want me to be happy, do you?"

Velma had to think about that. But the young girls were so noisy, she *couldn't* think. They were giggling and bouncing in the seats, making a racket. "These goddamn kids better shut up when this thing starts," she said. She heard Maddie sniffling beside her and thought, *Jesus. The kid's so sensitive.*

The velvet curtain rose, and a row of ballerinas twirled across the stage. All six little girls leaned forward, ooohing and aaahing.

"Be quiet," Velma scolded through clenched teeth.

"Mom, *shhh*."

"These tickets weren't cheap, Maddie," she whisper-shouted. "And I am not about to let these kids ruin my experience."

"What're you gonna do—*slap* them? That's assault, y'know?"

One of the young girls turned to another and said, "I'm the one in pink. Which one are you?"

And something pricked at Velma's heart. For a moment, she remembered having been small. Innocent. And hopeful. She'd also been two steps from the gutter when most girls were playing with dolls and wishing on stars. All she could hope for then was enough to eat and not to be left in another stranger's house. Dreams were a trick. She'd had some when she married Phil. The happily-ever-after sort. She wasn't programmed for dreaming anymore.

But what did she know? Maybe it *could* be different for Maddie. Maybe she'd be lucky enough to become *the one in pink* or whatever the hell it was she wanted. She patted her daughter's hand. "I'm not at my best right now," she told her. "Don't listen to me."

Her daughter didn't bother to acknowledge her. She simply sat there without a word or a glance and watched the stage. The girl never offered any support.

When the show was over, Velma thought Maddie would walk her to the subway. It was the least the kid could do after Velma came into the city and treated her.

Instead, Maddie quickly said goodbye and rushed off without even a kiss.

Velma tried with her. She really did. Maddie had become Phil's child. She thought her father was so perfect. *His* stupid ass was full of big dreams, too. One dream he had was that he was going to kick her out of the marriage and down into a ditch, but that would become his nightmare because Velma knew how to fight, and she was wired to survive. That pampered, spoiled, pussy-ass man never had to struggle like she did. He lived in the same big house with his mommy in the Bronx from birth until he left his first wife. Velma's rough ride had cultivated grit and stamina that Phil had no idea of. And she would sooner lick the devil's sweaty balls in hell than let that bastard beat her.

12.

New York, New York, 1980

Phil

Phil had been depositing Maddie's allowance in the bank on the corner of Fifth Avenue and Eighth Street. When the kid decided she didn't feel like visiting him anymore, he decided to let the funds run out.

That put a hasty end to her avoidance. She was on her way to his office now.

He'd just finished with his last patient for the day. As he leaned down, bringing his fingers to his toes to stretch his aching back, he considered having a drink before she got there. Then he thought better of it. He'd need clarity if she brought her teenage drama with her.

He'd discouraged Maddie from looking for a job this semester. The adjustment to the new environment and to taking classes would be enough for her to handle, he figured. But now, with Velma reneging on her portion of expenses and with his lawyer's fees mounting, Maddie would need to get something part-time in the new year. And she'd probably have to move into his office unless she wanted to stay with her grandparents in Harlem. He wouldn't press her about it yet. One thing at a time.

She rang the bell, though she still had keys. Ribald, his parrot, squawked for attention like he always did when Phil opened the door. She stood there, a mop of dark curls framing her baby face.

"Nice of you to make an appearance," he said, taking her in.

He leaned in to kiss Maddie's cheek, and she ducked away and moved around him into the apartment. Then, as if something caught her attention, without removing her hat or coat, she trotted past the noisy bird, through the waiting area, and straight into the open door of his office.

"Oh my God. That is so gross!"

"All right, enough, Ribald," he reprimanded the bird and followed Maddie into the room, where she stood gaping at the black-and-white eight-by-ten framed photo on his desk.

"Is that . . . Muriel's *ass*?"

It was. But it was an inarguably tasteful portrait. A fine art, body-in-nature nude of his lover in the woods. And her backside was perfect. Petite, unblemished, and without a trace of fat.

Maddie turned to him. "Why are you like this? You're so disgusting." She was crying.

This startled Phil. Tears? Over a photo?

"You knew I was coming," she went on. "You couldn't put that shit away?"

The bird continued to squawk in the other room.

Phil smiled now. She was so dramatic. "Oh, calm down," he said, pulling his silver money clip from his breast pocket. He peeled off a fifty-dollar bill. "Here."

Maddie stared at it for a second, then another, and another, and finally, she removed her mitten and took it.

Phil exhaled, unsure of why he felt so relieved. "Anika, the artist whose opening we went to, shot the photograph. She's working on a series, and she asked Muriel to model for it. She's going to paint it."

"Please don't buy that painting. *Please.*" Maddie put a hand on her cheek. "Nobody but you wants to look at that. Do you leave this thing out for your patients to see?" She puckered her face as if something noisome were in the room.

Phil laughed. "I know. I know. You don't want to think of your father having a girlfriend. That's why you've been avoiding me."

He watched her eyes rise to the ceiling. Then she looked around, seeming to take in the art: the amoeba-like biomorphic paintings by Abby of his and her entwined bodies, as well as the sculpture in the waiting room of the head bust tiled with tiny mirrors and the knife protruding from between its eyes, and the large portrait of himself suspended in clouds like a deity. Finally, her gaze landed on the parrot, who was now banging on the bars of his cage in the other room. She pocketed the money and put her mitten back on.

"I've got to get out of here," she said.

"Wait a minute." Phil blocked her path. "Am I right? I'm not supposed to date?"

"Dad . . ." She avoided his eyes by looking at the floor. "Is this—? This is the rug from our house." She glanced up at him again. "What's it doing *here*?"

"I bought it, Maddie. It's *mine.* Am I entitled to have some of my things?"

"Isn't it Mom's, too?"

Phil stared her in the face. "Did Mom just give you fifty dollars?"

Maddie stared back at him. "Thanks," she said. "I really need to go now. Could you please move?"

Phil ran both hands over the top of his newly close-cropped hair and then clasped them behind his neck. "Maddie, why does it have to be like this? You don't want to see your father?"

She covered her face with her mittened hands. When she lowered them, she looked at Muriel's eight-by-ten nude and then back at Phil. "I don't belong anymore. You're . . . different. I mean, look at your hair. And you have a new life . . . with your new white family. Anika should paint *that*."

Ah, he realized what the issue was. He could see how she might think he was transforming his life to exclude her. "I told you I'm not abandoning you. You're my family. That won't change. Listen, we're going skiing in Killington this weekend for the holiday. I'd like you to come."

Maddie blinked and shook her head. "We always go to Aunt Syl's for Thanksgiving." She eyed the Turkish rug again. "And I can't leave Mom alone. She'll be mad. Livia will be with *her* mother. And you have Muriel and Amy."

Phil felt his nostrils flare. "I said, *this weekend*, didn't I? Why can't you go with your mother on Thanksgiving and then come with us on Friday?"

"Killington's in Vermont, right?" She exhaled. "I don't really want to."

Phil's back teeth hurt as they pressed together. He needed a cigarette. If he moved to his desk to get one, she might walk out. "Look," he said. "I'm paying for your tuition, your dorm room, your meal plan, *and* I give you spending money. You think I'm just supposed to fork out for all your expenses, and you get to say, *Sure, I'll take your dough, Dad, but screw you*?"

"Don't most parents pay things for their kids when they're my age?"

"Do they? Tell that to your fucking mother. In fact, you know what? You want to stay with her the whole weekend? Get your money from her from now on, too."

Maddie's face reddened. "Why do you even want me to go with you?"

"To include you in my life, Madeline." Phil couldn't wait another second. He reached for the pack of cigarettes on his desk. "Muriel's bringing *her* kid. I want mine there, too."

13.
New York, New York, 1980
Livia

Livia had dinner with Phil on Thanksgiving Eve at a jazz supper club on University Place. Before their meal came and as her father talked about his new relationship, she listened politely and doodled parallelograms on a red cocktail napkin with a Montblanc fountain pen—a gift from the partners at her firm. The food was adequate. The music, however, was too loud, and Livia didn't enjoy jazz. She'd told Phil this on more than one occasion, and each time she did, it passed through the sieve of his mind and fell straight out like flour.

She was *not*, as he insisted, an ardent fan who appreciated the music. The improvisations went on too long. Drum solos banging and clanging gave her a headache. The worst were the saxophone players. Invariably full of themselves, they took twice as long as other musicians to get on with their self-indulgent diversions and return to the actual song.

Livia preferred music played as written. That notwithstanding, she sat opposite her father, whose yellow silk tie and pocket handkerchief matched, and she dutifully ate her shrimp scampi without complaint because she'd long known there was no remedy for her father's mental glitch. Once Phil believed something, that "thing" burrowed itself into the man's brain, and nothing, not even facts, could dislodge it.

She first became aware of this when she was five, and for the second year in a row, he got her mother's birth date wrong. It was the *eleventh* of May, but Phil gave her mother a gift on the *tenth*. Though Dorothy corrected him, it happened again the following year. He'd even quarreled with her, insisting her birth date was, in fact, the tenth. Livia watched with incredulity as Phil argued his erroneous case. He got the date wrong yet again the following year when Livia was seven, and soon after that, he moved out.

There were other examples. Her stepmother loved art nouveau jewelry, but Phil mistakenly believed art deco was her style of choice, and back when he and Velma still exchanged gifts, he'd buy her deco pieces, which she would receive without enthusiasm. Grandma Emily was the art deco aficionado, not Velma, but Phil could not—or *would* not—process this and update it in his mind. Velma stopped correcting him and resorted to selling the deco jewelry in her shop. Likewise, though her feelings were hurt, Livia no longer bothered to give Phil the satisfaction of reminding him that she didn't share his other daughter's zeal for the purported great American art form. She suspected, though she couldn't confirm, that there was a dark component to his forgetfulness, one intended to foster rancor and competition, but since she lived in Boston and intentionally saw him infrequently, it wasn't worth it to engage.

They'd just returned to his apartment when the doorbell rang. Phil tried plying Ribald with sunflower seeds to get him to stop screeching as Livia opened the door. Madeline carried an oversized army-green duffel bag, and she was bundled in a scarf and ski jacket. Livia kissed the pumpkin on the cheek and stepped aside to let her in. After setting her bag down, her sister stuck her fingers in her ears. The bird's screeching *was* annoyingly loud.

Maddie's tightly curled hair was thick and touched her shoulders. It was essentially an Afro, though, she wore it parted in the center and with bangs. Livia, too, had sported an Afro when she was just a bit older than Maddie. These days, as a corporate lawyer, she kept it long, shiny, and perpetually straight. The conservative look suited her. The wild-child Afro phase had been inspired by a boyfriend who'd been inspired by the times. That ex-boyfriend was a banker now. Livia saw him occasionally at alumni events in Cambridge. Aside from their hair, she and Maddie resembled one another physically, though Livia was taller. Slimmer, too. Intellectually, she saw little similarity at all.

"Did you see that thing?" Maddie's pointy chin jutted in the direction of their father's desk and the frame that housed the hideous photo. Her fingers remained lodged in her ears.

The obstreperous bird had not relented.

Livia nodded. Of course she'd seen it. One couldn't miss it, but the bare derriere in the woods wasn't something she cared to discuss. She preferred to ignore their father's perversions.

"He says it's 'art,'" Maddie said. "You're the artist. What do you think?"

What Livia thought was that their father had eccentricities in abundance. Nothing surprised her. He moved to a peculiar beat that he alone could hear, and neither of them would change that.

Livia stepped closer to the inner office threshold and glanced at his walls. None of her paintings hung there, though she'd gifted him many over the years. She feigned indifference. "It doesn't matter what I think," she said. "Art is subjective. He collects what he likes."

The bird finally stopped screeching and spoke the words, "The bitch has me trapped!" He then banged his beak clamorously against his metal cage before repeating the phrase.

"Oh, be quiet, Ribald," their father said with bluster.

Maddie put her face in her hands. Livia wasn't sure if she was laughing or weeping.

Phil finally stepped away from the parrot and joined Livia and Maddie in the office.

In her peripheral vision, Livia saw him watching her as she stared at his paintings.

"I know *you* can appreciate good art, right, Liv?" he said, gesturing to two repulsive biomorphs on the wall opposite his psychoanalytic couch. "Those are by Abby Goldberg. Remember her?" The sly smile he launched at Livia was akin to a conspiratorial wink.

She did not return the smirk. Livia had seen the paintings. They'd hung there since she was in college. She refused to give their father a reaction.

"Her work is all about our sex life," he continued proudly.

Maddie cringed, her shoulders rising to her ears. She and Livia exchanged a look.

Livia was embarrassed for him. Her eyes met Maddie's. "Ready to hit the road?"

"*Yes*," Maddie exclaimed without hesitation.

Their father was supposed to drive Madeline to Monroe that night. The new girlfriend demolished that plan when she decided she wanted to spend Thanksgiving in the city to show her daughter the Macy's parade and the holiday lights on Fifth Avenue. This was likely prompted by Phil, as these were things he'd done with Livia and Madeline in the past. Since Livia was heading to her aunt's house in New Paltz, where her mother would be, she offered Maddie a ride home.

In the car, Livia asked, "So, how are you doing with all that's going on?"

Maddie shrugged without looking at her. "Why is Daddy such a sex maniac? *Elch*."

Livia watched the glowing red brake lights on the countless cars ahead of them. Traffic was thick with city dwellers fleeing for the holiday. "Who knows?" she said. "He's always been a libertine. Do you know what that means?"

"A dog?"

"Exactly. And let's face it—if Daddy wasn't educated and hadn't come from a decent family, he'd be locked up somewhere."

Maddie smiled sadly. "Probably," she said, nodding in agreement. "My mother's crazy, too. You're lucky you don't have to deal with *that* scorned woman's fury. Did you know she was adopted?"

"Yes, pumpkin."

Maddie turned to Livia. "How come you never told me?"

Livia maintained her gaze through the windshield as they inched north on the West Side Highway. "Because she didn't *want* me to tell you. And because she *is* crazy."

Maddie turned toward her window. Lights from the tall apartment buildings twinkled to their right like a constellation.

"You know, Daddy left *my* mother, too, Maddie. And I was only in second grade. If anyone's lucky, it was you. You got the big houses and all those trips abroad that I didn't get. And ballet, voice, and piano lessons . . . I didn't get any fricking lessons." Though Livia was aware of the GW Bridge illuminated in the distance, she wasn't really seeing it. As she stared in its direction, she remembered visiting her daddy in his beautiful home, in his well-to-do-life, and each time she'd want to stay and wasn't allowed to.

"At least you got this car," Maddie said.

"What?" Livia gripped the wheel of the beat-up Chrysler Newport sedan.

"Daddy promised to teach me how to drive in this car, and then he gave it to you, which makes no sense because you're rich now, and I know you have another car. And he wouldn't teach me in his new car, because it's a stick shift. That's why I don't have a license."

"No, I don't have another car because I'm paying off loans and investing in real estate, and because I walk to work, Miss Know-It-All. You got *everything*. And I got this ramshackle piece of shit, and you think I shouldn't even have that? Un-fucking-believable. You've always acted like I shouldn't exist."

"No, that was *you* who didn't want *me* to exist. In all those sketches you drew of family holidays, I'm in exactly none of them. I was glad you existed. I wished you *did* live with us. But you should be happy you didn't have to grow up in vanilla-ville. Did you ever have to be the only Black kid in your class, or your Girl Scout troop, or on the cheerleading squad? You think that was fun?"

Both girls stared through the windshield.

"When you were three," Livia said, "you opened *every* present under the Christmas tree."

"There was no family," Maddie said.

"Including all of *mine*," Livia said.

"You had all the cousins in the Bronx," Maddie said. "And you had Uncle Lawrence and Grandma Emily. I had nobody."

"When you were five, you asked Daddy which one of us he loved more. When you were six, you said, '*I'm* thin and beautiful, and you're fat. *I* take ballet lessons, and you just sit.' At your seventh birthday party, you said I wasn't invited and told me to get out. When you were eleven, you knocked the cake off the table and ruined my graduation party." Livia was shouting now. "You were always spoiled. And you spoiled everything!"

Maddie was quiet for a while before she said, "I'm sorry. Guess I was jealous. All the relatives love you best. Especially Grandma Emily."

"Oh, shut up. No, she doesn't."

Maddie faced her. "She *told* me, Livia."

"She did *not*."

"I was visiting, and she had a picture of you as a toddler on her dresser, next to the mirror tray, and I thought it was me, and she told me it wasn't, and I asked why she didn't have one of me, too, and she said, "Because Livia's my first grandchild, and she's the one I love best."

"Damn," Livia said as if that was unfortunate, and yet the thought made her smile.

"Remember what Daddy told us when I asked who he loved best?" Maddie said. "He was driving, and we were in the back seat of the blue Chrysler. He told me to look at my hand, and he said that asking him which child he loved the most was like asking him which finger he loved most. He said we were both a part of him, and he loved us more than he could measure."

Livia grunted and left it at that. She loved their father, and she knew Maddie needed to love him, too. And so she didn't offer her opinion, which was that Phil was flawed. He loved them not for themselves but in the limited way his flaw allowed, as mere extensions of himself.

They made it to the house. Though Livia was apprehensive about seeing Velma for the first time since the split with Phil, she couldn't very well avoid her now that she was there. She'd show her face and then leave quickly. After all, this stop had already made her late in getting to her aunt's house.

She helped Maddie lug her duffel bag up the stone steps to the porch and through the door. They set it down, and both were immediately stunned to find no furniture in the foyer. No paintings on the walls. No photos. Nothing. They peeked into the living room. Same. Stripped bare. Empty walls and floor. Every piece of furniture was gone, including the piano.

Livia whispered, "What the fuck?"

"Mom," Maddie yelled, "where are you? What the hell happened?"

They found Velma in the kitchen, opening a box of Mueller's elbows for her macaroni and cheese. "My girls," she squealed, turning toward them in a full face of makeup and her gray sweat suit, arms open for hugs.

Livia was surprised to see the good old oak table and chairs in the room since it felt, from what she saw, that the entire house had been cleared out.

"Where's all our stuff?" Maddie's voice trembled.

Velma's pretty smile flattened as she crossed her arms without embracing either of them. She growled, "That asshole started taking things out of this house. *Stealing* from me to give to that bitch. Let me tell you both something." She pointed at them now. "Your father may not have respected me in this *marriage*, but he's gonna respect me in this *divorce*."

A chill rippled through Livia. She would have turned to see Maddie's reaction, but Velma took a step forward, and Livia realized she was glaring straight at her.

Velma cocked her head. "I heard you offered him money to help buy me out of this house."

Livia swallowed. Shit. How'd she know? Rare was the occasion when Livia's mind failed to deliver words to her mouth. This was one such occasion. Phil declined the offer. Had he been moronic enough to tell someone? Did Velma have his phone tapped?

"You save your money, girly," Velma said, her lips moving over closed teeth. "'Cause I'm not going any-damn-where. You understand me?"

Livia nodded. "Okay," she said, patting Maddie on the shoulder as she backed out of the kitchen. "Good seeing you, Velma. Happy Thanksgiving. Bye." Livia trotted quickly through the empty foyer and out the front door, jogging the rest of the way to her car.

14.
November 26, 1980
Maddie

Lucky me. My desk, bed, and nightstand are still in my room after my mother cleared out almost our entire house.

"I kept my own bedroom set, too," the maniac said as she lurked in my doorway earlier. "Everything else is in storage until the divorce is settled."

"Even my piano, though?" I said. "Daddy would never take that."

"You don't know what he'd do," she snapped. "And stop whining like a baby. You'll get it back when all this is over."

I sat on my bed, hating her guts. She's so selfish. And stupid. I wish she'd just agree to the settlement, get out, go away, and take her meanness with her.

I kicked off my boots and flung one into the wall. Then I lay back on my bed and said, "Great. So now, on top of everything else, there's no home to come home to either."

"What did you say?" My mother squinted for a moment. Then she sprang from the threshold, right at me, her hands clenched in raised fists.

I watched this insane bully coming for me. And I felt my own anger rise like an ocean wave. The many times she hit me when I was too little to fight back flashed through my mind. I drew my knees to my chest, and as she reached me, I kicked my legs straight into her, feet to flesh, banging her ribs with all the force and fury I had.

I saw her lift into the air and levitate in what seemed like slow motion before she finally slammed to the floor across the room, butt first. She gaped up at me, face stretched in astonishment, as her trembling hands rubbed the space between her breasts.

It was the first time I ever fought back.

And I could see in Velma's face that *she* could see that I would not back down. I'd fight her with everything I had, if need be. For *years* I wanted to stand up for myself. Now, I was big enough, and the fear in that woman's face sent a surge of excitement through me like a current. I was bolstered by my power. At last, Velma was getting a taste of what she'd been serving all these years.

I eyed her on the floor and waited to see what she'd do. When she didn't move, I stood up and looked down at her.

"If I'm old enough to know I have family you never bothered to mention, I'm old enough to stop taking your shit."

She got up with a hand on her heart, whimpering as if my kick had not only hurt her flesh and bones but her feelings, too. She trundled from the room without a word.

My confidence quickly deflated, seeping out like air from a punctured tire. I locked my door and bolted it with the desk chair.

Now I'm lying in my bed, terrified. And I feel guilty, but I shouldn't, right? She was about to punch me. My only other option would have been to let her. Still, I'm shaking, and I don't think I'll be able to sleep.

I get that she had a traumatic childhood and a bad marriage, and I'm sorry. But she's supposed to be my mother. Shouldn't I be able to trust that she won't take it out on me?

November 27, 1980
Maddie
It's Thanksgiving. I heard Velma in the kitchen early this morning. Sounded like she was packing up the macaroni and cheese. There was the crinkle of tin foil and the ping of a Pyrex dish hitting the counter. *She's leaving without me*, I thought, which she would absolutely do.

I didn't want to deal with her, but I didn't want to stay here alone and miss dinner at Aunt Sylvia's and the chance to see my cousin Suzy. I swished with Listerine, tied my frizzy hair into an Afro puff, and dressed as fast as I could. I didn't even eat breakfast before following her out to the car.

Velma drove her “new” (used) pea-green station wagon. She pretended I didn’t exist. She refused to speak and wouldn’t look at me either—punishment for the night before. I had no plans to apologize. I’ve been her persona non grata many times since I was a toddler, and I’m used to it. Actually, it’s a good respite. I was glad not to hear her constant complaining. I put on my headphones and listened to the soundtrack from *Fame* on my Walkman.

The drive down the Palisades was okay until there was a disturbing rattling sound from the car. Then it started to wobble. That got worse until finally, it felt like we were rocking in a boat. I braced one hand on the dashboard, grabbed the roof loop with the other, and said, “Mom, would you stop? I don’t wanna die.”

She still wouldn’t speak. She pulled to the side of the parkway. It turned out a wheel was loose. A state trooper showed up, drove us to a service station, and then arranged for a tow to a garage, which was closed. From there, we got a ride to a car rental place. I thought we were headed to Suzy’s house, but when we got back on the Palisades, I noticed Velma was driving north. When I asked why, my mother gave me that look she gives when she curses at you with her eyes. We ended up back in Monroe. No family. No turkey. No fun.

I called Suzy but didn’t say all I wanted to say in case Velma was listening on the line.

Suzy proceeds to go on and on about how great Howard University is, how great it is to have a boyfriend, how there are so many fine guys, and she tells me more about running into Zeke Odom. According to her, he says he wishes he and I could be friends.

“I don’t want to hear about anyone from Monroe, Suzy. And Zeke may be all into Black schools and Black girls *now*, but he liked plenty of white girls before he even noticed I had a pulse.”

“Maddie, it’s not like he had a choice. That’s all there *was* in Monroe.”

"There was me. And he treated *this* Black girl like trash."

"Oh, you're Black again, now? Thought you were half Russian or some shit."

"One quarter, not half. And I'm Black enough to be too Black for this town. I'm so glad I don't have to care what anyone from here thinks of me anymore, including Zeke. Screw him. If you see him again, don't tell me."

She goes, "You still go to a white school. You're probably too Black for there, too. You should transfer. Come to the Mecca, Maddie. It's amazing."

"I *like* New York City."

"Humph," Suzy goes. "Got a boyfriend yet?"

Silence on my end.

"Of course, you don't. You *would* if you went to Howard. I'm tellin' you, you need to come down here and stop being so scared of Black people."

"Oh, I'm not scared. I used to be scared of someone, but I'm not anymore."

"What? Who? What're you talking about?"

"I'm hanging up. I'm about to treat myself to some Breyer's chocolate ice cream and then get rid of it so I don't gain a pound."

Suzy goes, "What?"

I go, "Bye," and click the receiver.

15.
Monroe, New York, 1980
Velma

It was still dark when the honking outside woke Velma. She sat up in bed, and through the window, she saw Phil and that fucking slut parked in her driveway. Then she heard Maddie dragging her stuff into the foyer.

Velma ran down the stairs and stopped on the last step as Maddie headed to the door. "You're really gonna leave me and go off with him and that home-wrecking whore?" she said.

Maddie didn't answer. Her giant sack was slung over her shoulder as she dragged her ski bag along the carpet.

"Guess you enjoy letting him flaunt that white woman in your face," Velma said.

Maddie opened the door. "At least he doesn't try to put his *fists* in my face," she said.

Velma jumped off the bottom step and shoved the door shut. She held her hand against it and leaned into Maddie's face. "Ooh. You think he's better than me, huh?"

The car beeped outside again.

"Think your daddy loves you more?"

"I have to go, Mom. Move."

"Your darling daddy who's trying to put your own mother in the street? You wanna know what Dr. Low-Life loves? Your father loves the way you kiss his ass. Look at you—you're kissing it right now by going on this trip to insult me. What business do you have traipsing off with him and his mistress? For what?"

"For *money*. He won't give me any unless I go."

"Get a *job*, you spoiled brat."

"Since you dislike me so much, let me *leave*."

"Oh, and what're you gonna do? *Watch*?"

"Get out of my way," Maddie said, her eyes burning into Velma's.

She didn't move. Velma remembered now that her hair was in rollers, and her unmade-up face revealed lingering discolorations from the accident. She turned her head to stare at the empty room. "No matter what he does, you go right ahead and do whatever the hell he says." Tears crept into her voice. "I used to tell you to forgive his crap because I wanted you to have a relationship with him, but that selfish sleazebag only loves himself."

Outside, the horn beeped longer and louder than it had before.

"Got it," Maddie said. "My father doesn't love me. And *you're* better. Great. Now, move."

Velma looked at her and let out a sob. "Please. Let's talk this out." She flung her arms around Maddie.

"They're gonna leave me!" Maddie yelled.

Velma felt her daughter trying to wriggle away. She held tighter and realized she was trying to squeeze something out of Maddie to keep it from that bastard. "Please," she said. "You're all I have."

"Get off me." Maddie wedged her arms between Velma's and broke herself free. "That's not how you felt yesterday when you wouldn't talk to me. Or the day before when you tried to punch me. I'm all you have? You don't give a damn about me." She yanked the door open and lugged her stuff outside.

When Phil took her away like that, Velma was out of her mind with rage.

She could've . . . She was thinking some dark thoughts, but she knew Maddie and Livia would never forgive her if she murdered their father. Then she thought about killing herself. They should both be ashamed of what they did to her. *But why should I kill myself?* she thought. *No. If I'm gonna kill somebody, it'll be Phil. Or maybe that tramp Muriel. Or both.*

She knew she wasn't right in the head, and that made her want to kill Phil even more because he did that to her, just to show that he could.

Later, she found herself in Maddie's room. There was a notebook on the nightstand. A journal for her writing class. When Velma flipped through it, she saw complaints about *her*. Maddie couldn't stand her. She was mean, stupid, and abusive, and she wished Velma would just get out of the house. And after she'd read every terrible word Maddie had written about her, that's when the real crazy kicked in.

16.

Monroe, New York, 1980

Phil

Phil began to sweat behind the wheel of the Mercedes when Maddie climbed in. The car had been Morty's before he died. Would she judge him? Riding in this luxury sedan had to be better than riding in the hatch of his RX-7. Maybe she'd see the positive. As he rolled out of the driveway, he said, "Glad to see you, love. How was your Thanksgiving?"

Maddie grunted a nonreply and settled into the plush back seat. Phil guessed she was tired. She wasn't a morning person, nor was he, and so he understood. She'd be able to rest. There was plenty of space between her and Muriel's annoying nine-year-old, who was playing a noisy lap-sized video game that sounded like an entire arcade.

In the rearview mirror, he saw Maddie slouch and dig her Walkman out of her jacket. The girl did love her music. He was delighted she'd be occupying herself with that so he could focus on Muriel. One of his hands was on her inner thigh as he drove, and one of hers was on his cock, resting there casually, as if this were an everyday thing. It wasn't, and if there'd been no kids in the car, he could've pulled over and gone at it on the side of the road.

Phil knew this delicious phase of their relationship wouldn't last forever, and he was savoring each drop. When his hard-on poked up and made a teepee in his ski pants, Muriel giggled like a little girl. He caught Maddie's eyes in the mirror, piercing his like spikes. Christ. With her headphones on, she stared out the window. He gave Muriel an admonishing look and turned up the radio. Maddie didn't like his girlfriend. She probably didn't appreciate that she was white, but Phil couldn't imagine that Maddie would be any happier if he'd chosen a Black woman. She was a daddy's girl who wanted him all to herself.

17.
November 30, 1980
Maddie

We got to the ski center in Killington, Vermont, early Friday afternoon. My father hadn't bothered to tell me that neither Mousy nor Amy had ever been on skis. He didn't make a run with me at all. He babysat them. I skied by myself for about an hour. It was cold and not particularly fun, so I went to the lodge. There was a fireplace, a pool table, and—to my delight—a piano. No one was playing it. I sat on the bench. No one told me to get up. I played a few chords. No complaints. So, I sang "Out Here on My Own" from *Fame*, which I've been practicing because I'm in a holiday show coming up at school.

I kept my ski cap on. Hat hair on an Afro is not attractive. I stuck out in this place like a mountain in the sky. Vermont has to be among the whitest places in the entire world. The snow, the sky, and the people, too. But no one said anything mean to me. There was even a smattering of applause when I finished.

The ass model and her kid had had enough of the slopes in less than two hours. Maybe Phil was too tired from the driving and after teaching his little family not to kill themselves on the slopes, but I wished he had skied with me at least a little while. Nope. We left. After stopping for takeout and a few groceries, the four of us ended up at a condo that belongs to Muriel's friend, who wasn't there. It was decorated in beige shades with inexpensive but okay furniture, and I thought it was nice enough until I learned I'd be sharing a room with Amy.

That night I woke to the sounds of squeaking bedsprings and moaning. Muriel and my father. Doing it. In the next room. Ew.

Every muscle in my body knotted up as I lay in the single bed.

Oh-oh-oh-oh. Unh-unh, yeah baby, get it.

I thought, *Are you fucking kidding me*? So much anger coursed through my veins. Why the hell did he invite me on this trip? To hear *this*? I covered my head with a pillow.

Across the room, Amy started crying. She sounded so distraught. I was distraught, too, but Amy's just a little kid.

"You all right?" I asked.

"They're doing that sex thing again," Amy whispered through soft sobs.

Again? I thought. *Yikes*. The sounds kept coming. I imagined kicking their door open and bashing them in their horny heads with a ski pole. Assholes.

I got out of bed and walked over to her. I leaned down and put my hand on Amy's back. One half of her face was pressed into her pillow, and her head was turned toward the wall away from me. Her long blonde hair shimmered down the side of the bed like moonlight.

"Cover your ears," I told her.

"I miss my daddy," she wailed.

I knelt beside her and rubbed her back. And as I did, I felt a sob rise inside my own chest. But I'm grown. I couldn't cry like a fourth-grader just because I missed my daddy, too. The non-sex-maniac version of him. I did not know what to say to soothe the child. Her sobs got louder. Then she began hyperventilating.

And they were still at it, oh-ohing and yeah-babying. Finally, I got up, grabbed my ski boot off the floor, and banged on the wall three times.

The moaning stopped.

Fifteen seconds later, Muriel burst into our room in her bathrobe and asked Amy what was wrong. Amy didn't move or respond.

"She said she missed her daddy," I told her.

Amy rolled over to face her mother and said, "Maddie hit me with her boot."

Muriel's head whipped toward me.

Of course, I hadn't hit her, but I was standing near the wall, the ski boot still in my hand. "No, I didn't!" I said. "She heard you. You woke her up, and she started crying."

My father appeared in the doorway, and Muriel looked at him. "I don't trust Maddie," she shouted. "Get her out of my daughter's room. Now."

I could not believe *this* was what I was doing with my time, my weekend, my life.

I dropped the boot with a thud and pushed past Phil into the living room. Muriel slammed the door.

Phil stood in the hallway, hands on his hips, in his baggy Fruit of the Looms. I wanted to say, Put a fucking robe on; would you, please?

I sat on the sofa and pulled the sleeves of my pajama top over my cold hands. "She heard you two," I said. "*That's* why she was crying. You think I'd hit her?"

"I think you're trying to sabotage my relationship," he hissed. "That's what I think. But it's not going to work, so stop it." He went back into their room and pushed the door closed.

Fucking connard. I think that's asshole in French.

I was shivering. Part of it was the cold, but it seemed my whole body was quaking with rage now. I was on the verge of exploding, the way I'd seen my mother blow like a volcano. I truly wanted to bash my father's face in with that ski boot. I got up and paced barefoot back and forth across the shag carpet. I punched the air, furious with myself for falling for his shit again.

The man has been telling me something. Not overtly, but in the way I've been learning to read beneath the lines in a play. In that moment, I saw it. He told me when he set me up to walk in on them in the apartment. He told me again at that art opening, when he ignored me, and then couldn't even get my name right. And he was saying it again now: I don't matter. He was shoving my nose in just *how much* I don't matter.

I looked at the sofa. No pillow, no blanket. I sat down and hugged my knees to my chest. His bottle of scotch was across the room on the kitchen counter. I thought of numbing myself with it. There was also ice cream in the freezer. Butter pecan. His favorite. Muriel had bought it after skiing. I knew I wouldn't be able to sleep. I was too angry, but I could eat that ice cream. I could eat it all if I wanted to. I could take it in and then eject it, as if it had never been there at all.

The next morning, my father stood over me and said that he and Muriel were taking Amy to the slopes. His voice was brittle when he added, "You can stay here."

I unfurled out of the ball I'd curled myself into and sat up on the sofa. Muriel was already at the front door in her red wool hat. She radiated pure enmity from her light eyes. What were they? Hazel? Green? Whatever. Amy stood there, clinging to her mother's hip.

I rose to my feet and hugged myself for warmth. "You know why you were crying, Amy," I said. "Tell them the truth."

"Shut up," Muriel bellowed. "Don't you talk to her."

"She heard the sounds you two were making, and she told me she's heard you before."

"You be quiet!" my father shouted. He opened the front door, ushered his little family out of the condo, and left me there.

You be quiet, I thought. If you'd *been* fucking quiet, this wouldn't have happened.

I wondered how I could get home. Bus? Was there a train? Then I thought, but where's home? *What* home? The only place for me to go back to was the dorm, and no one was there because of the holiday.

I pushed open the door to the bedroom I'd been kicked out of the night before. My plan was to write in this journal. Then I rooted around in my duffel bag, and it wasn't there. I realized where I'd left it: beside my bed at the house. The thought gave me a headache.

Of course, my nosy-ass mother would read it. She's been reading my diary since I first had one. Fuck.

I spent the time in bed daydreaming of Gustavo and thinking up song lyrics. Still working on one. Here's the first verse:

Take me in, be my home.
I'm alone.
Wanna begin to build a place
Where I feel safe to dream again.

I thought of that time he and I walked home together, and he encouraged me. If I can finish it, and he hears it one day, I wonder if he'll know he was my inspiration.

I fell asleep and had a dream that I was at my grandparents' apartment in Harlem. The buzzer rang, and when I pulled the door open, a woman was standing there in a sparkly silver dress made of tiny mirrors. She wore a bun on top of her head like the singer Alberta Hunter. Then I saw that it *was* Alberta Hunter. She had warm, soulful eyes that I stared into, and she stared back at mine. Somehow, I knew she was my grandmother, the real one. She stood there facing me and sang a verse from "Out Here on My Own." Her voice was smooth, rich, and filled with emotion. The lyrics ask for support. They summon someone to be there for the subject of the song, who feels lost, alone, and doesn't fit in.

When Alberta finished singing the verse, she gestured to me as if to say, *Your* turn.

And then I sang the second verse. It's full of yearning, longing for home, and a guide to help navigate the way there. When I finished my part, my real grandma smiled and nodded, and her eyes shined with tears. She leaned across the threshold and gave me a tight hug.

I could still feel it when I woke up.

Yeah, it's unlikely Alberta Hunter is my real grandmother, but since I don't know what she looks like, I guess it helps to have someone to picture, and Miss Hunter is the best person I can think of because I already kind of love her, even though I don't know her. I think I love my real grandmother, too, and I don't know her either.

When my father and his white girls got back, I closed the bedroom door. Muriel flung it open, stomped in with her ski boots on, and ordered me out. My father appeared in the doorway.

"Muriel, leave her alone. You don't know for sure that Amy was telling the truth."

"Of course, she was." Sheer contempt rose off Muriel like waves of heat. "You said yourself the girl's just like your crazy ex-wife. Why would you believe her?"

I shot my father a look that I hoped would hit him like a punch. His face drooped under the hood of his yellow parka.

Tears steamed in my eyes as I pushed past him and moved to the sofa. How, exactly, am I just like my mother? Because I don't want him having sex in my face? Because I don't want to see pictures of his girlfriend's butt? What's he talking about?

"Well, Maddie," he said. Then he sighed a long sigh. "This is certainly a tumultuous time." The cushion sank under his weight as he lowered himself beside me. "And your father's not managing it very well." His voice faded as if he were about to fall asleep.

I think he was expecting me to say, *It's okay, Daddy*, like I have sometimes in the past. What I said was, "Why do you call yourself 'your father,' like that's some *other* asshole?"

He stared at the air in front of him. Silent.

Then Muriel went into the kitchen, opened the refrigerator and then the freezer, and then she turned toward me. "What happened to the ice cream I bought?"

"You all left me here all day. There was nothing but coffee, creamer, scotch, and that ice cream."

Her lips were a thin straight line. "You couldn't wait until we got back? Your father brought you a burger and fries." She pointed to a white bag on the counter.

"How was I supposed to know when you'd be back? Or that anyone would bring me something?"

"So you just ate the *whole* half gallon?" she yelled. "*All* of it? What the fuck is wrong with you?"

"All right, Muriel. Enough," Phil said like he meant it.

I didn't admit that I binged and purged it. I *did* feel bad. I didn't admit that either. I know I shouldn't have done it. But I don't think what I did was as bad as what they did to me.

Muriel marched into their room and slammed the door.

Phil looked down at his hands and said, "I'll get you your pillow and blanket."

This morning, the two of them weren't speaking, and it was snowing as we left what's become my least favorite state. Last time I was in Vermont, it was springtime, and my father offered me a joint in our hotel room after dinner in front of my mother, even though he and I never *once* got high together, ever. He did it to mess with her. She went on a tirade *and* had a hot flash at the same time. I thought she was going to stroke out. As you might imagine, the trip ended pretty much like this one was ending now, with no one talking to each other because of some stupid shit my dad did.

Muriel drove. Amy sat beside her, playing Ms. Pac-Man. Phil slumped in the back with me. I didn't speak, except to announce when I had to pee.

When we finally got to the house in Monroe, it was getting dark. Muriel pulled all the way up into the long driveway and stopped behind the garage. She ordered my father out, too, even though his car was back at her place. The two of us began unloading our skis and bags from the trunk when something slammed into the hood of the Mercedes, making a loud bang.

Muriel screamed from behind the wheel. I grabbed my duffel bag, looked up, and saw my mother in her gray sweat suit, lurking above us on the porch. I watched in stunned amazement as she held a terra-cotta flowerpot in her hand and pulled it through the air behind her, like a football player ready to throw.

Then she hurled it toward *me*. I ducked behind the open trunk as the pot missed and shattered in the driveway. Amy was wailing now.

"God dammit, Velma," my father yelled. He dropped his ski bag and dashed in her direction.

Velma said, "Get that bitch off my property!" She picked up another pot and hurled it at him. It missed by mere inches and smashed on the blacktop.

Muriel revved the engine. She backed up over Phil's skis and mine and almost hit me before I jumped out of the way. Then she peeled off with the trunk wide open and with my father's suitcase still inside it.

He pumped his arms in his bright yellow parka as he lunged up the stone steps toward my mother. I wondered what he planned to do if he caught her.

"I live here, you piece of shit," Velma shouted. "Keep your skanky hoes away from my fucking house."

He reached the porch and chased her inside. My heart jack-hammered as I followed. I watched from the empty foyer as they ran into the kitchen. She picked up a caned oak chair and pointed its legs at him like a lion tamer.

He stepped back. "You ever pull anything like that again," he said, "and I'll beat the living crap out of you."

"Yeah? You do, and they'll never find your body."

"Fuck you," he said.

She took a step toward him. "You've shitted on me for years, and you're not getting away with it anymore. Now get the hell outta my house."

"*Your* house? I'm the one paying for the fucking house." He stretched his arms wide toward the white-tiled walls, as if to claim them.

"Listen, Philip, I don't want to leave your girls without a father," she growled, "but I *will*."

"Don't you threaten me."

"My brother's been here," she said. "You understand what I'm telling you?"

My father's face turned the color of raw meat. Beneath the yellow hood, sweat glistened on his forehead. My mother's brother is a New York City cop. Who owns guns. Uncle Aubrey probably could make a body disappear.

My own fear was quaking in my stomach when I said, "We should leave. Let's just go, Dad." I turned down the hallway to grab the stuff I'd left in my room.

Behind me, I heard the nervousness in my father's voice. "Velma, leave that kid alone."

When I turned, she was on my heels. I sprinted into my bedroom and tried to close the door. She stopped it with her foot.

"Get away from me," I said.

"Why?" she said, with her eyes open so wide the full irises were visible. "I can't hurt you. You can fight back, right?"

"You tried to kill me outside."

"I was trying to kill Muriel. Not you."

"You're crazy."

She nodded. "I am. And your father made me that way. Don't ever let anyone disrespect you the way he disrespected me. That man stomped on my dreams." She reached out to touch my cheek. "You go for yours."

I backed away from her into the edge of my bed. Over her shoulder I could see my father in the hallway, looking like Big Bird in his canary-colored coat.

"I know you think I'm stupid," my mother said. "And selfish."

"No, I don't," I said.

"Yeah, you do. You wrote it in your book." She flung her chin at my journal on the wicker night table.

I stared straight into her scary eyes. "Okay, *that's* disrespectful. *You're* disrespectful. And that's not even real. It's for a class. I write stuff in there I don't even mean."

"Oh, you meant it. You're sick of me. You think I should get out of the house."

"I don't know what you should do."

"Velma, leave her alone," Phil said from the hallway.

If my mother heard him, she didn't care. She didn't take orders from Phil when they were together. Why would he hold sway now?

She folded her arms and clutched her shoulders. "When I saw you drive away with her, I felt, she's not only taking my husband but my baby, too."

I struggled not to smile. "Your *baby*? Are you being serious right now? You don't even *like* me. And nobody *took* your husband. He *left* you. As miserable as you make each other, you ought to be glad."

My father got me a taxi to the Shortline Bus station in Monroe, and from there, I rode into the city. The divider was stretched across the room when I walked in. I didn't mind. I came into the bathroom with my journal. Jennifer could've been having an orgy with men, women, and a bunch of bears, and I would've been no less pleased to be back.

18.

Los Angeles, California, 1996

Maddie

Typically *not* much of a drinker, Maddie has polished off most of a bottle of Malbec. She's been in therapy before, lots of it, but reading about that time in her life explains even more than her various shrinks have.

Of course, she's had difficulty in relationships. Look at the models she had. She knows she can't blame her parents for her choices, and she has to take responsibility for her own life, but she can't help but feel that if they'd been more mature and less self-involved, she might have fared better in love and in life.

She's doing fine now, though that's relative. At least she's making a living as a singer and not struggling like she was in her twenties when she still had to clean her father's apartment for extra cash. She's able to pay for this wedding. And she loves Rolando and believes in him. She hopes they'll be happy. But she isn't sure. She wishes she *could* be sure, but lots of marriages fail, so who *is* certain when they marry? He's younger, not yet established in his career, though he's getting there, she thinks. He's funny and sweet and mostly kind.

Her therapist says she picks "fixers" that she has to take care of and people-please for, because she doesn't believe she deserves better. She's been conditioned to accept less. To not have needs. Parents like hers do this unconsciously, she's been advised. What their kids want or feel doesn't matter. They prioritize themselves and their own desires.

Maddie listened during her sessions, but she wasn't convinced of where her poor choices and difficult relationships had come from. She thought she was simply attracted, unluckily, to difficult people. After all, she didn't know in advance that they'd turn out to be selfish or lack empathy. Yet the pages she's reading pretty persuasively make the therapist's point. She *does* find herself worrying about what Rolando wants and how *he* feels without checking in with herself. Is that always bad, though? Isn't it kind and generous to think about one's partner's needs before one's own? She's not sure she would know what she wants if she asked herself. She doesn't ask. She takes what comes and hopes for the best.

19.
New York, New York, 1980
Phil
The regular bartender at Bradley's was off, and the fill-in got Phil's drink wrong. *Everything* was wrong. He was so damn tired of trying to please women. They never stopped complaining. He visited his mother and gave her some money for her rent. All she could manage to say was that he'd failed at marriage again and how he'd broken another family, and he was selfish. Selfish, after he paid her fucking rent.

Livia was being standoffish, and he had no idea why. He understood the other kid's grievance. Maddie still wasn't speaking to him. Muriel had billed him for the motherfucking dent Velma made in the Mercedes, and she was threatening to charge his daughter with assault. What a pain in the ass. The woman was convinced that since Maddie was abused, she, too, was abusive.

Phil had known too many women who never treated patients or even studied psychology and yet wanted to tell him how it worked. He sipped his drink and shook his head. The vermouth mixed with scotch was sweet when it was supposed to be dry.

Velma was causing paranoia. The woman was some kind of psychic demon. His lawyer had looked at him like he was a halfwit earlier that day when her lawyer said, "And what about the Swiss bank account?"

How the fuck did she know about that? The statements came to the city. And why should she get half his money? Did she do half his goddamn work? Marriage was usury. He'd never do it again. Never. Not even if he met a rich woman.

He glanced around. The brunette he'd chatted up the other night was sitting near the stage. She hadn't looked his way once. At least the music was good. The pianist, John Hicks, hit those keys with such elation. He was practically dancing as he played. They said he drank, but so what if he did? Didn't diminish his genius. Phil wished Maddie were there. She said Hicks's playing stuck with her and made her imagine flying through stars. What a good companion. Muriel didn't get jazz. One day Maddie would sing here. She'd forgive him. He was the one who pushed her to pursue her aspirations. *And* financed them. Who else was going to encourage her? She'd come around. She needed her dad.

20.

December 11, 1980

Maddie

Some lunatic shot John Lennon just a few miles uptown from here. I still can't believe he's gone. The day after it happened, when Jen and I walked down our hallway on the way to breakfast, we heard Lennon songs coming from multiple rooms. Students were crying in the lobby and in the dining hall. I had my History of Performance class that morning, and when I got back, Jennifer played and rewound "Imagine" on her boom box over and over and over. She's into punk bands, but the Beatles were part of her childhood. Mine, too. I used to play *Abbey Road* all the time, and my dad had their greatest hits albums. And last spring I performed in a showcase with my voice coach, and I sang "Yesterday." When I told my cousin Suzy about it, she said I needed a Black vocal coach so I won't sing like a white girl. I don't know. The teacher I have here at school is Black, and her technique isn't much different from my other teacher.

I wonder if Suzy cares about Lennon's death. Or if it's even a big deal at Howard, like it is at NYU. Suzy's made fun of me for liking some white music. But then she loved Kraftwerk's "Trans-Europe Express," and she bought the soundtrack from the movie *Grease*, which confused me. I still don't understand the rules of what music is cool to like if you're Black and what you're supposed to shun. John Lennon was great, no matter what her opinion. He was my favorite Beatle.

The lyric "living life in peace" is on a loop in my mind like it doesn't want to leave. I'd love to live in peace. Wish my parents would consider it, too. I haven't talked to either of them since Thanksgiving weekend. They, too, are in my thoughts and won't leave—and not in a good way. I feel dread when I think of either of them.

December 17, 1980
Maddie
The other night my stomach fluttered, and I couldn't stop smiling when Gustavo walked me home from class. At the same time, a nervous terror had my entire body under siege. I was practically shaking with desire and a fear that I'd say or do something dumb. The more I like him, the more stressed out I feel around him. I really want him to like me—to pick me. I've never been in love, but I so want to be. Maybe what I'm feeling is almost love. The world is beautiful when he seems into me.

During our walk, the sun ducked behind the buildings, bathing them in a bronze glow. Streetlights began blinking on. Snow flurries floated down, shimmering like fairy dust in the fading light. Even the junkies in Union Square seemed choreographed and magical, like they were dancing, not nodding. I may not be sure I'm in love with Gustavo, but I am definitely in love with this dazzling city.

He checked me out in my designer jeans as we crossed Fourteenth Street onto Broadway.

"You're losing weight," he said. And under his hat, his dense eyebrows rose in approval. "Just don't lose that cute booty."

I grinned and tingled everywhere.

He winked. Then he told me his breakup with his ex was official. "Terminado," he said.

Cool, I thought. Until he sighed, and in a melancholy, high-pitched voice I've never heard him use, he said, "I really wanted me and Raquel to stay friends."

Ugh. He seemed so bereft that it felt wrong to be happy, even though I'd wanted the breakup to happen.

"My papi's pissed at me, too," he went on. "'Cos Raquel's mami's his chef, and every day she's threatening to quit now. Ai, Papi says loyalty's everything."

Is it?

So, Gustavo should stay with someone he doesn't want to be with out of loyalty? To whom? His dad? Raquel? Or because Raquel's mother is loyal to his dad? Any variation seems wrong.

A few years ago, I knew my dad didn't want to be married to my mother, but I still wanted him to stay and be a better husband. I wanted a normal family. And my mother wouldn't agree to the divorce. But things are worse than ever now, so I get it. If someone wants to be free, I think it's better to let them.

We ate dinner at Beefsteak Charlie's. He treated. It was flirty and fun, and he told me a lot about his childhood, his parents' breakup, and his experiences on movie sets. He didn't ask about me so I didn't talk much. And then he came back to my room, and we cuddled on my twin bed. Jennifer grinned at us lying there, and she put the room divider up.

I have this unfortunate issue where when I make out with a guy, at first, I get super-nervous. It happened with Zeke Odom, too. My heart starts beating fast, and I feel scared. I know it's irrational. I try to control it, but someone overpowered me once when I was a little girl. My parents left me with a babysitter during a vacation—a man—and I couldn't stop him from doing what he did, and now, when a guy gets close, I guess part of my brain remembers that until I push the memory away and focus on the present.

I don't think Gustavo even noticed, though he might have heard my heartbeat. We made out for a while and then stripped to our underwear. He kissed almost every inch of my body. I enjoyed it. Except when I was worrying that I'd do something wrong. He massaged me, and it was as if he were playing my back and butt like an instrument. It was a song. And then he stopped. Abruptly. I took that as a cue to kiss *him* all over, and when I did, he pulled me up to lie beside him. He drew the covers over us, kissed me on the lips, and then turned my body sideways to spoon me.

"Good night, Maddita," he whispered in my ear.

I thought, *That's it*? What happened? Did I kiss badly? Did I smell? His *body* wasn't turned off. A certain part of him was definitely not turned off. But soon, he was breathing deeply, falling asleep or pretending to, and I lay there bewildered.

He was gone when I woke the next morning. I wasn't sure if he'd spent the night. I went downstairs before Jennifer and saw him in the dining hall with his roommate, Vijay, a cute Indian American guy from Long Island who always wears a blue Yankees cap and black Converse All Stars.

When I sat next to Gustavo, he and Vijay were discussing the Scorsese film *New York, New York*, which, of course, I'd seen because of the jazz. I mentioned that I knew the man who coached De Niro's wife Diahnne Abbott on "Honeysuckle Rose," which she sings in the movie. Vijay's face brightened like he might be interested, but Gustavo didn't even look my way. He didn't even say hello. He was talking about the complexity of De Niro's performance. How convincing he was going from charming to hothead. I didn't agree, though I love De Niro. But I didn't say anything.

When Gustavo was done talking and eating, he got up, put his coat on, and said, "Hasta luego," without meeting my eyes. He left with Vijay.

I sipped my coffee, sat there, and tried keep from blinking so tears wouldn't fall. I had no idea what I'd done wrong. He obviously didn't want his roommate or anyone to know we were together, and it stung like a slap.

From the corner of my eye, I saw Frannie stalk by on her way out of the dining hall. I was glad she didn't see the broken look on my face.

Jennifer appeared. Her smile was sunny and so wide it included every one of her very even teeth. She sat her skinny self down directly across from me. "So," she purred, "how's it going?" Her cheery shine dimmed when I told her what didn't happen with Gustavo the night before and what did happen just before she got there.

"Aw, I'm so sorry, roomie." She gently squeezed my arm with her black-polished fingernails. "Boys are assholes. Why do you think I sleep around? I have my fun, and never do I give them even a bit of my soul."

"But I don't wanna keep my soul all to myself," I said. "I wanna share it. I want him to be my boyfriend."

She thumbed a tear off my cheek and lowered her voice. Her darkly outlined eyes were especially gentle as she said, "I know. You will have a boyfriend. If that's what you want. Even if it's not him." She leaned back in her chair. "As for me, I don't believe in romantic love. It doesn't last. My parents, your parents—so many people get divorced. Just enjoy what you can, and don't get your heart hurt." She patted my arm. "It's not worth it."

"If it's not worth it, why does everyone want it so badly?"

"Ooh." She sighed and sat for a moment, thinking. Then she shrugged. "Conditioning? From TV, books, and movies. Cultural brainwashing?"

She didn't sound very confident, and I thought, even if she's right, I still want to love and be loved. And finally getting laid would be nice.

In the lobby, there was a note at the front desk from my father, "demanding" that I return his call. I crumpled it and tossed it in the trash. Then I walked through the park toward class. Thoughts of Gustavo and of my insane parents turned over and over in my mind, falling into each other like clothes in a dryer. I heard someone call my name.

I turned back and blinked, confused to see a guy I briefly liked in high school coming my way. What was Ron, the Viking from Monroe, doing in Washington Square Park? His blond hair was longer, skimming his shoulders now, and he'd gained a little weight. His mischievous smile with his slightly chipped front tooth and his friendly blue-green eyes were exactly the same. And I was surprised by how fast my mood lifted at seeing him.

Then I saw that Frannie was with him. Ugh. When Ron hugged me, he smelled like Tic Tacs and Musk by English Leather, the way he had in school.

He kept his hands on my shoulders and beamed at me. "I'm here for one night on my way back to Florida." His voice brimmed with enthusiasm. "Good to see you, lady. Come have dinner with us later. We're going to Shakespeare's on MacDougal."

My eyes met Frannie's with mutual dislike. I almost laughed. "Ah—I don't think so," I said. "But let me give you my number." I tore off a piece of notebook paper, scribbled the digits, and handed it to him. "Maybe we can meet up after?"

Ron hugged me again before Frannie yanked him away. He glanced back over his shoulder and pantomimed holding a phone to his ear before he and the segregationist slid back into the stream of students and disappeared.

In History of Performance, I had to perform a song in a scene from Yiddish theatre in front of the class. It was with a group, but I sang the solo. I didn't understand what all the Yiddish words meant exactly, but the teacher had given us a vague translation that suggested a tough-spirited woman urging others to get it together and be tough, too. I adopted the posture of a strong matriarch. The character seemed to overtake me, as if she'd swooped in to inhabit my body.

When the song was over, our professor, a renowned theatre scholar rumored to date students, stood and applauded. His eyes were wide, as was his mouth, apparently stunned. He said he couldn't be more impressed with my adept portrayal of the Jewish character. I thought, *Right on; hopefully, I'll get an A in this class.*

I was gracious and grateful, but I did wonder if his surprise was due to my race. Would he have found the performance equally amazing if I were white? Then it occurred to me that maybe there *was* something curious about my ability to inhabit the character. Could the genetic memory of my biological grandfather Liberov have been roused? Hm.

In any case, I had a run-through that evening for a holiday show I'm singing in at the acting school, and though the professor's praise had boosted my confidence earlier, I wasn't at my best that night. My voice cracked when I got emotional. Our singing teacher had a show that night, so our acting teacher sat in on the rehearsal, and he frowned during my song. Gustavo's not in the show. There's no one of color in it but me, and it seemed like I was the only one Victor scowled at, though I could be imagining it.

When I got back to the dorm, it was dinnertime. Gustavo was in the lobby getting his mail at the desk. I approached from behind and tapped him on the back of his suede coat. When he turned, he didn't return my smile. "Ai, you can't be up in my face all the time, chica. It's too much."

Ouch.

When I took in his words, his attitude toward me, it was like he'd used a sledgehammer to bash whatever inner scaffolding held me up. I cracked and caved into myself.

He sighed, as if my crumbled expression inconvenienced him.

I slumped toward the stairwell, broken.

"Oh, c'mon," he said, following me. "I'm still buggin' about Raquel and how mad she is. Maybe I need a minute before I'm ready for another nena."

I turned to face him. "But you were in my bed last night. You were kissing me."

"'Cos I like you, Maddita. But, mira, even though me and Raquel are over, it feels like I'm cheating when I'm with you."

I ran up the stairs.

Of course, it's a waste to shed tears over someone who's not interested or ready or whatever. I cried in the shower anyway. But I cut my session of sobs short, dried off, moisturized, applied mascara and lip gloss, and then strode back out of the dorm in a short leather jacket and Jordache jeans. I strutted my stuff over to Shakespeare's in the West Village, hoping the Viking was still there.

On the way, the wind whipped up my damp curls like a kitchen mixer. I knew I looked disheveled and tried to pat my hair back into presentability as I peered through the window of the restaurant. Then I remembered how Ron used to like me to look wild. Unlike most Monroe folks, who seemed put off by the texture of my hair, he complimented the kinky curls. "Don't straighten them," he said. "They're pretty when you let them be."

Inside, I spotted him in the center of the room, leaning across the wooden table toward Frannie. His top lip appeared to be curled in anger as he spoke. I headed in their direction. Frannie saw me first. She stood and walked out.

"Man," Ron said. "Great timing, Mad. Thanks." He covered his face with his hands.

I sat down and asked what happened. He shook his head. It took him a moment to collect himself before he leaned back in his chair and smiled. "I'm really glad to see you, lady."

“Are you two dating?” I asked

“God, no,” he said, closing his eyes briefly and laughing. He combed a hand backwards through his long bangs. “We’re not even friends. My pop bowls with hers and told him I’d be in the city this week.” His head tilted toward the ceiling. “Wait ’til he finds out I called her a fucking idiot.”

When he looked at me again, I lifted my shoulders, dropped them, and tried not to grin. “I’m sure you had your reasons.”

He wanted to visit the Empire State Building, and off we went. I found it easy to hang out with Ron the Viking. He’s the kind of companionable guy who creates fun wherever he goes. On the subway, he told a silver-haired woman in a Persian lamb coat across from us that we were high school sweethearts reunited. Not exactly true; not a total lie either. When the woman saw him take my hand and kiss it, her eyes gleamed behind her funky lime-green glasses, and she squealed like we were cute little puppies.

Ron swung our arms as we walked up Thirty-Fourth Street. “I’m moving here one day,” he said. “I like the open-minded people.” He squeezed my fingers.

When I asked what he meant, he looked surprised, as if I should’ve been following his train of thought. “Don’t you remember how people looked at us when we held hands at school?”

I nodded.

“See anyone looking at us that way now?”

No one was looking at us *at all*, which made his point, though it wasn’t a fair example because no one knew us here. Everyone knew us in high school. We’d both been in the same district since kindergarten. And though Manhattan is more liberal than Monroe, it’s not devoid of racism. Still, I didn’t challenge him. I love it here, too.

It occurred to me that it was time to stop calling Ron “the Viking.” I’d never say it to his face. It was something I started with

Suzy, and I'm ashamed. Would I appreciate it if I found out he had a comparable name for me? The Black? Or more appropriately, the Mongrel? The Mulatto? The Mutt?

He's studying architecture in Miami, and he was excited to see the landmark building. He talked about its panels, canopies, and glass-enclosed bridges. He got nerdy with it, the way I do with jazz singers.

On the observatory deck, I was freezing. Ron wasn't. He wrapped his Burberry scarf around me, and I watched him take in New York, joy glittering on his face like all the city lights we could see. I was glad for him and a little envious, too, because I don't have that kind of happiness.

He took my hand and twirled me as if we were in the middle of a dance. Then he kissed me. He wanted to make out, and I wished I could be in the moment with him, the way he seemed to want to be in it with me, but I couldn't stop thinking of the guy who *didn't* want to be with me. And so, we didn't kiss for long.

Later, we walked down Fifth Avenue in the cold. He held my hand and said, "You know you can tell me what's going on."

As I looked at him, he knit his brows. I didn't say anything.

"It's like you're weighed down with a shawl of sorrow," he said. "Let me help you take it off."

That sounded oddly forward, and I wasn't sure if he was consoling, teasing, or flirting. I didn't ask. I filled him in on the lunatics who were supposed to be my parents and told him about Gustavo. He listened without interrupting.

I said, "Even though college should be a great time in my life, it feels impossible to be happy." And I started to cry.

He put his arm around me. "When you start feeling down, Maddie, try to shift your focus. Okay? Think of something else. Meditate on what makes you smile."

He made it sound easy.

We walked all the way down Fifth Avenue to the dorm, and when we got there, I didn't want to leave him. "Where are you staying?" I asked.

His blond eyebrows went high, low, then high again, as if he had a fun secret. "A townhouse around the corner on Eleventh Street," he said. "It's amazing."

I was impressed. He'd come in the day before for a lecture at Columbia that his professor, who's also his mom's cousin, gave. The professor-cousin went back to Miami and left Ron the keys to stay another night.

I really wanted Gustavo to be my first. As it turned out, my mother was right. You get what you get. And it's never what you hoped for.

Maybe I'm not a dreamer anymore.

Still, Ron was sweet. He used a condom. I had anxiety, the way I do when someone approaches me in that way. He knew what it was because I'd told him about the babysitter in the past. He was patient and gentle and kept asking if I was okay. And it didn't hurt that much. The look on his face was tender when he played with my curls and whispered, "You'll never forget me."

He's right. I won't. He hinted at having a relationship, and I won't do that either. If his father is friendly with Frannie's—a man who wouldn't allow me to come to his house because of my color—Ron's father isn't someone I want to know. I'm done with Monroe and those attitudes.

I didn't fall asleep. Ron did. His face was peaceful, as if he were enjoying a sweet dream, when I tiptoed out before the sun rose.

21.

New York, New York, 1980

Livia

Livia came into Manhattan for the holidays and had dinner with her father at another one of his jazz spots, the Knickerbocker, on

University Place. She was still furious with him for betraying her confidence about the offer to help him buy Velma out, and she was waiting for the right moment to bring it up. If ever. She struggled with confronting this man who'd left her when she was a child and never fully integrated her into his new life.

Between sips of his dry Rob Roy, he prattled on about how he was taking Muriel to Verbier, Switzerland, for Christmas. Livia listened, though her eyes traveled to the wood-paneled walls and the white tablecloths. As she saw it, her father appeared disproportionately proud to be seeing this woman. The way he boasted, it was as if he believed she improved him in some way. The woman's education was mediocre. She didn't come from a prestigious, powerful, or wealthy family. Nor did she have a career to speak of. She'd been a housewife. She was of European descent. That was it.

Unlike her sister, Livia hadn't met Muriel. She had no idea if the woman was even attractive. She'd never seen her face, only her bare buttocks in the photo he kept on his desk, which, due to its arrogance and gross exhibitionism, had not made a positive impression.

She wished he would stop. Livia detested hearing or knowing about her father's illicit romantic life. She'd been well aware that he was unfaithful to her stepmother. During her first semester of college, she'd unwittingly met one of the mistresses, Abby, the artist. That meeting was Livia's fault. But he could have refused. He *should* have. Livia and her then-boyfriend showed up at Phil's office one night, uninvited, interrupting their tryst.

And he'd let them in.

They'd had the decency to get dressed, though they might as well have done it in front of them; it was so apparent what was going on.

Years later, her father brazenly brought a *different* woman with him when he visited her in Cambridge during law school. They were invariably white. Velma knew, and she referred to them collectively as "the bow-wows." As his daughter, Livia took care to withhold any opinion on Phil's mistresses' appearances, though her stepmother was not incorrect. She remained silent if Velma brought it up. Livia only tolerated exposure to this aspect of his life because there was no possibility of a relationship with him otherwise.

When Phil finally stopped bragging about Muriel's approbation of his attributes—his intelligence, his looks, his worldliness, his success, and the prowess he, thankfully, only alluded to—she prepared to broach her grievance, but before she could get the words out, he furrowed his brows and asked, "Have you heard from Madeline?" He was suddenly chagrined, serious, and sad. He reached into his tweed sports jacket and pulled out a cigarette.

She eyed him. "What did you do now, Daddy?"

He struck a match and lit up. "What have you heard?" After discarding the match in a glass ashtray atop the white tablecloth, he drew on the cigarette and exhaled, avoiding her gaze.

Livia brushed her hair off her shoulders, as if this could prevent it from taking on the stale smell of smoke that clung to her whenever she spent time with Phil. "Nothing recent. Weeks ago, she told me about what happened at your apartment. And I have to say, it sounded like you wanted it to happen."

"Of course I didn't want it to happen," he said with a scoff. He tapped his ashes and then stared at his other hand resting on the table.

His nails were buffed to a sheen, as were his impeccably polished shoes. Dr. Philip Arrington, the ladies' man, prided himself on being well-groomed.

Livia picked at the wedge of iceberg lettuce on her plate. "You couldn't just tell her you were seeing someone? You had to *show* her?"

"I was going to tell her." He realized he was too loud and smiled over at the bartender apologetically. Then he dropped the smile and lowered his volume when he looked back at her. "How was I supposed to know she'd show up?"

She leaned toward him. "She said you gave her the keys. You sure you didn't want her to?"

"Oh, Livia, that's nonsense." He flicked his manicured hand in a haughty gesture, turned away, and puffed on the cigarette.

The back of Livia's neck began to perspire under her hair and silk blouse. She'd been silenced. Her father frequently denied her observations. And if she criticized, he'd counter with an attack. She stared at her plate slathered in Roquefort dressing and tried to quell her emotions. There was a buzz of inaudible conversations around them. Cutlery clinked on dishes. She summoned her courage because fuck him. "Is it, though?" she said. "Nonsense? Think about what you do when you want out of a relationship. Think about what you did to my mother. And to Velma. You made sure they knew. And that they saw."

Phil growled, "Oh, and you're so kind to your boyfriends when you want to break up?" He crossed his legs, turning farther from the table, and continued to smoke.

Livia smiled inside. "We're not talking about me."

"There's no equivalence," he hissed. "I'm not trying to end my relationship with Madeline."

"I think you expected her to walk in. You gave her the key to your apartment, Dad. *I* don't have one, by the way."

He leaned toward her and snapped, "Because you don't live here, Livia."

She gave a slight, head-tilted nod and a pursed-lipped face that suggested it was a fair point. But his reason was rubbish. And she felt a dull ache in her chest. She came into the city from Boston occasionally. If one daughter had a key, why shouldn't she?

She couldn't ask.

There was still a wounded part of her that avoided the reality of being the perpetual outsider. "You wanted her to go to NYU," she said. "You didn't expose her to any other schools."

Phil discarded a log of ashes. He sucked his teeth. "She wanted to go, Livia." He looked around as if searching for the waiter, like he was done with her. She wasn't worthy of his attention.

"Because that's all she *saw*," Livia pressed on. She was Phil's child, and old patterns held firm, but she was also a trained attorney. She'd won arguments with men far more formidable. "You hung out with her here in the Village and let her drink with you like an adult. Like she was your confidant. She's seventeen. She's not your peer. Or your partner."

He continued avoiding her eyes. An annoyed smirk smeared across his face as he gazed at the ceiling and smoked his cigarette down to the butt.

It wasn't that Livia cared so deeply about the mistakes he made with her half-sister. It was the fact that he wanted Maddie close. Livia was never given that option. She raised her voice. "Didn't you tell me Grandma made Uncle Lawrence her partner after your father died?"

Phil eyed her now and squinted. "Is that relevant?"

"You said Grandma used him—your words—for emotional support."

He whispered tersely, "What are you getting at, Livia?"

"Your relationship with Maddie is inappropriate. You don't have boundaries."

Phil caught the black-and-white–attired waiter's eye and signaled to his empty drink with a smile. "Oh, you're being ridiculous. Stop. I know you resent my not spending as much time—"

"*You* stop. I know exactly who's ridiculous. You didn't encourage Maddie to go away to school because you wanted her around for *you*. Not because it's what's best for her."

"Oh, you think you know so much." Phil uncrossed his legs and squared himself with the table to lean toward her. "I didn't send her away because she wants to learn how to act." He stubbed out the cigarette and glared into her eyes. "This is New York City. How is it not the best place for her?"

A young piano player, who'd been on a break, began his next set, tinkling the keys.

Livia lowered her voice to be respectful of his playing. "You don't need Maddie to be your companion anymore and go to jazz bars and plays and movies and museums and wherever you go because you have someone. And so, you showed her. Didn't you?"

"Christ," he said. "Thanks for your support. Glad to know you hold your father in such high esteem."

Their waiter placed Phil's third Rob Roy on the table, along with their entrees—steak and scalloped potatoes for him; broiled fish and green beans for her.

Her foot itched in her black leather boots in a spot too far down to reach. "If you don't want to hear what I think, don't ask me anything. Don't *tell* me anything. And don't involve me. My job is demanding, and I have a life of my own."

"Yes, I know," he said, cutting his meat with a steak knife. "And I'm very proud of you."

"And I don't want your shit compromising mine," she said pointedly.

He was focused on his food and gave no indication he'd even heard what she said. Did he know what she meant? Why was she so afraid to confront him about disclosing her offer to help buy Velma out? Her heartbeat thrummed in her ears.

"Yes, yes, you're so successful." He smiled as if she'd told a joke.

He was mocking her. The son of a bitch. She *was* successful. She was at a large Boston firm, living beneath her means, and saving boatloads of money. She knew he was proud of the way her accomplishments reflected on him. She'd heard him brag to his friends. And yet, there was a constant air of amused dismissal in his tone with her.

And that was it. She hesitated to bring up his betrayal of her confidence because she wouldn't be able to handle it if he met it with indifference. Which he would. He'd deny or dismiss it. He'd snap at her with some attack. He'd play the victim and make her wrong for daring to disapprove.

He spoke while chewing. The man's manners weren't nearly as genteel as he believed. "Your father appreciates that you make the time to visit, being that you're so busy. But your analysis is without merit, Livia." He chuckled.

She could point out how condescending he was and how she'd like to hurl her hunk of lettuce at his head, but energy was a limited commodity and she'd wasted enough. "How's your lawyer working out? Do my thoughts on *that* have merit?"

Color flooded his cheeks and read as embarrassment, though Livia didn't know why. Her colleague hadn't discussed his case with her.

"He seems very confident," Phil said, nodding. "Thank you for the recommendation." He cleared his throat and stared at his plate.

She watched as his forehead tensed. She detected fear. The divorce was worrying him. As it should.

"Take my advice," she said. "Let the lawyer be the asshole now. You've done more than enough to antagonize Velma. Stop acting out. Stop boasting. Keep quiet. Keep everything, including your sex life, to yourself. Think you can do that?"

He winced for a moment before closing his eyes. When he shook his head slightly, she realized he wasn't saying no to the question. He was thinking about something he'd already *done*. Probably whatever calamity had caused her sister to stop speaking to him.

"What? What did you do, Daddy?" she asked, though she realized she probably did not want to know.

22.
December 20, 1980
Maddie

I had to hand in my class journal last week. It felt weird, even though the professor said she wasn't going to read them closely. From talking to other people, I think mine was a lot more personal than it was supposed to be. Anyway, I've started this new one.

Last night during the holiday concert at the Lee Strasberg Theatre Institute, I stood onstage in a spotlight. Every soloist had an accompanist, so there was no piano to hide behind. I performed "Out Here on My Own" to a packed crowd of students, faculty, and friends.

It was awesome. I sang through tears, and for the first time, my voice never cracked. And everything clicked—the tone, the emotional honesty, the way my body settled and relaxed. It was like something was guiding me, telling me I was meant to be on that stage.

Gustavo sat in the front row with Jen and her girls, Racine and Mia. He leaned forward and looked up at me with an open-mouthed face. When the last note ended, he jumped up and shouted, "Brava. Brava!" It was almost embarrassing. Jennifer and her girlfriends stood and applauded too, though, and then everyone did.

Everyone.

It was crazy. Like a dream. I was so amazed, my heart clapped in my chest like it was cheering back.

Afterward, all the performers came out and took their bows. As soon as the house lights came on, the magnificent Anna Strasberg herself—Lee's glamorous, much-younger wife—swirled up to me like a poised tornado. She said, "You have remarkable stage presence." Her eyes shined at mine. "Lee must see you sing."

I was so excited I practically jumped into her arms. Then I noticed Victor standing right beside Anna. She gave him a sideways glance and said, "She studies with you? Talented girl." Then she whirled away in her flowing skirt and scarf and vanished into the crowd like vapor.

Victor's intense, dark eyes lasered into mine. He said nothing. Only shrugged, as if unimpressed. Then he walked away, checking Jennifer out as she approached. Victor was a predictable jerk, but even he and his disdain for me couldn't ruin this night.

Gustavo swooped in and embraced me—and not in the baby-burping, half-assed way he used to hug me. "Dios mío," he said. "That was fierce. You gotta sing at our restaurant."

As people surrounded me, my father appeared. He looked dapper in his black cashmere coat. I didn't even know he was in the audience.

"Madeline," he said, raising his voice over the hubbub of my friends' chatter. "I need to speak with you."

My stomach felt like it had fallen off a roof. I hadn't talked to him since Thanksgiving weekend. I'd never reminded him about the show and didn't think he'd be there. I gestured to the swarm of bodies around me. *Can't you see I'm busy?*

He pointed a finger at me and gritted his teeth. "I *said*, I need to speak with you." He flicked the finger toward the exit.

I didn't want to, but I gave in.

Outside on Fifteenth Street, he lit a cigarette and dropped the match on the sidewalk. "I haven't been able to reach you."

I exhaled and made huge white plumes in the cold air. "What do you need to talk about?"

He sucked on his cigarette. Smoke glowed in the streetlight. "I always knew you had talent. That's why I've invested in you," he said sternly, as if reminding me how I owed him.

"Thanks." I hugged myself and shivered in my thin silk dress. "Is that it?"

"You did a good job, honey." He brushed a hand over his head. His hair had grown in enough to show its curl again. "Listen, Amy made up some nonsense about me, too. Muriel wants to apologize. She's in the car."

I stared him in the eye for several seconds, wondering why he'd interrupt *my* night with this bullshit. "I'm going back to my friends." I turned toward the door.

"She's sorry," he said. "Give her a chance." He followed me and grabbed my shoulder.

I spun around. "A chance for what? She's your problem, not mine."

"I miss you. I miss hearing about what you're up to. I like being your dad, you know?"

I looked down at my pointy-toed pumps. That might have been the kindest thing he's ever said to me, but I did not want to see something in his eyes that would cause me to get sucked back in. I don't want to be part of his new family. I don't want to be subjected to any of that ever again. "Thank you for coming," I mumbled. "But you should go."

A few bodies spilled out of the building, Gustavo among them. He was carrying my bag and my recently cleaned camel-hair coat, which he draped around my shoulders. I introduced them. As they shook hands, my father smiled and tried to charm Gustavo like nothing was amiss. "I have my car," he said. "Let me give you kids a ride back to Fifth Avenue."

"No, thank you." I was firm. There was no way I was stuffing my body into that horrible glass trunk. Did he expect Gustavo to cram in there? "We'll walk," I said.

A short way down the block, I saw Muriel climb out of my father's Mazda RX-7 in a long red fur. She moved toward us, taking awkward steps on high-heeled boots, tottering like a toddler. "You made me want to sing again," she shouted, touching both hands to her chest. "Remember when you came over that time, and I sang the Buffy Sainte-Marie song?"

"Fuck off, Muriel," I said.

She froze. Her eyes snapped wide open like the pop-up headlights on my father's car.

Gustavo stifled a laugh with his hand.

Muriel was red-faced and near tears.

My father put his arm around her. "I remember," he said, consoling her. "'Until It's Time for You to Go.'"

"And that's our cue!" Gustavo said. "Vamanos." He grabbed my hand. "Hasta la vista."

"Bye." I waved.

My father frowned as Gustavo tugged me away from them. I felt a rush of relief at my escape.

Victor emerged from the school. Jennifer, Mia, and Racine were right behind him. When the girls saw me, they started singing the chorus from "Out Here on My Own," and Gustavo joined in. He and I dove in line behind the girls as they marched west toward Park Avenue South.

Victor was just ahead of them and I watched Jennifer ease her way up to him. Mia and Racine remained a few lengths behind. They began counting out loud. I wasn't sure why until they got to forty-five, and Jen linked arms with Victor. The girls laughed. I did not. What if she brought him back to our room? But then Jen and the ex–movie star headed north instead of south, and I said, "Hope she grinds his heart to a pulp, rolls it up, and smokes it."

Gustavo gave me a disapproving look. "Don't let these fools make you bitter, Maddita. Stay sweet."

My feet were cold, sore, and practically crying by the time we made it back to the dorm. He invited me to his room for a foot massage. Christmas lights glowed on his headboard. He had champagne in his mini refrigerator. And on the bed sat a small gift box wrapped in star-covered paper.

This was weird since just the other day, he'd told me to back off. I hadn't expected a gift. Nor had it occurred to me to get him one. I mean, it's not like we were a "thing," so . . .

"Don't worry about it," he said and waved the concern on my face away with a hand.

Inside was a shimmering silver chain and a pendant with the comedy/tragedy masks. I loved it. He sat beside me and fastened it around my neck.

I was puzzled by his abrupt change and by the fact that days earlier, being with me made him feel he was betraying his novia, and now, suddenly, he was treating me like I was his girl. I wondered if he'd bought the necklace for Raquel and decided to give it to me. I thought all of this, though I didn't ask any questions. I was afraid to hurt Gustavo's feelings so I went with what happened next.

"Vijay's gone," he said. "I wanted to make this special for you."

For me? I thought. I still couldn't quite believe this. He rubbed my feet and then unzipped my dress. He kissed me everywhere. We did everything. And he was sweet the entire time. When he said he was honored to be my first, guilt shuddered through me, but I smiled and let him think it was true.

We spent the night together, and when I woke the next morning with his body wrapped around mine, it felt like belonging. And I really wanted to belong. I took it all in. The buttery smell of his skin, the way I felt sheltered in his arms, my butt against his groin, his chest pressing into my back, and the sound of his breath in my ear. I memorized it all to save for the next time I needed to smile.

December 25, 1980
Maddie
On the way to Harlem, on the A train, this morning I started feeling sick. By Fifty-Ninth Street, my nose had begun to run. When I got off at 145th, I was sneezing, and the backs of my eyes ached. I trudged up the hill toward Convent Avenue against the wind, carrying a bag of inexpensive gifts bought at Azuma on Eighth Street. The money came from me playing for the other students in the holiday show who rehearsed in the piano room. I had my down coat on but wished I hadn't forgotten my scarf. When I finally made it to my grandparents' building, got buzzed in, and entered the warm lobby, the stinky smell of chitterlings almost brought my breakfast up. There were five flights to climb.

After four locks clacked open, the door did as well, and my grandfather placed a perfunctory peck on my cheek.

He was dressed like a dandy in a wool vest and bow tie over his white shirt. "She's in the back," he said, before disappearing through the French door into the large kitchen and its aroma of cornbread and bacon, which my one clear nostril could smell.

I hadn't seen my mother since she'd hurled flowerpots at me from the porch and read my journal. With trepidation, I dragged myself down the plastic runner in the long, dark hallway and stopped at the open door to the den.

Velma turned and saw me standing there. She was seated in my grandfather's leather recliner, watching television and munching on peanuts from a cut-glass dish on a TV tray. Her face brightened in what appeared to be genuine pleasure. She pushed the tray aside, stood, and came toward me.

I managed to smile before sneezing three times in a row.

She stopped still before reaching me. "Bless you," she said, eyeing me with suspicion. "What's wrong?"

"I feel sick."

"Well, go lie down on Grandma's bed."

I leaned through the door and handed over the bag of gifts. "Think I might have a fever." I rubbed my forehead because it began to hurt.

Velma set the bag on the carpet. "Oh, Maddie, please. You've still got your coat on, and it's hot as the devil's asshole in here. We all feel like we're running a temperature." She pulled on the collar of her black turtleneck.

"I have a headache and my throat hurts, too," I said. "I think I should go back downtown."

She made a tsk sound with her tongue. "Stop being a hypochondriac. I know you don't wanna visit with me. You'd rather be on a ski trip with your father, who you think is so perfect. But your cousins are gonna be here any minute. Don't you wanna see them?"

My grandfather appeared in the hallway behind me. "Madeline Ann," he said, handing me a tissue, "your mother had no Thanksgiving. This is not a day to let her down."

I took the Kleenex and sneezed into it.

Grandma waddled toward us in a sleeveless housedress and slippers, her ample hips and arms shimmying with each step. She touched my forehead with her palm. "The chile's on fire, Pop." She turned to my grandfather. "Now, if she's not feelin' well, why you want her to stay and get errybody sick? Give her some cab fare." She caressed my cheek. "I'll pack you a plate, baby." She jiggled back down the hall.

"Maddie, just go lie down for a while," Velma said. "You're fine."

I glanced toward the hallway and the front door.

"I drove into the city to see you," she said, folding her arms. "Your cousins are coming in from the Island. But go right ahead and do whatever you want. Like you always do. Merry Christmas." She turned away and went back to the recliner.

I stared at her for several seconds before I said, "Yeah, you, too."

23.
New York, New York, 1980
Suzy

When I get there, Grandpa and Aunt Velma are talking all kinds of shit about Maddie. He calls her self-centered and says she thinks she's grown. Thinks she's too good for everybody. Thinks she's white, like her wanna-be-white father. Aunt Velma says Maddie needs to learn how to treat family. She says lying, cheating, low-down Phil's been a bad influence on her. She says Maddie needs some sense slapped into her.

Me, my mom, and Nana don't agree. All three of us tell 'em to stop, but you can't tell those two anything. Nana Althea gets up and walks to the kitchen, shaking her head and saying, "Have mercy," as she goes.

My mother follows to check on the peas and rice. My brother Treavor's out on the fire escape, hurrying to finish a joint before Five-O-Uncle Aubrey and his nosy wife and kids show up.

I sit there and wait for Grandpa to talk to me. He's actually my mother's half-brother, but he was like a dad to her, and my brother and I call him Grandpa. He doesn't ask me about school, about DC, or about my boyfriend. The man asks me nothing, just consoles Aunt Velma, as if Maddie leaving because she's sick is some kind of tragic criminal offense.

I go into the kitchen and tell my mother I'm going downtown to check on my cousin. She and Nana fall silent for a second because they've been gossiping about Uncle Phil and his white woman. Then Mom starts to give me an attitude about my plans.

I say, "Y'all have a whole house full of people here. Maddie's alone. And Aunt Velma's not the only one going through stuff."

Nana Althea says I'm right. "But don't get too close to her now," she says. "And careful not to eat behind her."

She gives me a can of Lysol, packs me a bag of food, and sends me on my way. She also slips me cab fare, but you can't get a real taxi in their neighborhood, only gypsy cabs. I keep the cash and take the A train.

Maddie's dorm looks like it's for old people. It used to be some kind of hotel, and it has a grand, old-timey, white-folks feel. The place is damn near empty, too, and pin-drop quiet. Aside from a couple of foreign students, Maddie's probably the only one there.

She's shocked to see me, and we don't hug, because she's contagious. Her nose is red and runny, and even in her sweatpants, she looks the skinniest I've ever seen her. She tells me I can sit on her roommate's bed to be safe from her germs. After I take off my coat and boots and curl up across the room, she stares at me like she's not sure if I'm real.

She sniffles and keeps blowing her nose, and she thanks me for coming to see her.

"Of course, I came," I tell her. "Couldn't let you spend the day all by yourself."

She sneezes and thanks me again. Then she starts to cry.

I say, "Why're you crying?" I don't know why I ask, though, 'cause it's pretty obvious. Who'd want to spend Christmas alone in a dorm room?

"I'm not," she lies. "My nose is running, that's all." She's losing her voice. And she's definitely crying.

I don't want to embarrass her, so I change the subject. "Hey, what did you mean when you said you were eating ice cream and then 'getting rid of it'?"

She says nothing. Her eyes are on her socks.

"Maddie. Look at me. You better not have that bulimia mess. Do you?"

She shrugs.

"You know that's some white girl's foolishness, right? Wish you'd come to Howard. Me and my crew go running to stay in shape. Do that. Exercise if you want to lose weight, but you need to stop 'getting rid' of food that way. I heard it could damage your throat."

This gets her attention. She grabs the top of her neck under her chin and holds it, looking like she's gonna choke herself.

I say, "You're trying to be a singer, right? How are you going sing if your throat's all jacked up? Maddie, Maddie, Maddie, Maddie, Maddie. Stop that shit, okay? Don't do things to hurt yourself."

I talk, and she lies there and creaks with barely a voice. I tell her about my cool professors and all the cute dudes I could introduce her to. I show her pictures of Marcel and me. And of the Yard at Howard, which is the joint, with all of its beautiful Black people sprawled across the grass.

She nods but doesn't say much. Her eyes seem sad. There's definitely no place like the Yard at NYU. Maddie's still a minority here, same as she was where she grew up. At Howard, she'd blend in.

She doesn't have any pictures of this Gustavo dude. I question whether he even exists. And then he calls while I'm there. I watch Maddie on the phone. She giggles and her cheeks get some color, and even though she's not feeling well, her eyes look so jazzed it's like they're dancing.

Later, when we're eating the plates Nana fixed, I find out that not only has he been the dude to do the deed, but he's her boyfriend now. *And* she's spending New Year's Eve with him at his family's restaurant. And she's gonna be singing. *For money*. Wish I could go, but I have plans with Marcel. And here I was, thinking Maddie's life was miserable. She's doing fine, despite her wack-ass parents.

24.
December 31, 1980
Maddie

I was recovering and alone, really alone, for days. Everyone's home with their families, and I didn't want to go to Monroe. Gustavo did call a few times, but Suzy's the only person I saw. When she was here, a part of me wanted to tell her about Ron, and I couldn't. I knew she wouldn't approve. And I wasn't about to be shamed for going through a rite of passage with someone outside the tribe. I love my cousin, but she's always telling me what to do and how I'm supposed to do it.

Christmas was Thursday. The worst of my symptoms were over by Sunday. That left only two days to rehearse in the piano room for my gig at Gustavo's father's place. Most of the songs were ones I'd already practiced with my coach. The new one I *wrote* was the one making my insides quiver. I'd never performed my own stuff before. The thought of it was terrifying yet exhilarating, too.

I was almost out of food yesterday and low on funds. The dining hall's been closed since the last day of finals and won't open until the new semester. I've been living on canned tuna, bananas, and some cornbread Suzy left from Grandma Althea.

My father was in Switzerland with his ass-model, but when I checked his apartment, there was nothing to eat there but some salted nuts. For a second, I almost considered tossing the noisy bird into a pot and making soup out of him. I'm kidding. The poor thing was lonely, and it's not his fault he's badly trained. Instead, with the little money I had, I treated myself to a pint of vanilla Häagen-Dazs. I ate only half and did not throw it up. I want to stop doing that. I know it's bad for me. And I don't want to hurt my voice. But sometimes I can't help it. I go into a frenzy, like a frenetic trance, where I can't stop eating. I gorge myself like mad and lose control. Then the vomiting somehow calms me down, and I feel normal again, once everything's up and out. In this case, I didn't need to get rid of the calories. Between being sick and being broke, my loose clothes say I've lost about five pounds.

This morning my father called and said he was back in the city. He wanted to know what I was doing. When I told him I was singing tonight in Washington Heights, he wanted to come. I balked at the idea of Muriel being there, but because he pays for my voice lessons and reminds me of that constantly, and he does support my shows, I felt obligated to tell him where it was and when.

"That's far," he said. "I'll drive you."

"That's okay," I said. "I'll be dressed up."

"What does that have to do with anything?"

"I can't ride in your trunk, Dad."

"Did you hear me say anything about riding in the trunk?" he yelled. "What time do you need to be there?"

We took the FDR Drive toward the Harlem River Drive, and he told me he and Muriel fought in Verbier. "I'm done with that relationship," he said.

I thought, *Yippee*. But I didn't say anything. I leaned toward the rearview mirror and fluffed my curls with my fingers.

"You're not going to say anything?" he said.

"Nope." My lips looked dry, and I applied some gloss to them.

"You could at least say, 'That's too bad.'"

"Humph," I grunted. "I *could*."

"I see." He smiled smugly. "You're pleased to have your father to yourself again."

I stared through the windshield. Was I? I didn't really think so. I fingered the comedy/tragedy pendant Gustavo gave me. I think I was just glad I wouldn't have to see that lady and her lying little kid again. And I think my father shouldn't be telling me what I feel.

A red awning boasted the name Leonardo's. The restaurant was on the first floor of a well-kept brick building. Two leafless trees decorated with small yellow lights framed the entrance. According to Gustavo, his father owned the business with his mother until they divorced, amicably, as I could only dream mine would.

Leonardo appeared at the door in a tailored black suit and welcomed us inside before the place opened. His wavy dark hair was threaded with silver, and his honey-brown face was clean-shaven. He was so handsome he made me nervous. I might have blushed. I thought if Gustavo were to one day grow into *that*, it would be worth the wait. And oh my God, the sound of the older man's accented English, when he told me what time I'd be introduced, made my knees weak. He grew up in Cuba and sounded different from Gustavo, who was raised here. Leonardo said I'd be on toward the end of the first seating. Then he invited my dad and me to stay as his guests for the Latin jazz band that would play during the second seating and past midnight, when there would be salsa dancing. I stood there and gawked at his gorgeous face without responding. He had to ask if I understood. Embarrassing.

Gustavo appeared and was almost as fine as his daddy. His dark curls skimmed the collar of a white dress shirt, which he wore with no tie under a charcoal-gray suit. He hugged me tight, kissed me on the lips, and said hello to my father. Then he took my hand and led us deeper into the restaurant.

It was covered with framed photographs of street scenes in Havana and oil paintings of beautiful Cuban women. There were lots of plants everywhere—some in pots on the floor and others hanging, with leaves draping the walls like long hair. Brown-wicker ceiling fans spun throughout, which made the space feel like a tropical island, even in winter. Latin music, with spritely trumpets, trilled from the speakers.

We came into the main room, where a magnificent black baby grand gleamed near the opposite wall. It took my breath away. As Gustavo seated my father and hung our coats, I walked over to it and sat down to check its tune. My stomach was knotted with nerves. I was planning on playing my new song first to get it out of the way.

I heard a woman's voice grumble from the kitchen, "Why her? Can she even sing in Spanish?"

A man with no accent shushed her. "At least half our regulars don't speak Spanish, Graciela."

Soon, families began arriving, sitting, and eating. Gustavo was moving from table to table, chatting with everyone. I sat with my father. Though I realized I had to be hungry, I didn't feel it. I was too anxious to eat. He drank enough mojitos and ate enough black-bean soup, plantains, and pork and rice for both of us.

When it was time, Gustavo took me by the hand, led me to the piano, and introduced me as his "friend" from NYU. He told the crowd, "I've heard her sing, and she is special."

I don't remember us even exchanging a look. He gave a little bow to the crowd and exited stage right.

I sat, blew out a nervous breath, then touched the keys and began.

Take me in, be my home.
I'm alone.
Wanna begin to build a place,

where I feel safe
to dream again.

As I went into the chorus, I looked at my father and saw his eyes shining back at me. He seemed proud. I glanced over at Gustavo, and he gave me thumbs-up.

Old walls have tumbled down.
Solid ground's
just a relic from the past,
when I had faith
in love that lasts.

The song went fine. For a first performance, I was pleased. The audience applauded with enthusiasm and didn't seem to realize or care that it was my original piece. I took that as a good sign and thought the rest of my set would be easy. I started to relax and then realized I was *ravenous*. I could hardly wait to eat.

As I began the next song, a Donna Summer ballad, "On My Honor," a phenomenally gorgeous young woman, curvaceous in a clinging plum-colored dress, clicked into the main dining room in stilettos and no coat. Thick curly hair cascaded down her back to her butt, and I immediately envied it. Her face, though flawless, was tense—visibly distressed.

I kept singing and watched the woman glance around and then make a beeline to Gustavo's table with her arms wide, as if demanding a hug.

His eyes filled with fear. Raquel. Of course, it was.

I saw him glance at me and then back at his ex.

Honestly, I couldn't even blame him for being into her. I mean, who wouldn't be? Gustavo shook his head, refusing to hug her. Then he muttered something I couldn't hear. It seemed he was telling her to leave.

She raised her voice. "This is how you treat me, Tavo?"

Now people were looking, murmuring. I kept singing, though no one was listening to me. All eyes, even my father's, were on Raquel and Gustavo.

A middle-aged Latina entered from the kitchen in a white chef's coat and hat and stood beside Raquel. I knew this had to be the mother. She was statuesque and had skin as smooth as the dinner plates on the table.

I was still singing as Leonardo approached Raquel, kissed her cheek, and placed a hand on her back. He said something in her ear and gestured toward the entrance. Then the mother began fussing at Leonardo in Spanish. She got in his face. He was pleading with both women, his arm pointing to the room full of patrons. Raquel held her ground. Then she turned and barked something at me in Spanish.

Fuck, I thought. My heart pounded. I kept playing and singing because, you know, the show must go on. Raquel gave me a piercing frown, and I didn't know what to do. I felt like a fool, and I assumed I looked like one, too, because some diners began to laugh.

The chef-mama pointed at me. Then she faced Raquel and spat a few Spanish words, which included "culo," and I knew she was telling her daughter to kick my ass.

Even though I didn't do anything to the girl, I understood their anger. I was Muriel, disrespecting their territory, and Raquel was Velma. But in my opinion, Gustavo was the one they should've been angry with. He invited me.

I continued singing as Raquel glared in my direction, like she was considering an attack. But she sighed and with what sounded like exasperation, she turned to her mother and said, "Mami, I'm pregnant."

Gustavo leapt out of his seat. "¿Qué? ¡Coño!"

Her mother shrugged and said, "Eh, only a little."

That's all I caught. There was a lot of shouting in Spanish after that, and I finally gave up on the song.

Gustavo paced and yelled, and he seemed ready to cry.

Leonardo apologized. He placed a hundred-dollar bill in my hand and then led me away from the piano. He gave my father and me our coats and again said he was sorry. Gustavo was so busy arguing with Raquel and her mother that I didn't interrupt him to say goodbye.

On the way downtown, my father filled the RX-7 with cigarette smoke. "You okay?" he asked.

I rolled down my window and stared at the East River. "I'd be better if I could breathe."

He ignored me. "I'm not dating any more women with kids," he said. "All Muriel could talk about was how Amy was feeling. Who the fuck cares?" He shook his head and smoked. Then he continued in a mocking tone. "She's grieving; she's lonely; the relationship is causing her stress."

I closed my eyes.

He patted my knee. "That's too bad about your boyfriend. But you've got lots of life ahead of you. There'll be other men. In the meantime, you have your dad, and this night is for you. Should we stop by Bradley's?"

I massaged my eyebrows, unsure of whether I even wanted to go. "Can we get in? Without a reservation? It's New Year's Eve."

He screwed up his face as if my questioning him was absurd. "Maddie. I'm a regular."

We got there before ten. It was packed full of bodies, filled with smoke, and there were no empty seats. Fortunately, the music had swing. It was so good I would have danced if I hadn't been sad and there was space to move. We were crunched near the bar, and there was no way to see past the many bodies to view the musicians. I was still starving and gorged on handfuls of peanuts. My father bought me a glass of wine. He spoke into my ear. "Your new song wasn't bad. Keep at it."

At the time, I took it as a compliment and thanked him. Writing this now, I'm not so sure. Anyway, we stood side by side, listening to the music, bopping our heads. I appreciated being there, having his company and something to focus on besides the earlier part of the evening.

A tall blonde with ample cleavage in a red sequined dress waved to Phil from a cluster of people closer to the stage. I saw his face brighten as she pushed her way toward him through the crowd.

Without a glance in my direction, he elbowed me aside to make room for her. And she shoved into the narrow space between us. He angled his body toward her and chatted into her ear. I waited to see if he'd introduce me or invite me to join the conversation or even acknowledge my presence again. I finished my wine and ate more nuts.

I am an idiot, I thought. How many times will I let myself fall for this shit? Yes, he's financing my education but this is . . .

I don't know what it is, but it's not cool.

After a moment, I pushed my way in between him and the woman, leaned close, and said, "I'm not doing this with you anymore, Dad. J'ai fini avec toi."

He frowned as if I were a nuisance for interrupting. And that was his only response.

I stumbled outside, woozy from the wine, and hugged my bag to my grumbling stomach. Lively jazz greeted me on the sidewalk, though not from Bradley's, where I'd just been.

It was coming from across University Place a couple of blocks south. A marquee announced that Alberta Hunter was headlining at the Cookery. Light-headed, I ambled over there in my heels.

Ms. Hunter's rich, sweet, and salty voice flowed into the street. I watched through the window and took in her songs like sustenance. She wore her signature gray bun, and she was small and old. But her sparking eyes and expression bore an infectious, girlish gleam. Her sound, delivery, and phrasing suggested she'd experienced many highs and lows. Her life hadn't always been easy. Yet she was celebrating it.

The joy radiating from her was the hug I needed tonight.

It struck me that people who've experienced sorrows can feel the good times maybe even more profoundly because they've known hard times. This showed me that I, too, could be an artist. Even with all that's broken in my life right now, someday I can sing my comedies and tragedies and turn them into more.

When the cold got to be too much, I headed back to the dorm and this quiet room. I kicked off my shoes and turned the TV to *New Year's Rockin' Eve.* And even though I can't say this has been a good night, I'm not unhappy to come home to myself. It's better than being with people who make me sad. Without them, it's easier to envision good things to look forward to.

I'm smiling because I know now that no one can crush me unless I let them. Not my parents, not some guy, or a teacher who doesn't like me, or bigots in the town I come from. I'm still standing, alone but content, in my little portion of this city aglow with dreams. Imagine.

Daughtered Out

BOSTON, 1988

Livia

You're growing your first child inside; it's a girl, and your father is visiting for Thanksgiving. He wears a chocolate-brown ascot with a white shirt under a multicolored Pucci jacket. You wonder when he began wearing ascots, and you curse under your breath because you've already purchased his Christmas gifts, which include an insanely expensive silk tie you took forty minutes to select on the first Saturday of November when, one rare occasion, you weren't working. Why didn't he tell you he'd switched to ascots?

He sits across from you and your handsome husband in downtown Boston, where you live, intentionally, away from the rest of your family. In your formal dining room, under the chandelier you designed and had custom-made, your father takes a matchbook from his breast pocket and reads from its inside flap the names Phillis, Phillipa, Philomene, and Philomena.

Your back teeth grind together, and you set down your fork. You've made lists of dozens of names, none of which begin with "Phil." Something pulls tight in your chest. You feel your husband, seated to your right, smiling as he says nothing and sips his Beaujolais.

If your father is unnerved by your silence, he doesn't show it. He restows his matchbook and resumes chewing and swallowing large bites of the roasted duck à l'orange you prepared at his request, even though you work upwards of seventy hours a week at a law firm. Planning this meal required precise scheduling of shopping, chopping, measuring, and mixing in advance.

He eyes you directly and, without a trace of irony, tells you he has no one to carry his name. No sons. He's been "daughtered out," he says, his voice tinged with complaint, as if it's your fault you were born female.

You feel like he's thrown something hot in your face.

You've earned two summa cum laude Harvard degrees and financed significant portions of your undergraduate and law school tuition with scholarships and loans, while your father groused about the living expenses he paid, which afforded you a shared basement apartment infested with water bugs. You ate canned generic beans on a regular basis for seven years.

Your head stills as your eyes narrow to the thin edge of a knife. You contemplate the antediluvian phrase "daughtered out," which at one time meant a father couldn't pass on his surname or bequeath property to his female offspring.

Has this troglodyte with whom you share DNA not noticed that you've kept your last name? *His* last name? And that you're a junior partner in a notable firm, you're under thirty-five and earn nearly what he does at fifty-five, and that you purchased the apartment he's dining in before you married?

Daughtered out?

A knot tightens in the back of your neck as you're reminded how *you* were left out, time after time, after he divorced your mother and remarried and had a new daughter, who had the privilege of living with him in posh homes in white neighborhoods while you were left in the Bronx.

Your frills-free urban upbringing notwithstanding, you were the one accepted to top schools. You became a professional. You got married. Now you're expecting, and the years are unfurling exactly as planned; meanwhile, his other daughter blows through life aslant and fucks loser Lotharios who'll never marry her. Maybe Maddie can be a single mother and have a boy and name it Philip-fucking-Arrington.

Your father can give *her* the responsibility of saving him from the fate of being daughtered out. He's given her everything else.

You think all this, but you set your face into a pleasant-as-possible mask, and you say through closed teeth, "Yes, I'll consider those names. Absolutely, Daddy."

And a little piece of you dies inside. It joins a cluster of buried pieces that accrete each time you meet his demands at your own expense.

Your head shakes. Or it *doesn't*. You feel it does because it should. This baby will need all of your heart. She'll need you to put her needs before yours for approval.

Your daughter should have a name you and *her* father choose, one that's hers alone, not *your* father's, because she doesn't owe him.

Your mind leaps to the way he'll feel slighted and how his displeasure will cause an unbearable ache in you. But bearing it will be your responsibility because you'll be someone's mother.

After not offering to help you and your husband clear the table, your father retires to your tidy guest room, the way you used to withdraw to his. You were always the temporary presence in your father's house. Never the forever girl.

Once the dishwasher is loaded, next on your agenda is time in the master bath, which you've commandeered for yourself, leaving your spouse the smaller guest bathroom because he can't keep his things where they belong.

You sit down to relax in your sunken tub, and as you soak, you remember how your father spoke often of being the odd one out when his father died.

He became the son who wasn't loved.

Then he made your family. And you loved him *best*. He knew it, and it didn't matter.

You were seven, and you were stunned the day he sat you in your grandmother's kitchen, held your dirty little hand, and told you he was leaving. Something popped inside you, a burst, like a big bang, and you felt shattered in a place you couldn't reach, so you couldn't fix it.

With the globe in your parents' bedroom, your father had taught you about Pangaea—how the once-solid supercontinent split apart into smaller pieces. That was you that day—a piece broken off. An island. Stranded. Alone.

You sink into the fragrant bubbles and close your eyes, and you're sitting at Grandma Emily's table, staring at the sugar cubes in their shallow dish set on the doily. A jagged hole from a missing screw on the chair leg tickles your big toe, and lacy white curtains behind you brush your back with the breeze. Your hands are filthy from drawing pictures out front on the sidewalk with chalk and dirt.

You wish you'd washed them before your father held one in his and told you he wasn't happy; he was moving out; he and your mother were getting divorced.

You couldn't move after the awful crack inside your chest. The room dimmed and so did you, as clouds wiped the sun. You slumped forward in the chair, your eyes connected to his, hoping maybe it wasn't really happening, but you could see your grandmother behind him, her tears shimmering at you from the doorway.

Was there something you could do? you asked. If you were better, would that make him stay? He closed his eyes, and you wondered, what if you were cleaner, smarter, more obedient?

He squeezed your fingers. You were ashamed of the grime caked under their nails. He said he loved you and that you'd still see each other. But, no, he couldn't stay. He wouldn't be there to read to you, kiss you good night, or tell you to have a good day at school. You'd never do things as a family again.

Never. At seven, the word was hard to fathom, like death. There were things you were never *supposed* to do—talk back, play with matches, cross the street alone, bother your mother when she was busy. But you *could* do them. If you really wanted to.

Oh, how you longed to keep your family together. You wanted and wished with all the force you had. When you figured out you couldn't, no matter how you yearned and prayed, you understood that, like death, "never" meant gone, over, not coming back. Ever.

What did remain was the inexorable grief of that summer day. A constant companion, it lives in the space that cracked open inside you. Still.

In the days that followed, which turned to months and years and decades, the world went on without your family. And you made your place in it, mostly alone, learning that, like a landmass broken from a continent, you could survive and even flourish.

You're fine. And though you know it's best to look forward, you've looked back, again and again, and wondered if your father hadn't noticed how your mother didn't want to do motherly things. Did he not see how she wouldn't play with you or take you to the zoo, kiss you good night, or listen when you talked about your day at school? You thought he knew, that he *saw* how your mother was not unlike the mother he said *he* had. You thought he knew that *he* made your family because he was the one who wanted to spend time with you. He was the one who called you a branch to his tree.

Then why didn't he take you?

It's not how things were done back then. You know that. You also know your father didn't follow social mores of *any* time. He did what he wanted. Always.

He didn't take you because he didn't want to. You've never said this out loud, but you think it—often.

You fell down the front stairs once after he left. You were carrying a sketch you'd drawn for your mother. You bumped your head and back, and you crumpled the drawing. For a long time, you lay in pain, crying on the hardwood floor below the bottom step, which was right outside the room where she was. You knew your mother heard you. You wailed, and she didn't come. Finally, you picked yourself up, rubbed the bump on your head, walked into the parlor, and found her working on her own drawing. You asked why she didn't come to see if you were all right. She didn't look at you when she said, "You were crying, so I knew you weren't dead or unconscious."

You had your grandmother but only briefly because she was *his* mother, and your mother wasn't going to keep living with his mother without him. So, you moved out, and another piece of you broke off.

You sit in the tub with that. A stab of pain is warm in your chest, and you sense your strength pulsing all around the sore spot. That's the thing; you didn't choose to stay broken. You are, but you put yourself back together, imperfectly perhaps, and you sketched out and executed the creation of your life, carefully, purposefully, like an artist. On the surface, you're a kind of masterpiece.

That's why your father flaunts you, when he can, to his colleagues, like one of his accomplishments—his Ivy League, high-powered, self-sufficient progeny.

Then why do you give him such power to leave you feeling the sting of imperfection? Of not being male? Not being enough?

You sense your baby inside imploring, *Don't carry your childhood into motherhood.* She'll need you to fight for her the way you couldn't for yourself. The way your parents wouldn't.

Unlike them, you walked down the aisle because you wanted to. They were kids. Nineteen when they married, with you already on the way.

Children should be prepared for. You plan everything in advance.

Your daughter will be hugged and kissed with every bump and hurt feeling. She'll know she's loved. Wanted. You'll never leave her.

When you step out of the tub onto your marble floor, you feel a twinge of uneasiness. You rub your rounding belly before slipping into your Turkish robe.

In the hallway, you stand outside the guest room and knock. From behind the door, your father says he's not dressed. You tell him you have something to say, and you hear him grumble, his feet hitting the floor. He opens the door while tying his bathrobe. "What is it?" he asks, as if you've interrupted something important.

You stare down at his bare feet. Like yours, they're large, and the second toe is longer than the first. "I don't want to name her any derivative of Philip," you say. Then you lift your face level with his. "Her father and I have our own choices."

His face wilts. Your words have drained a little life out of him. "Fine. They were only suggestions," he says with a sliver of pain in his voice.

It pierces you like you knew it would. You stand straight and try not to let it show. "Thanks for understanding," you say.

"Sure." He leans in and kisses your cheek. "I'm glad you invited me. Y'know, parents *do* like to see their children once in a while." His eyes smile. "Good night." The door clicks closed.

What? Was that a dig? Oh, *now* he wants to see you? Now that you're grown and busy and have a life of your own?

You stand in the hallway, eyes on his door, and then you feel a flutter in your belly, a tiny cartwheel, as if your baby is happy because you took a step. You put your own family first. And that's your plan going forward, even if it makes your daddy unhappy. Even if he pulls away. A broken branch can still grow.

You hear a whisper in your mind: *No. Wash your dirty hands.* Seven-year-old you. She's still there.

You walk down the hallway toward your bedroom and toward your husband, and you whisper back that you hear her. You tell her your hands are fine, and the two of you are going to celebrate because joy is on its way. And if you'd never known sadness, you couldn't appreciate the elation you feel in looking forward to your new girl and how brightly she'll shine.

This Side and That

BRONX, NEW YORK, 1989

Emily

When I pass on, my second son will arrive more than twenty minutes late to my funeral. With wild, dyed hair in need of a cut and his Burberry overcoat rumpled, Philip will drag open the door to the stone chapel, causing it to creak and scuff against the slate gray floor.

He'll stand there, stiff, wide-eyed, and bewildered, as each head in every pew turns to stare at him, while my niece May reads the obituary that I'll have written myself.

Sighs and rolling eyes will shame him on my behalf as they add this offense to others: the time he went silent and shunned me for months, the many times he raised his voice, and the time he left me to die in a subpar nursing home when he could have afforded better. But I'll receive his last act of aggression toward me without resistance or dismay because, in the end, I'll observe and accept, and I'll let things be.

Philip's unshined shoes will flap up the aisle, followed by Madeline's thin heels clicking behind them. My granddaughter, too, will be late because when I pass on, she'll still be young enough to hope her father will do what he says: get her to the church on time. Stop breaking the hearts of those who try to love him.

Lawrence, my first son, will glance at his lovely wife of thirty years and grit his teeth when his brother's foot loudly bumps the pew across from Velma, Phil's second ex, who'll frown at Phil and tell herself she's there only to support her daughter and stepdaughter. This will be untrue. Velma will be there for herself. I'll understand. She once belonged and then she didn't, and exclusion was more than she could bear.

I'll neglect to name her among those I've left behind because she won't be family when I go, but she will be there because she'll refuse not to be, and eventually, tenacity will win, and she'll belong.

It'll be October. Cool and sunny rays will shine through the Tiffany stained-glass windows. I might be resting in one of those rays, watching everything and hearing all.

Philip will slouch next to Madeline and behind his first daughter, Livia, who'll have risen before dawn to drive to the Bronx from Boston with her baby and spouse, letting nothing—not her prestigious job or her husband's, not infant car sickness or soiled, smelly diapers—keep her from arriving on time.

Philip's stomach will growl, though his morning tea with scotch and toast will have contributed to his lateness. He'll feel too warm in his suit. And he'll note with surprise all the people—so many—who'll be there to pay respects. He'll think ahead to when it's his time and wonder, *Who will show?*

Family will be seated everywhere he looks, along with neighbors, friends, and members of my church, a community I'll have cultivated over six decades. He'll see, but not want to see, that though my way wasn't his way, it didn't amount to less than his. When it's over, he'll see my little life had meaning.

He'll marvel at how I'll have stuck with those he fled because he wished for things the white world had, like tennis clubs and homes with grounds and swimming pools, Swiss Alps ski trips, and women with slight buttocks. He believed those things were better.

When I pass on, Philip will tell himself his choice to leave one wife and then another was right for him. But a voice inside his head will ask *What if?* What if he'd stayed, put down roots, and watered them? What if he'd not destroyed two families? Would life have been worse had he nurtured the lives he made or stuck with the community he came from?

The choir, dressed in blood-red robes, will sing somber hymns I'll have chosen myself before my demented mind slipped too far to reach.

With a ponderous face, Philip will sit, legs crossed, his fingers stroking the hair on his chin, and he'll think that if his choices were mistakes, he can trace them back to me. He'll remember the many times I pushed him away and days when my words were unkind. He'll believe I favored his brother, and sometimes I did. The music and voices that fill the church won't soften his ire or quell his clanging thoughts of my transgressions.

The melodies will, however, seep inside my granddaughters and slip through fissures in armor they'll have cloaked around hearts, wounded by the ways their parents failed them, too. They'll tow resentments piled in childhood, but unlike their father, Livia and Madeline will long to let theirs go. When I pass on, they'll still be tender enough inside to hope they *can* release them.

I'll have done all I could to make things right with Philip. I will have offered apologies, written notes and letters, crocheted afghans, prayed, and made late-night calls to say I love you, before my earthly mind forgets the name and face I gave him, and he puts me in a place where mothers of bitter sons wait to shed their shells and dance in the new dimension.

Before I lose my memory, I will have learned that in mothering there is no making up for the love you don't give. What you do or don't do with your offspring—the good and bad—makes the mold that shapes them.

Philip will work in a profession that talks endlessly about these molds. He'll lean back in his leather office chair, chain-smoke cigarettes, and analyze them, but the truth is, once set, they don't change. Still, he'll endeavor to mend the minds and hearts that yield from the shoddy molds (his own included), so they might shine in the world.

When I pass on, I'll learn that in the living, these defects, while sometimes ameliorated, are rarely fully healed or prayed away.

If this isn't the truth for all families, it will indeed be for ours. Wounds passed from my parents to me and from me to mine will pass to theirs and so on. And I'll watch from this realm, helplessly, as my brood ticks forward in time with its pain.

After my burial, Philip will hug Livia and her baby goodbye. And after Madeline leaves for the subway, he'll carry his wrinkled coat, draped over the arm of his tailored suit, into the post-service repast, where he'll linger longer than he planned to.

He'll ignore Velma across the room, chatting easily with my first son and his family. He'll sit on a plastic folding chair and eat a second, then a third cucumber finger sandwich off a white paper plate. He'll make inconsequential conversation with those he deems unsophisticated because he'll have taken the day off, and he'll have nowhere better to go. And because, though he won't admit it, he'll miss me.

Long-forgotten images will crack across his closed mind like lightning. He'll see me in my blue hat, smiling in the front row at his high school graduation. He'll recall the lemony scent of my 4711 cologne and the fresh smell of our kitchen when I made mint jelly from scratch. He'll feel me rubbing his tired ten-year-old feet with witch hazel after he's walked home from school in the rain. He'll remember how I held his little hand in the hot Bermuda sun when we skipped down the cobblestones past the tall steps of St. Peter's Church on the way to my mother's house.

He'll think I must be there somewhere among the simple people, sending these memories, and perhaps I will be, but the past will blaze in his thoughts because longtime friends and family from our neighborhood—sweet-smelling ladies wearing hat pins and carrying hard candies in their latch-top purses—will regard him warmly and remind him of me, a me who's never done him wrong.

Philip will live alone at the time in his tiny Greenwich Village flat, where his daughters will visit infrequently, and he'll serve them Jack Daniel's coffee on a table stacked with matchbooks and mail. He'll boast of his numerous romantic conquests, and at the same time, he'll be seeing a thin white woman from his other world Upstate. She'll be married, and soon she'll crush and discard him like a cigarette stub.

Not once will he visit my grave. He'll forget my birthday and speak ill of me. I won't hold it against him. He'll mistreat women continually. Sometimes he'll realize—more often he won't—that though I'll be long gone, he'll never stop trying to get back at me for all that I didn't give him.

Toward his own end, his girls will come to accept their father's flaws, though not condone them. When his mind goes, its decline will stir up past hurts. Neither daughter will abandon him, nor will they take him in when he needs constant care. By then, he'll have a new sweetheart, pale and thin, like those before her. This one will be unmarried and live in the city, and she'll be kind. To Madeline and Livia's astonishment, she'll keep him, bedridden and babbling, in her high-rise uptown until the day he's carried away.

One Monday morning in March, his sweetie will leave for work, and he'll go into cardiac arrest with only an unlicensed home nurse from the Bronx, by way of Jamaica, to witness his soul's departure. She'll holler curses and prayers in patois and call 911, and the paramedics will restart his heart.

Though he'll have left his body to breathe via machine, he won't be ready to come when I call him. He'll think he still has things to do.

His girls will arrive by Tuesday morning. They'll sit with his brain-dead flesh and bones until Thursday evening, when the tubes are removed.

That afternoon, Velma will take the bus from Upstate New York into Manhattan. Wearing gold earrings, bright lipstick, and heels, she'll be reading her local paper in the ICU waiting room as Livia and Madeline say goodbye.

After the body expels its last breath, Velma will join the girls, the girlfriend, and the home nurse from the Bronx as they all walk east from Tenth Avenue to have dinner in a skyscraper above Columbus Circle.

Velma will chat nonstop, enjoy the view and the high-end meal, and not notice Livia and Madeline's silence. Despite having known their father's end was coming, its reality will stun them both.

Fond memories of his presence at their graduations and weddings and the times he took them on adventures will light their minds in the days ahead, though not be bright enough to outshine the dark ones. They'll think of him with love while still wishing he could have been better to them and to their mothers.

When he finally gets where I am, he'll have had no homegoing at all, just a small gathering the girls arrange at a restaurant on Waverly Place. He'll have frequented its bar for years, sitting late into the night with his Dewar's on ice, writing an entire book on yellow legal pads. A few friends will attend, though only two from Monroe, his chosen, white home away from home. Some of the small-town connections will have passed on before him. Others will turn out to have not been true friends. I won't mention this when I see him.

Velma will insist on being in attendance after first insisting she be included in his obituary. This I *will* comment on, and we'll share a good giggle.

A colleague will call the psychoanalytic theory he developed fascinating, audacious, and a work of genius. A few family members from the Bronx and elsewhere will tell amusing stories of him rumbling with the gangs from Mount Vernon, hitting on pretty girls with boyfriends, and sneaking out his window and onto the roof at night to stare at the stars. And while it won't be for me to understand, Philip will watch with glee and be profoundly pleased with his send-off, miniscule though it may be.

When he arrives here, I'll be the second to embrace him and smile into his eyes after his father, and he'll be amazed to find he's no longer angry with me. You can't be when you get here, because the scars made in life don't travel with you. Nothing hurts. And there's only love. As far as what happened and what's still happening on the other side, all you can do is observe, accept, and let things be. Together, we'll wait for the rest of our beloveds, and we'll look forward to nothing but goodness to share with them when they arrive.

Acknowledgments

My immense gratitude to Crystal Wilkinson for her guidance and this wonderful opportunity with Screen Door Press. Thanks also to Margaret Kelly, Ashley Runyon, Jackie Wilson, and the whole team at the University Press of Kentucky.

Thank you to my wonderful agent, Danielle Chiotti.

Parts of this collection were developed in various workshops at Callaloo, the Prague Summer Program for Writers, One Story Summer Conference, Hurston/Wright, the Atlantic Center for the Arts, and Kimbilio. I'm grateful for the support these spaces provided.

Thank you to the journals, anthologies, and editors who published versions and excerpts of these stories: *Aunt Chloe: A Journal of Artful Candor*: Elyce Strong Mann and Sharan Strange; *Serving House Journal*: Duff Brenna; *Fiction Magazine*: Mark Mirsky, Ruth Mirsky, Chris Bonfiglio, and Sonja Killebrew; *Vida Review*: Feliz Moreno; *Moria Online*: Linda Dove and Sarah Olmedo; *Coachella Review*: Yennie Cheung and Collin Mitchell; *Accolades: A Women Who Submit Anthology*: Tisha Marie Reichle-Aguilera and Rachael Warecki; *Transformation: A Women Who Submit Anthology*: Lorinda Toledo.

I'm so grateful for colleagues and friends who read parts of this collection and offered feedback and support: My trusted first reader Kate Maruyama, Richard Torres, Eriq LaSalle, Dara Hyde, Roxane Gay, Kristin Gentry, Jabari Asim, Jacinda Townsend, Ravi Howard, Will Allison, Stuart Dybek, Valerie Ann Burns, Allen Jones, Mary B. Sellers, Caleb Klitzke, Grace Bydalek, Nafissa Thompson-Spires,

Marame Guyere, Kiiettii Walker-Parker, Stephanie Early Green, Shirley Asano Guldimann, Ian Caskey, Kelly Fordon, Peter Demarco, Whitney Bryant, Beth Levine, Elise Gallagher, Joy Ntoma, Hadassah Williams, Jeannetta Craigwell-Graham, Darlene Taylor, Regina Brayboy, Jennifer Shannon, Brianna Johnson, Hana Wulu, Ebonya Washington, Deesha Philyaw, Minda Honey, Latria Graham, Jazmin Witherspoon, Deidra White, David Haynes, Ryane Granados, Corinne Brinkley, Oluabambi Ige, Camile Forbes, and Alyssia Gonzalez.

Thanks to my fabulous Zoom room Blackbird writing group: Cynthia Bond, Jan Ford, Kim Sykes, Tchaiko Omawale, Nana-Ama Danquah, Adrienne Crew, Tonya Pinkins, Wanda Belle, Brandi Collins-Dexter, and Colly Vaughan. Big thanks to Women Who Submit and to David Rocklin for the opportunity to read parts of these stories publicly.

Many thanks and all my love to Leonard Chang.

About the Author

Toni Ann Johnson won the Flannery O'Connor Award for her linked story collection *Light Skin Gone to Waste* (UGA Press, 2022), which was selected for the prize and edited by Roxane Gay. The book was nominated for a 2023 NAACP Image Award for Outstanding Literary Work and shortlisted for the 2024 Saroyan Prize. A novella, *Homegoing*, won Accents Publishing's inaugural novella contest in 2020 and was released by the press in 2021. Johnson's first novel *Remedy for a Broken Angel* (2014) was a finalist for a 2015 NAACP Image Award for Outstanding Literary Work by a Debut Author. A two-time Pushcart Prize nominee, Johnson's short fiction has appeared in the *Coachella Review*, *Hunger Mountain*, *Callaloo Journal*, *Fiction Magazine*, and many other publications. She earned an MFA in creative writing at Antioch University Los Angeles. She's been a Kimbilio fellow (2024), a Hurston/Wright fellow (2021), and a Callaloo Writing Workshop fellow (2016), and she's received support for her writing from the One Story Summer Conference, the Prague Summer Program for Writers, the Sundance Screenwriter's Lab, and the Atlantic Center for the Arts.